Balsamo the Magician

Alexandre Dumas

Balsamo the Magician

The present edition is a reproduction of previous publication of this classic work. Minor typographical errors may have been corrected without note; however, for an authentic reading experience the spelling, punctuation, and capitalization have been retained from the original text.

ISBN: 978-1-63637-979-1

CONTENT

CHAPTER I

THE GRAND MASTER OF THE SECRET SOCIETY

On the left bank of the Rhine, near the spot where the Selz rivulet springs forth, the foothill ranges rise of many mountains, of which the bristling humps seem to rush northerly like herds of frightened buffaloes, disappearing in the haze. These mountains tower over a deserted region, forming a guard around one more lofty than the rest, whose granite brow, crowned with a ruined monastery, defies the skies. It is Thunder Mount.

On the sixth of May, 1770, as the great river wavelets were dyed in the rainbow hues of the setting sun, a man who had ridden from Maintz, after a journey through Poland, followed the path out of Danenfels Village until it ended, and, then, alighting and leading his steed, tied it up in the pine woods.

"Be quiet, my good Djerid (javelin)," said the horseman to the animal with this Arabian name which bespoke its blood, and its speed; "and good-bye, if we never meet again."

He cast a glance round him as if he suspected he were overheard.

The barb neighed and pawed with one foot.

"Right, Djerid, the danger is around us."

But as if he had made up his mind not to struggle with it, the venturesome stranger drew the charges from a pair of splendid pistols and cast the powder and bullets on the sward before replacing them in the holsters. He wore a steel-hilted sword which he took off with the belt, and fastened it to the stirrup leather so as to hang from the saddle-horn point down.

These odd formalities being done, he ungloved, and searching his pockets produced nail-scissors and pocket-knife, which he flung over his shoulder without looking to see whither they went.

Drawing the longest possible breath, he plunged at random into the thicket, for there was no trace of a path.

He was a man about thirty, taller than the average, but so wonderfully well built that the utmost strength and skill seemed to circulate in his supple and nervy limbs. He wore a black velvet overcoat with gilt buttons; the flaps of an embroidered waistcoat showed below its lowest buttons, and the buckskin riding breeches defined legs worthy to be a sculptor's models; the elegant feet were cased in patent leather boots.

His countenance was a notable mixture of power and

1

intelligence, with all the play of Southern races; his glance, able to display any emotion, seemed to pierce any one on whom it fell with beams that sounded the very soul. His cheeks had been browned by a sun hotter than that of France. His mouth was large but finely shaped, and parted to reveal magnificent teeth, all the whiter from his dark complexion. His hand was small but muscular; his foot long but fine.

Scarcely had he taken a dozen steps within the glade before he heard faint footsteps. He rose on tiptoe and perceived that unseen hands had unhitched Djerid and were leading him away. He frowned slightly, and a faint smile curled his full cheeks and choicely chiseled lips.

He continued into the heart of the forest.

For a space the twilight guided him, but soon that died out, and he stood in gloom so dense that he had to stop lest he blundered blindly.

"I reached Danenfels from Maintz," he said, aloud, "as there was a road. I reached this forest as there was a path: I am here as there was some light: but I must stop now as I have no sight."

Scarcely had he spoken, in a dialect part French, part Sicilian, than a light flashed out only fifty paces off.

"Thanks! I will follow the light as long as it leads."

The light at once moved onward, regularly and steadily, like a stage lamp managed by the lime-light operator.

At a hundred paces, a breath in the adventurer's ear made him wince.

"Turn and you die!" came this whisper.

"All right," answered the stranger.

"Speak, and you die!" whispered a voice on the left-hand.

He bowed without speaking.

"But," said a voice seeming to issue from the bowels of the earth, "if you are afraid, go back to the plain, by which it will be clear that you are daunted, and renounce your errand."

The traveler waved his hand to imply that he was going ahead, and ahead he went.

But it was so late and the shade so deep that he stumbled during the hour the magic light preceded him, but he did not murmur or show any tremor in fear, while he heard not a breath.

All of a sudden, the light went out!

He had passed through the woodland, for on lifting his eyes, he could see a few stars glitter on the darksome sky.

He kept on in the same direction till he saw loom up the somber mass of the ruins of a castle—its spectre. At the same time his foot met its fallen stones.

2

A clammy thing wound itself round his forehead and sealed his eyes. He could no longer see even the shadows. It was a wet linen cloth. It must have been an expected thing, for he made no resistance to being blindfolded. But he put forth his hand silently as a blinded man naturally does to grope. The gesture was understood, for on the instant a cold, dry, bony hand clutched his fingers. He knew it was a skeleton's, but had it possessed feeling, it must have owned that his own hand no more trembled.

For a hundred yards the seeker was dragged forward rapidly.

All at once the bandage was plucked aloof, and he stopped; he had reached the top of the Thunder Mount.

Before him rose the moldy, mossy steps of the portico of the old Castle of Donnerberg. On the first slab stood the phantom with the osseous hand which had guided him thither. From head to foot a long shroud enwrapped it; through a slit the dead eyes peered without luster. The fleshless hand pointed into the ruins where the goal seemed to be a hall too high up to be viewed, but with the collapsed ceiling flickering with a fickle light.

The traveler nodded in consent. Slowly the ghost mounted the steps one by one, till amid the ruins. The man followed with the same solemn and tranquil pace regulating his walk, and he also entered.

Behind him slammed the principal door as noisily as a ringing bronze gate.

The phantom guide had paused on the threshold of a round hall hung with black and illumined with greenish hues of three lamps.

"Open your eyes," said the ghastly guide.

"I see," replied the other, stopping ten paces from him.

Drawing a double-edged sword from his shroud with a swift and haughty gesture, the phantom smote with it a brazen column which boomed a note like a gong.

Immediately, all around, the slabs of the hall floor rose up, and countless ghosts like the guide, stole in with drawn swords and took posts on steps where they stood like statues on their pedestals, cold and motionless. They stood out against the sable drapery.

Higher than the steps was a dais for seven chairs; on these six ghosts took place, leaving one seat vacant; they were chiefs.

"What is our number, brothers?" challenged one of the six rising in the middle.

"Three hundred is the right tally," answered the spectres, with one voice thundering through the hall and dying amid the black hangings.

"Three hundred," said the presiding chief, "representing each ten thousand associates; three hundred swords worth three millions of daggers. What do you want, stranger?" he demanded, turning to the intruder.

"To see the Light," was the rejoinder.

"The paths leading to the Mountain of Fire are hard and toilsome—fear you not to tread them?"

"I fear nothing."

"You can not turn back once you start. Bear this in mind."

"I mean to stop only at the goal."

"Are you ready to take the oath?"

"Say it and I will repeat."

The president lifted his hand and slowly and solemnly uttered these words:

"In the name of the Master Carpenter, swear to break all carnal bonds tying you to whomsoever, and above all to those to whom you may have pledged faith, obedience or service."

The new-comer in a firm voice repeated what was pronounced.

"From this out," continued the president, "you are absolved from plights made to native land and rulers. Swear to reveal to your new leader what you have seen and done, heard or learned, read or guessed, and further to spy and discover all passing under your eyes."

On his ceasing the novice repeated.

"Honor and respect the Water of Death," went on the president without a change of voice, "as a prompt means in skilled hands, sure and needful, to purge the globe by the death or insanity of those who strive to stifle the Truth or snatch it from our hands."

An echo could not more faithfully repeat the vow.

"Avoid Spain, Naples, and all accursed lands; and moreover the temptation to let out what you learn and hear—for the lightning is less swift to strike than we with our unseen but inevitable blade, wheresoever you may flee. Now, live in the name of the Supernal Three!"

In spite of the final threat, no emotion could be descried on the novice's face, as he reiterated the words with as calm a tone as he used at the outset.

"Now, deck the applicant with the sacred ribbon," said the president.

Two shrouded figures placed on the bent brow of the stranger a sky-blue ribbon with silver letters and female figures; the ends of the badge were tied behind on the nape. They stepped aside, leaving him alone again.

"What do you want?" asked the chief officer.

"Three things: the iron hand to strangle tyranny; the fiery

sword to drive the impure from earth; and the diamond scales to weigh the destinies of mankind."

"Are you prepared for the tests?"

"Who seeks to be accepted, should be ready for everything."

"The tests!" shouted the ghosts.

"Turn round," said the president.

The stranger faced a man, pale as death, bound and gagged.

"Behold a traitor who revealed the secrets of the Order after taking such an oath as you did. Thus guilty, what think you he deserves?"

"Death."

"Death!" cried the three hundred sword-bearers.

Instantly the unhappy culprit, despite superhuman resistance, was dragged to the back of the hall. The initiated one saw him wrestling and writhing in the torturers' hands and heard his voice hissing past the gag. A poniard flashed in the lamplight like lightning, and after it fell, with a slapping sound of the hilt, the dead body landed heavily on the stone floor.

"Justice has been executed," observed the stranger, turning round to the terrifying circle, whose greedy eyes had gazed on him out of their grave clothes.

"So you approve of the execution?"

"Yes, if the slain were truly guilty."

"And would you drink the downfall of any one who sold the secrets of this Ancient Association?"

"In any beverage."

"Bring hither the cup," said the arch-officer.

One of the two executioners drew near with a skull brimming with a warm and ruddy liquid. The stranger took the goblet by its brass stem and said, as he held it up: "I drink to the death of all false brothers." Lowering the cup to his lips, he drained it to the last drop, and calmly returned it to the giver.

A murmur of astonishment ran around the assemblage, as the phantoms glanced at one another.

"So far well. The pistol," said the chief.

A ghost stole up to the speaker holding a pistol in one hand, and powder and ball in the other, without the novice seeming to deign a glance in that direction.

"Do you promise passive obedience to the brotherhood, even though it were to recoil on yourself?"

"Whoso enters the household of the Faithful is no longer his own property."

"Hence you will obey any order given you?"

"Straightway."

5

"Take this firearm and load it."

"What am I to do with it?"

"Cock it."

The stranger set the hammer, and the click of it going on full cock was plainly heard in the deep stillness.

"Clap the muzzle to your temple," ordered the president, and the suppliant obeyed without hesitating.

The silence deepened over all; the lamps seemed to fade, and the bystanders had no more breath than ghosts.

"Fire!" exclaimed the president.

The hammer fell and the flint emitted sparks in the pan; but it was only the powder there which took fire and no report followed its ephemeral flame.

An outcry of admiration burst from nearly every breast, and the president instinctively held out his hand toward the novice.

But two tests were not enough for some doubters who called out: "The dagger!"

"Since you require it, bring the dagger," said the presiding officer.

"It is useless," interrupted the stranger, shaking his head disdainfully.

"What do you mean?" asked several voices.

"Useless," repeated the new-comer, in a voice rising above all the others, "for you are wasting precious time. I know all your secrets, and these childish proofs are unworthy the head of sensible beings. That man was not murdered; the stuff I drank was wine hid in a pouch on his chest; the bullet and powder I loaded the trick-pistol with fell into a hollow in the stock when the weapon was cocked. Take back the sham arm, only good to frighten cowards. Rise, you lying corpse; you cannot frighten the strong-minded."

A terrible roar shook the hall.

"To know our mysteries, you must be an initiate or a spy," said the president.

"Who are you?" demanded three hundred voices together, as a score of swords shone in the grip of the nearest and were lowered by the regular movement of trained soldiers toward the intruder's bosom.

Calm and smiling, he lifted his head, wound round with the sacred fillet, and replied:

"I am the Man for the Time."

Before his lordly gaze the blades lowered unevenly as they on whom it fell obeyed promptly or tried to resist the influence.

"You have made a rash speech," said the president, "but it may have been spoken without your knowing its gravity."

"I have replied as I was bound," said the other, shaking his head and smiling.

"Whence come you, then?" questioned the chief.

"From the quarter whence cometh the Light," was the response.

"That is the East, and we are informed that you come from Sweden."

"I may have passed through there from the Orient," said the stranger.

"Still we know you not. A second time, who are you?"

"I will tell you in a while, since you pretend not to know me; but, meantime, I will tell you who you are."

The spectres shuddered and their swords clanked as they shifted them from the left to the right hands again to point them at his breast.

"To begin with you," said the stranger, pointing to the chief, "one who fancies himself a god and is but a forerunner—the representative of the Swedish Circles—I will name you, though I need not name the others. Swedenborg, have not the angels, who speak familiarly with you, revealed that the Man you expect was on the way?"

"True, they told me so," answered the principal, parting his shroud the better to look out.

This act, against the rule and habit during the rites, displayed the venerable countenance and snowy beard of an old man of eighty.

"And on your left," continued the stranger, "sits the representative of Great Britain, the chief of the Scottish Rites. I salute your lordship. If the blood of your forefathers runs in your veins, England may hope not to have the Light die out."

The swords dropped, for anger was yielding to surprise.

"So this is you, captain?" went on the stranger to the last leader on the president's left; "in what port have you left your handsome cruiser, which you love like a lass. The Providence is a gallant frigate, and the name brings good luck to America."

"Now for your turn, Prophet of Zurich," he said to the man on the right of the chief. "Look me in the face, since you have carried the science of Physiognomy to divination, and tell me if you do not read my mission in the lines of my face?"

The person addressed recoiled a step.

"As for you, descendant of Pelagius, for a second time the Moors must be driven out of Spain. It would be an easy matter if the Castilians have not lost the sword of the Cid."

Mute and motionless dwelt the fifth chief: the voice seemed to have turned him to stone.

7

"Have you nothing to say to me?" inquired the sixth delegate, anticipating the denouncer who seemed to forget him.

"Yea, to you I have to say what the Son of the Great Architect said to Judas, and I will speak it in a while."

So replied the traveler, fastening on him one of those glances which pierced to the heart.

The hearer became whiter than his shroud, while a murmur ran round the gathering, wishful to call the accused one to account.

"You forget the delegate of France," observed the chief.

"He is not among you—as you well know, for there is his vacant place," haughtily made answer the stranger. "Bear in mind that such tricks make them smile who can see in the dark; who act in spite of the elements, and live though Death menaces them."

"You are a young man to speak thus with the authority of a divinity," resumed the principal. "Reflect, yourself—impudence only stuns the ignorant or the irresolute."

"You are all irresolute," retorted the stranger, with a smile of supreme scorn, "or you would have acted against me. You are ignorant, since you do not know me, while I know ye all. With boldness alone I succeed against you, but boldness would be vain against one with irresistible power."

"Inform us with a proof of this power," said the Swedenborg. "What brings ye together?"

"The Supreme Council."

"Not without intention," went on the visitant, "have you come from all quarters, to gather in the sanctuary of the Terrible Faith."

"Surely not," replied the Swede; "we come to hail the person who has founded a mystic empire in the Orient, uniting the two hemispheres in a commonalty of beliefs, and joining the hands of human brotherhood."

"Would you know him by any token?"

"Heaven has been good enough to unveil it by the intermediation of its angels," answered the visionary.

"If you hold this secret alone and have not revealed it to a soul, tell it aloud, for the time has come."

"On his breast," said the chief of the Illuminati, "he wears a diamond star, in the core of which shines the three initials of a phrase known to him alone."

"State those initials."

"L. P. D."

With a rapid stroke the stranger opened his overcoat, coat and waistcoat and showed on the fine linen front, gleaming like flame, a jeweled plate on which flared the three letters in rubies.

"HE!" ejaculated the Swede: "can this be he?"

"Whom all await?" added the other leaders, anxiously.

"The Hierophant of Memphis—the Grand Copt?" muttered the three hundred voices.

"Will you deny me now?" demanded the Man from the East, triumphantly.

"No," cried the phantoms, bowing to the ground.

"Speak, Master," said the president and the five chiefs, bowing, "and we obey."

The visitor seemed to reflect during the silence, some instants long.

"Brothers," he finally said, "you may lay aside your swords uselessly fatiguing your arms, and lend me an attentive ear, for you will learn much in the few words I address you. The source of great rivers is generally unknown, like most divine things: I know whither I go, but not my origin. When I first opened my eyes to consciousness, I was in the sacred city of Medina, playing about the gardens of the Mufti Suleyman. I loved this venerable old man like a father, but he was none of mine, and he addressed me with respect though he held me in affection. Three times a day he stood aside to let another old man come to me whose name I ever utter with gratitude mixed with awe. This august receptacle of all human wisdom, instructed in all things by the Seven Superior Spirits, bore the name of Althotas. He was my tutor and master, and venerable friend, for he is twice the age of the oldest here."

Long shivers of anxiety hailed this speech, spoken in solemnity, with majestic gesticulation and in a voice severe while smooth.

"One day in my fifteenth year, in the midst of my studies, my old master came to me with a phial in hand. 'Acharat,' he said—it was my name—'I have always told you that nothing is born to die forever in this world. Man only lacks clearness of mind to be immortal. I have found the beverage to scatter the clouds, and next will discover that to dispel death. Yesterday I drank of this distillation: I want you to drink the rest to-day.'

"I had extreme trust in my teacher but my hand trembled in taking this phial, like Eve's in taking the apple of Life.

"'Drink,' he said, smiling. And I drank.

"'Sleep,' he said, laying his hands on my head. And I slept.

"Then all that was material about me faded away, and the soul that solitarily remained lived again, like Pythagoras, for centuries through which it had passed. In the panorama unfolded before it, I beheld myself in previous existence, and, awaking, comprehended that I was more than man."

He spoke with so strong a conviction, and his eyes were fixed heavenward with so sublime an expression that a murmur of

9

admiration hailed him: astonishment had yielded to wonder, as wrath had to astonishment.

"Thereupon," continued the Enlightened One, "I determined to devote my existence at present, as well as the fruit of all my previous ones, to the welfare of mankind. Next day, as though he divined my plan, Althotas came to me and said:

"'My son, your mother died twenty years ago as she gave birth to you; for twenty years your sire has kept hidden by some invincible obstacle; we will resume our travels and if we meet him, you may embrace him—but not knowing him.' You see that all was to be mysterious about me, as with all the Elect of heaven.

"At the end of our journeys, I was a Theosophist. The many cities had not roused my wonderment. Nothing was new to me under the sun. I had been in every place formerly in one or more of my several existences. The only thing striking me was the changes in the peoples. Following the March of Progress, I saw that all were proceeding toward Freedom. All the prophets had been sent to prop the tottering steps of mankind, which, though blind at birth, staggers step by step toward Light. Each century is an age for the people. Now you understand that I come not from the Orient to practice simply the Masonic rites, but to say: Brothers, we must give light to the world. France is chosen to be the torch-bearer. It may consume, but it will be a wholesome conflagration, for it will enlighten the world. That is why France has no delegate here; he may have shrunk from his duty. We want one who will recoil from nothing—and so I shall go into France. It is the most important post, the most perilous, and I undertake it."

"Yet you know what goes on there?" questioned the president.

Smiling, the man called Acharat replied: "I ought to know, for I have been preparing matters. The king is old, timid, corrupt, but less antiquated and hopeless of cure than the monarchy he represents. Only a few years further will he sit on the throne. We must have the future laid out from when he dies. France is the keystone of the arch. Let that stone be wrenched forth by the six millions of hands which will be raised at a sign from the Inner Circle, and down will fall the monarchical system. On the day when there shall be no longer a king in France, the most insolently enthroned ruler in Europe will turn giddy, and spring of his own accord into the gulf left by the disappearance of the throne of Saint Louis."

"Forgive the doubt, most venerated Master," interrupted the chief on the right, with the Swiss accent, "but have you taken all into calculation?"

"Everything," replied the Grand Copt, laconically.

10

"In my studies, master, I was convinced of one truth—that the characteristics of a man were written on their faces. Now, I fear that the French people will love the new rulers of the country you speak of—the sweet, clement king, and the lovely amiable queen. The bride of the Prince Royal, Marie Antoinette, is even now crossing the border. The altar and the nuptial bed are being made ready at Versailles. Is this the moment to begin your reformation?"

"Most illustrious brother," said the supreme chief to the Prophet of Zurich, "if you read the faces of man, I read the features of the future. Marie Antoinette is proud and will obstinately continue the conflict, in which she will fall beneath our attacks. The Dauphin, Louis Auguste, is good and mild; he will weaken in the strife and perish like his wife, and with her. But each will fall and perish by the opposite virtue and fault. They esteem each other now—we will not give them time to love one another, and in a year they will entertain mutual contempt. Besides, brothers, why should we debate on the point whence cometh the light, since it is shown to me? I come from out of the East, like the shepherds guided by the star, announcing a new birth of man. To-morrow, I set to work, and with your help I ask but twenty years to kill not a mere king but a principle. You may think twenty years long to efface the idea of royalty from the hearts of those who would sacrifice their children's lives for the little King Louis XV. You believe it an easy matter to make odious the lilyflowers, emblem of the Bourbon line, but it would take you ages to do it.

"You are scattered and tremble in your ignorance of one another's aspirations. I am the master-ring which links you all in one grand fraternal tie. I tell you that the principles which now you mutter at the fireside; scribble in the shadows of your old towers; confide to one another under the rose and the dagger for the traitor or the imprudent friend who utters them louder than you dare—these principles may be shouted on the housetops in broad day, printed throughout Europe and disseminated by peaceful messengers, or on the points of the bayonets of five hundred soldiers of Liberty, whose colors will have them inscribed on their folds. You tremble at the name of Newgate Prison; at that of the Inquisition's dungeon; or of the Bastile, which I go to flout at—hark ye! We shall all laugh pity for ourselves on that day when we shall trample on the ruins of the jails, while our wives and children dance for joy. This can come to pass only after the death of monarchy as well as of the king, after religious powers are scorned, after social inferiority is completely forgotten, and after the extinction of aristocratic castes and the division of noblemen's property. I ask for

11

a generation to destroy an old world and rear a new one, twenty seconds in Eternity, and you think it is too much!"

A long greeting in admiration and assent hailed the somber prophet's speech. It was clear that he had won all the sympathy of the mysterious mandatories of European intellect. Enjoying his victory just a space, the Grand Copt resumed:

"Let us see now, brothers, since I am going to beard the lion in his den, what you will do for the cause for which you pledged life, liberty and fortune? I come to learn this."

Silence, dreadful from its solemnity, followed these words. The immobile phantoms were absorbed in the thoughts which were to overthrow a score of thrones. The six chiefs conferred with the groups and returned to the president to consult with him before he was the first to speak.

"I stand for Sweden," he said. "I offer in her name the miners who raised the Vasas to the throne—now to upset it, together with a hundred thousand silver crown pieces."

Drawing out tablets, the Hierophant wrote this offer. On the president's left spoke another:

"I am sent by the lodges of England and Scotland. I can promise nothing for the former country, which is burning to fight us Scots. But in the name of poor Erin and poor Scotia, I promise three thousand men, and three thousand crowns yearly."

"I," said the third speaker, whose vigor and rough activity was betrayed beneath the winding sheet fettering such a form. "I represent America, where every stick and stone, tree and running brook, and drop of blood belong to rebellion. As long as we have gold in our hills, we will send it ye; as long as blood to shed, we will risk it; but we cannot act till we ourselves are out of the yoke. We are so divided as to be broken strands of a cable. Let a mighty hand unite but two of the strands, and the rest will twist up with them into a hawser to pull down the crowned evils from their pride of place. Begin with us, most venerable master. If you want the French to be delivered from royalty, make us free of British domination."

"Well spoken," said the Hierophant of Memphis. "You Americans shall be free, and France will lend a helping hand. In all languages, the Grand Architect hath said: 'Help each other!' Wait a while. You will not have long to bide, my brother."

Turning to the Switzer, he drew these words from him:

"I can promise only my private contribution. The sons of our republic have long supplied troops to the French monarchy. They are faithful bargainers, and will carry out their contracts. For the first time, most venerated Master, I am ashamed of their loyalty."

12

"Be it so, we must win without them and in their teeth. Speak, Spain!"

"I am poor," said the grandee, "and have but three thousand brothers to supply. But each will furnish a thousand reals a year. Spain is an indolent land, where man would doze though a bed of thorns."

"Be it so," said the Grand Master. "Speak, you, brother."

"I speak for Russia and the Polish clubs. Our brothers are discontented rich men, or serfs doomed to restless labor and untimely death. In the name of the latter, owning nothing, not even life, I can promise nothing; but three thousand rich men will pay twenty louis a head every year."

The other deputies came forward by turns, and had their offers set down in the Copt's memorandum book as they bound themselves to fulfill their plight.

"The word of command," said the leader, "already spread in one part of the world, is to be dispensed through the others. It is symbolized by the three letters which you have seen. Let each one wear them in the heart as well as on it, for we, the Sovereign Master of the shrines of the Orient and the West, we order the ruin of the Lilies. L. P. D. signifies Lilia Pedibus Destrue—Trample Lilies Under! I order you of Spain, Sweden, Scotland, Switzerland and America, to Trample down the Lilies of the Bourbon race."

The cheering was like the roar of the sea, under the vault, escaping by gusts down the mountain gorges.

"In the name of the Architect, begone," said the Master. "By stream and strand and valley, begone by the rising of the sun. You will see me once more, and that will be on the day of triumph. Go!"

He terminated his address with a masonic sign which was understood solely by the six chiefs, who remained after the inferiors had departed. Then the Grand Copt took the Swede aside.

"Swedenborg, you are really an inspired man, and heaven thanks you by my voice. Send the cash into France to the address I shall give you."

The president bowed humbly, and went away amazed by the second sight which had unveiled his name.

"Brave Fairfax," said the Master to another, "I hail you as the worthy son of your sire. Remind me to General Washington when next you write to him."

Fairfax retired on the heels of Swedenborg.

"Paul Jones," went on the Copt to the American deputy, "you have spoken to the mark, as I expected of you. You will be one of the heroes of the American Republic. Be both of you ready when the signal is flying."

Quivering as though inspired by a holy breath, the future capturer of the Serapis likewise retired.

"Lavater," said the Master to the Swiss, "drop your theories for it is high time to take up practice; no longer study what man is, but what he may become. Go, and woe to your fellow countrymen who take up arms against us, for the wrath of the people is swift and devouring even as that of the God on high!"

Trembling, the physiognomist bowed and went his way.

"List to me, Ximenes," said the Copt to the Spaniard; "you are zealous, but you distrust yourself. You say, Spain dozes. That is because no one rouses her. Go and awake her; Castile is still the land of the Cid."

The last chief was skulking forward when the head of the Masons checked him with a wave of the hand.

"Schieffort, of Russia, you are a traitor who will betray our cause before the month is over; but before the month is out, you will be dead."

The Muscovite envoy fell on his knees; but the other made him rise with a threatening gesture, and the doomed one reeled out of the hall.

Left by himself in the deserted and silent hall, the strange man buttoned up his overcoat, settled his hat on his head, pushed the spring of the bronze door to make it open, and went forth. He strode down the mountain defiles as if they had long been known to him, and without light or guide in the woods, went to the further edge. He listened, and hearing a distant neigh, he proceeded thither. Whistling peculiarly, he brought his faithful Djerid to his hand. He leaped lightly into the saddle, and the two, darting away headlong, were enwrapped in the fogs rising between Danenfels and the top of the Thunder Mountain.

CHAPTER II

THE LIVING-WAGON IN THE STORM

A week after the events depicted, a living-wagon drawn by four horses and conducted by two postboys, left Pont-a-Mousson, a pretty town between Nancy and Metz. Nothing like this caravan, as show people style the kind, had ever crossed the bridge, though the good folks see theatrical carts of queer aspect.

The body was large and painted blue, with a baron's insignia, surmounting a J. and a B., artistically interlaced. This box was lighted by two windows, curtained with muslin, but they were in the front, where a sort of driver's cab hid them from the vulgar eye. By these apertures the inmate of the coach could talk with outsiders. Ventilation was given this case by a glazed skylight in the "dickey," or hind box of the vehicle, where grooms usually sit. Another orifice completed the oddity of the affair by presenting a stovepipe, which belched smoke, to fade away in the wake as the whole rushed on.

In our times one would have simply imagined that it was a steam conveyance and applauded the mechanician who had done away with horses.

The machine was followed by a led horse of Arab extraction, ready saddled, indicating that one of the passengers sometimes gave himself the pleasure and change of riding alongside the vehicle.

At St. Mihiel the mountain ascent was reached. Forced to go at a walk, the quarter of a league took half an hour.

Toward evening the weather turned from mild and clear to tempestuous. A cloud spread over the skies with frightful rapidity and intercepted the setting sunbeams. All of a sudden the cloud was stripped by a lightning flash, and the startled eye could plunge into the immensity of the firmament, blazing like the infernal regions. The vehicle was on the mountain side when a second clap of thunder flung the rain out of the cloud; after falling in large drops, it poured hard.

The postboys pulled up. "Hello!" demanded a man's voice from inside the conveyance, "what are you stopping for?"

"We are asking one another if we ought to go on," answered one postillion with the deference to a master who had paid handsomely.

"It seems to me that I ought to be asked about that. Go ahead!"

But the rain had already made the road downward slippery.

"Please, sir, the horses won't go," said the elder postillion.

"What have you got spurs for?"

"They might be plunged rowels deep without making the balky creatures budge; may heaven exterminate me if——"

The blasphemy was not finished, as a dreadful lightning stroke cut him short. The coach was started and ran upon the horses, which had to race to save themselves from being crushed. The equipage flew down the sloping road like an arrow, skimming the precipice.

Instead of the traveler's voice coming from the vehicle, it was his head.

15

"You clumsy fellows will kill us all!" he said. "Bear to the left, deuce take ye!"

"Oh, Joseph," screamed a woman's voice inside, "help! Holy Madonna, help us!"

It was time to invoke the Queen of Heaven, for the heavy carriage was skirting the abysm; one wheel seemed to be in the air and a horse was nearly over when the traveler, springing out on the pole, grasped the postboy nearest by the collar and slack of the breeches. He raised him out of his boots as if he were a child, flung him a dozen feet clear, and taking his place in the saddle, gathered up the reins, and said in a terrifying voice to the second rider:

"Keep to the left, rascal, or I shall blow out your brains!"

The order had a magical effect. The foremost rider, haunted by the shriek of his luckless comrade, followed the substitute impulse and bore the horses toward the firm land.

"Gallop!" shouted the traveler. "If you falter, I shall run right over you and your horses."

The chariot seemed an infernal machine drawn by nightmares and pursued by a whirlwind.

But they had eluded one danger only to fall into another.

As they reached the foot of the declivity, the cloud split with an awful roar in which was blended the flame and the thunder.

A fire enwrapped the leaders, and the wheelers and the leaders were brought to their haunches as if the ground gave way under them. But the fore pair, rising quickly and feeling that the traces had snapped, carried away their man in the darkness. The vehicle, rolling on a few paces, stopped on the dead body of the stricken horse.

The whole event had been accompanied by the screams of the woman.

For a moment of confusion, none knew who was living or dead.

The traveler was safe and sound, on feeling himself; but the lady had swooned. Although he guessed this was the case, it was elsewhere that he ran to aid—to the rear of the vehicle.

The led horse was rearing with bristling mane, and shaking the door, to the handle of which his halter was hitched.

"Hang the confounded beast again!" muttered a broken voice within; "a curse on him for shaking the wall of my laboratory." Becoming louder, the same voice added in Arabic: "I bid you keep quiet, devil!"

"Do not wax angry with Djerid, master," said the traveler, untying the steed and fastening it to the hind wheel; "he is frightened, and for sound reasons."

So saying, he opened a door, let down the steps, and stepped inside the vehicle, closing the door behind him.

He faced a very aged man, with hooked nose, gray eyes, and shaking yet active hands. Sunken in a huge armchair, he was following the lines of a manuscript book on vellum, entitled "The Secret Key to the Cabinet of Magic," while holding a silver skimmer in his other hand.

The three walls—for this old man had called the sides of the living-wagon "walls"—held bookcases, with shelves of bottles, jars and brass-bound boxes, set in wooden cases like utensils on shipboard so as to stand up without upsetting. The old man could reach these articles by rolling the easy chair to them; a crank enabled him to screw up the seat to the level of the highest. The compartment was, in feet, eight by six and six in height. Facing the door was a furnace with hood and bellows. It was now boiling a crucible at a white heat, whence issued the smoke by the pipe overhead exciting the mystery of the villagers wherever the wagon went through.

The whole emitted an odor which in a less grotesque laboratory would have been called a perfume.

The occupant seemed to be in bad humor, for he grumbled:

"The cursed animal is frightened: but what has he got to disturb him, I want to know? He has shaken my door, cracked my furnace, and spilt a quarter of my elixir in the fire. Acharat, in heaven's name, drop the beast in the first desert we cross."

"In the first place, master," returned the other smiling, "we are not crossing deserts, for we are in France; and next, I would not abandon a horse worth a thousand louis, or rather priceless, as he is of the breed of Al Borach."

"I will give you a thousand over and over again. He has lost me more than a million, to say nothing of the days he has robbed me of. The liquor would have boiled up without loss of a drop, in a little longer, which neither Zoroaster nor Paracelsus stated, but it is positively advised by Borri."

"Never mind, it will soon be boiling again."

"But that is not all—something is dropping down my chimney."

"Merely water—it is raining."

"Water? Then my elixir is spoilt. I must renew the work—as if I had any time to spare!"

"It is pure water from above. It was pouring, as you might have noticed."

"Do I notice anything when busy? On my poor soul, Acharat, this is exasperating. For six months I have been begging for a cowl to my chimney—I mean this year. You never think of it, though you

17

are young and have lots of leisure. What will your negligence bring about? The rain to-day or the wind to-morrow confound my calculations and ruin all my operations. Yet I must hurry, by Jove! for my hundredth year commences on the fifteenth of July, at eleven at night precisely, and if my elixir of life is not then ready, good-night to the Sage Althotas."

"But you are getting on well with it, my dear master, I think."

"Yes, by my tests by absorption, I have restored vitality to my paralyzed arm. I only want the plant mentioned by Pliny, which we have perhaps passed a hundred times or crushed under the wheels. By the way, what rumbling is that? Are we still going?"

"No; that is thunder. The lightning has been playing the mischief with us, but I was safe enough, being clothed in silk."

"Lightning? Pooh! wait till I renew my life and can attend to other matters. I will put a steel bridle on your electric fluid and make it light this study and cook my meals. I wish I were as sure of making my elixir perfect——"

"And our great work—how comes it on?"

"Making diamonds? That is done. Look there in the glass dish."

Joseph Balsamo greedily caught up the crystal saucer, and saw a small brilliant amid some dust.

"Small, and with flaws," he said, disappointed.

"Because the fire was put out, Acharat, from there being no cowl to the chimney."

"You shall have it; but do take some food."

"I took some elixir a couple of hours ago."

"Nay, that was at six this morning, and it is now the afternoon."

"Another day gone, fled and lost," moaned the alchemist, wringing his hands; "are they not growing shorter? Have they less than four-and-twenty hours?"

"If you will not eat, at least take a nap."

"When I sleep, I am afraid I shall never wake. If I lie down for two hours, you will come and call me, Acharat," said the old man in a coaxing voice.

"I swear I will, master."

At this point they heard the gallop of a horse and a scream of astonishment and disquiet.

"What does that mean?" questioned the traveler, quickly opening the door, and leaping out on the road without using the steps.

CHAPTER III

THE LOVELY LORENZA

The woman who was in the fore part of the coach, in the cab, remained for a time deprived of sense. As fear alone had caused the swoon, she came to consciousness.

"Heavens!" she cried, "am I abandoned helpless here, with no human being to take pity upon me?"

"Lady," said a timid voice at hand, "I am here, and I may be some help to you."

Passing her head and both arms out of the cab by the leather curtains, the young woman, rising, faced a youth who stood on the steps.

"Is it you offered me help? What has happened?"

"The thunderbolt nearly struck you, and the traces were broken of the leading pair, which have run off with the postboy."

"What has become of the person who was riding the other pair?" she asked, with an anxious look round.

"He got off the horses as if all right and went inside the other part of this coach."

"Heaven be praised," said she, breathing more freely. "But who are you to offer me assistance so timely?"

"Surprised by the storm, I was in that dark hole which is a quarry outlet, when I suddenly saw a large wagon coming down at a gallop. I thought it a runaway, but soon saw it was guided by a mighty hand, but the lightning fell with such an uproar that I feared I was struck and was stunned. All seemed to have happened in a dream."

The lady nodded as if this satisfied her, but rested her head on her hand in deep thought. He had time to examine her. She was in her twenty-third year, and of dark complexion, but richly colored with the loveliest pink. Her blue eyes sparkled like stars as she appealed to heaven, and her hair fell in curls of jet, unpowdered contrary to the fashion, on her opal neck.

"Where are we?" she suddenly inquired.

"On the Strasburg to Paris highway, near Pierrefittes, a village. Bar-le-Duc is the next town, with some five thousand population."

"Is there a short cut to it?"

"None I ever heard of."

"What a pity!" she said in Italian.

As she kept silent toward him, the youth was going away, when this drew her from her reverie, for she called him for another question.

"Is there a horse still attached to the coach?"

"The gentleman who entered, tied it to the wheel."

"It is a valuable animal, and I should like to be sure it is unhurt; but how can I go through this mud?"

"I can bring it here," proposed the stripling.

"Do so, I prithee, and I shall be most grateful to you."

But the barb reared and neighed when he went up.

"Do not be afraid," said the lady: "it is gentle as a lamb. Djerid," she called in a low voice.

The steed recognized the mistress's voice, for it extended its intelligent head toward the speaker, while the youth unfastened it. But it was scarcely loose before it jerked the reins away and bounded up to the vehicle. The woman came forth, and almost as quickly leaped on the saddle, with the dexterity of those sylphs in German ballads who cling to riders while seated on the crupper. The youth sprang toward her but she stopped him with an imperative wave of the hand.

"List to me. Though but a boy, or because you are young, you have humane feelings. Do not oppose my flight. I am fleeing from a man I love, but I am above all a good Catholic. This man would destroy my soul were I to stay by him, as he is a magician whom God sent a warning to by the lighting. May he profit by it! Tell him this, and bless you for the help given me. Farewell!"

Light as the marsh mist, she was carried away by the gallop of Djerid. On seeing this, the youth could not restrain a cry of surprise, which was the one heard inside the coach.

CHAPTER IV

GILBERT

The alarmed traveler closed the coach door behind him carefully, and looked wistfully round. First he saw the young man, frightened. A flash of lighting enabled him to examine him from head to foot, an operation habitual to him on seeing any new person or thing. This was a springald of sixteen, small, thin and agile; his bold black eyes lacked sweetness but not charm: shrewdness and observation were revealed in his thin, hooked nose, fine lip and projecting cheek bones, while the rounded chin stuck out in token of resolution.

"Was that you screamed just now,—what for?" queried the gentleman.

"The lady from the cab there rode off on the led horse."

The traveler did not make any remark at this hesitating reply; not a word; he rushed to the fore part and saw by the lightning that it was empty.

"Sblood!" he roared in Italian, almost like the thunder peal accompanying the oath.

He looked round for means of pursuit, but one of the coach-horses in chase of Djerid would be a tortoise after a gazelle.

"Still I can find out where she is," he muttered, "unless——"

Quickly and anxiously he drew a small book from his vest pocket, and in a folded paper found a tress of raven hair.

His features became serene, and apparently he was calmed.

"All is well," he said, wiping his streaming face. "Did she say nothing when she started?"

"Yes, that she quitted you not through hate but fear, as she is a Christian, while you—you are an atheist, and miscreant, to whom God sought to give a final warning by this storm."

"If that is all, let us drop the subject."

The last traces of disquiet and discontent fled the man's brow. The youth noticed all this with curiosity mingled with keen observation.

"What is your name, my young friend?" inquired the traveler.

"Gilbert."

"Your Christian name, but——"

"It is my whole name."

"My dear Gilbert, Providence placed you on my road to save me from bother. I know your youth compels you to be obliging: but I am not going to ask anything hard of you—only a night's lodging."

"This rock was my shelter."

"I should like a dwelling better where I could get a good meal and bed."

"We are a league and a half from Pierrefitte, the next village."

"With only two horses that would take two hours. Just think if there is no refuge nearer."

"Taverney Castle is at hand, but it is not an inn."

"Not lived in?"

"Baron Taverney lives there——"

"What is he?"

21

"Father of Mademoiselle Andrea de Taverney——"

"Delighted to hear it," smilingly said the other: "but I want to know the kind of man he is."

"An old nobleman who used to be wealthy."

"An old story. My friend, please take me to Baron Taverney's."

"He does not receive company," said the youth, in apprehension.

"Not welcome a stray gentleman? He must be a bear."

"Much like it. I do not advise your risking it."

"Pooh! The bear will not eat me up alive."

"But he may keep the door closed."

"I will break it in; and unless you refuse to be my guide——"

"I do not; I will show the way."

The traveler took off the carriage lamp, which Gilbert held curiously in his hands.

"It has no light," he said.

"I have fire in my pocket."

"Pretty hard to get fire from flint and steel this weather," observed the youth.

But the other drew a silver case from his pocket, and opening the lid plunged a match into it; a flame sprang up and he drew out the match aflame. This was so sudden and unexpected by the youth, who only knew of tinder and the spark, and not of phosphorus, the toy of science at this period, that he started. He watched the magician restore the case to his pocket with greed. He would have given much to have the instrument.

He went on before with the lighted lamp, while his companion forced the horses to come by his hand on the bridle.

"You appear to know all about this Baron of Taverney, my lad!" he began the dialogue.

"I have lived on his estate since a child."

"Oh, your kinsman, tutor, master?"

At this word the youth's cheek colored up, though usually pale, and he quivered.

"I am no man's servant, sir," he retorted. "I am son of one who was a farmer for the baron, and my mother nursed Mademoiselle Andrea."

"I understand; you belong to the household as foster-brother of the young lady—I suppose she is young?"

"She is sixteen."

He had answered only one of the two questions, and not the one personal to him.

"How did you chance to be on the road in such weather?" inquired the other, making the same reflection as our own.

22

"I was not on the road, but in the cave, reading a book called 'The Social Contract,' by one Rousseau."

"Oh, found the book in the lord's library?" asked the gentleman with some astonishment.

"No, I bought it of a peddler who, like others of his trade, has been hawking good books hereabouts."

"Who told you 'The Contract' was a good book?"

"I found that out by reading it, in comparison with some infamous ones in the baron's library."

"The baron gets indecent books, always costly, in this hole?"

"He does not spend money on them as they are sent him from Paris by his friend the Marshal Duke of Richelieu."

"Oh! of course he does not let his daughter see such stuff?"

"He leaves them about, but Mademoiselle Andrea does not read them," rejoined the youth, drily.

The mocking traveler was briefly silent. He was interested in this singular character, in whom was blended good and evil, shame and boldness.

"How came you to read bad books?"

"I did not know what they were until read; but I kept on as they taught me what I was unaware of. But 'The Contract' told me what I had guessed, that all men are brothers, society badly arranged, and that instead of being serfs and slaves, individuals are equal."

"Whew!" whistled the gentleman, as they went on. "You seem to be hungry to learn?"

"Yes, it is my greatest wish to know everything, so as to rise—"

"To what station?"

Gilbert paused, for having a goal in his mind, he wanted to keep it hidden.

"As far as man may go," he answered.

"So you have studied?"

"How study when I was not rich and was cooped up in Taverney? I can read and write; but I shall learn the rest somehow one of these days."

"An odd boy," thought the stranger.

During the quarter of an hour they had trudged on, the rain had ceased, and the earth sent up the sharp tang replacing the sulphurous breath of the thunderstorms.

"Do you know what storms are?" questioned Gilbert, after deep musing.

"Thunder and lightning are the result of a shock between the electricity in the air and in the earth," he said, smiling.

"I do not follow you," sighed Gilbert.

23

The traveler might have supplied a more lucid explanation but a light glimmered through the trees.

"That is the carriage-gateway of Taverney," said the guide.

"Open it."

"Taverney gate does not open so easily as that."

"Is it a fort? Knock, and louder than that!"

Thus emboldened, the boy dropped the knocker and hung on to the bell, which clanged so lustily that it might be heard afar.

"That is Mahon barking," said the youth.

"Mahon? He names his watchdog after a victory of his friend my Lord Richelieu, I see," remarked the traveler.

"I did not know that. You see how ignorant I am," sighed Gilbert.

These sighs summed up the disappointments and repressed ambition of the youth.

"That is the goodman Labrie coming," said the latter at the sound of footsteps within.

The door opened, but at the sight of the stranger the old servant wanted to slam it.

"Excuse me, friend," interposed the traveler; "don't shut the door in my face. I will risk my travel-stained garb, and I warrant you that I shall not be expelled before I have warmed myself and had a meal. I hear you keep good wine, eh? You ought to know that?"

Labrie tried still to resist, but the other was determined and led the horses right in with the coach, while Gilbert closed the gates in a trice. Vanquished, the servant ran to announce his own defeat. He rushed toward the house, shouting:

"Nicole Legay!"

"Nicole is Mademoiselle Andrea's maid," explained the boy, as the gentleman advanced with his usual tranquility.

A light appeared among the shrubbery, showing a pretty girl.

"What is all this riot; what's wanted of me?" she challenged.

"Quick, my lass," faltered the old domestic, "announce to master that a stranger, overtaken by the storm, seeks hospitality for the night."

Nicole darted so swiftly toward the building as to be lost instantly to sight. Labrie took breath, as he might be sure that his lord would not be taken by surprise.

"Announce Baron Joseph Balsamo," said the traveler; "the similarity in rank will disarm your lord."

At the first step of the portal he looked round for Gilbert, but he had disappeared.

24

CHAPTER V

TAVERNEY AND HIS DAUGHTER

Though forewarned by Gilbert of Baron Taverney's poverty, Baron Balsamo was not the less astonished by the meanness of the dwelling which the youth had dubbed the Castle. On the paltry threshold stood the master in a dressing gown and holding a candle.

Taverney was a little, old gentleman of five-and-sixty, with bright eye and high but retreating forehead. His wretched wig had lost by burning at the candles what the rats had spared of its curls. In his hands was held a dubiously white napkin, which proved that he had been disturbed at table. His spiteful face had a likeness to Voltaire's, and was divided between politeness to the guest and distaste to being disturbed. In the flickering light he looked ugly.

"Who was it pointed out my house as a shelter?" queried the baron, holding up the light to spy the pilot to whom he was eager to show his gratitude, of course.

"The youth bore the name of Gilbert, I believe."

"Ugh! I might have guessed that. I doubted, though, he was good enough for that. Gilbert, the idler, the philosopher!"

This flow of epithets, emphasized threateningly, showed the visitor that little sympathy existed between the lord and his vassal.

"Be pleased to come in," said the baron, after a short silence more expressive than his speech.

"Allow me to see to my coach, which contains valuable property," returned the foreign nobleman.

"Labrie," said Lord Taverney, "put my lord's carriage under the shed, where it will be less uncovered than in the open yard, for some shingles stick to the roof. As for the horses, that is different, for I cannot answer for their supper; still, as they are not yours, but the post's, I daresay it makes no odds."

"Believe me, I shall be ever grateful to your lordship——"

"Oh, do not deceive yourself," said the baron, holding up the candle again to light Labrie executing the work with the aid of the foreign noble; "Taverney is a poor place and a sad one."

When the vehicle was under cover, after a fashion, the guest slipped a gold coin into the servant's hand. He thought it a silver piece, and thanked heaven for the boon.

"Lord forbid I should think the ill of your house that you speak," said Balsamo, returning and bowing as the baron began leading him through a broad, damp antechamber, grumbling:

"Nay, nay, I know what I am talking about; my means are limited. Were you French—though your accent is German, in spite of your Italian title—but never mind—you would be reminded of the rich Taverney."

"Philosophy," muttered Balsamo, for he had expected the speaker would sigh.

The master opened the dining-room door.

"Labrie, serve us as if you were a hundred men in one. I have no other lackey, and he is bad. But I cannot afford another. This dolt has lived with me nigh twenty years without taking a penny of wages, and he is worth it. You will see he is stupid."

"Heartless," Balsamo continued his studies; "unless he is putting it on."

The dining-room was the large main room of a farmhouse which had been converted into the manor. It was so plainly furnished as to seem empty. A small, round table was placed in the midst, on which reeked one dish, a stew of game and cabbage. The wine was in a stone jar; the battered, worn and tarnished plate was composed of three plates, a goblet and a salt dish; the last, of great weight and exquisite work, seemed a jewel of price amid the rubbish.

"Ah, you let your gaze linger on my salt dish?" said the host. "You have good taste to admire it. You notice the sole object presentable here. No, I have another gem, my daughter——"

"Mademoiselle Andrea?"

"Yes," said Taverney, astonished at the name being known; "I shall present you. Come, Andrea, my child, and don't be alarmed."

"I am not, father," said a sonorous but melodious voice as a maiden appeared, who seemed a lovely pagan statue animated.

Though of the utmost plainness, her dress was so tasteful and suitable that a complete outfit from a royal wardrobe would have appeared less rich and elegant.

"You are right," he whispered to his host, "she is a precious beauty."

"Do not pay my poor girl too many compliments," said the old Frenchman carelessly, "for she comes from the nunnery school and may credit them. Not that I fear that she will be a coquette," he continued; "just the other way, for the dear girl does not think enough of herself, and I am a good father, who tries to make her know that coquetry is a woman's first power."

Andrea cast down her eyes and blushed; whatever her endeavor she could not but overhear this singular theory.

"Was that told to the lady at convent, and is that a rule in religious education?" queried the foreigner, laughing.

"My lord, I have my own ideas, as you may have noticed. I do not imitate those fathers who bid a daughter play the prude and be inflexible and obtuse; go mad about honor, delicacy and disinterestedness. Fools! they are like seconds who lead their champion into the lists with all the armor removed and pit him against a man armed at all points. No, my daughter Andrea will not be that sort, though reared in a rural den at Taverney."

Though agreeing with the master about his place, the baron deemed it duty to suggest a polite reproof.

"That is all very well, but I know Taverney; still, be that as it may, and far though we are from the sunshine of Versailles Palace, my daughter is going to enter the society where I once flourished. She will enter with a complete arsenal of weapons forged in my experience and recollections. But I fear, my lord, that the convent has blunted them. Just my luck! my daughter is the only pupil who took the instructions as in earnest and is following the Gospel. Am I not ill-fated?"

"The young lady is an angel," returned Balsamo, "and really I am not surprised at what I hear."

Andrea nodded her thanks, and they sat down at table.

"Eat away, if hungry. That is a beastly mess which Labrie has hashed up."

"Call you partridges so? You slander your feast. Game-birds in May? Shot on your preserves?"

"Mine? My good father left me some, but I got rid of them long ago. I have not a yard of land. That lazybones Gilbert, only good for mooning about, stole a gun somewhere and done a bit of poaching. He will go to jail for it, and a good riddance. But Andrea likes game, and so far, I forgive the boy."

Balsamo contemplated the lovely face without perceiving a twinge, wrinkle or color, as she helped them to the dish, cooked by Labrie, furnished by Gilbert, and maligned by the baron.

"Are you admiring the salt dish again, baron?"

"No, the arm of your daughter."

"Capital! the reply is worthy the gallant Richelieu. That piece of plate was ordered of Goldsmith Lucas by the Regent of Orleans. Subject: the Amours of the Bacchantes and Satyrs—rather free."

More than free, obscene—but Balsamo admired the calm unconcern of Andrea, not blenching as she presented the plate.

"Do eat," said the host; "do not fancy that another dish is coming, for you will be dreadfully disappointed."

"Excuse me, father," interrupted the girl with habitual coolness, "but if Nicole has understood me, she will have made a cake of which I told her the recipe."

"You gave Nicole the recipe of a cake? Your waiting maid does the cooking now, eh? The next thing will be your doing it yourself. Do you find duchesses and countesses playing the kitchen-wench? On the contrary, the king makes omelets for them. Gracious! that I have lived to see women-cooks under my roof. Pray excuse my daughter, baron."

"We must eat, father," rebuked Andrea tranquilly. "Dish up, Legay!" she called out, and the girl brought in a pancake of appetizing smell.

"I know one who won't touch the stuff," cried Taverney, furiously dashing his plate to pieces.

"But the gentleman, perhaps, will," said the lady coldly. "By the way, father, that leaves only seventeen pieces in that set, which comes to me from my mother."

The guest's spirit of observation found plenty of food in this corner of life in the country. The salt dish alone revealed a facet of Taverney's character or rather all its sides. From curiosity or otherwise, he stared at Andrea with such perseverance that she tried to frown him down; but finally she gave way and yielded to his mesmeric influence and command.

Meanwhile the baron was storming, grumbling, snarling and nipping the arm of Labrie, who happened to get into his way. He would have done the same to Nicole's when the baron's gaze fell on her hands.

"Just look at what pretty fingers this lass has," he exclaimed. "They would be supremely pretty only for her kitchen work having made corns at the tips. That is right; perk up, my girl! I can tell you, my dear guest, that Nicole Legay is not a prude like her mistress and compliments do not frighten her."

Watching the baron's daughter, Balsamo noticed the highest disdain on her beauteous face. He harmonized his features with hers and this pleased her, spite of herself, for she looked at him with less harshness, or, better, with less disquiet.

"This girl, only think," continued the poor noble, chucking the girl's chin with the back of his hand, "was at the nunnery with my daughter and picked up as much schooling. She does not leave her mistress a moment. This devotion would rejoice the philosophers, who grant souls to her class."

"Father, Nicole stays with me because I order her to do so," observed Andrea, discontented.

By the curl of the servant's lip, Balsamo saw that she was not insensible to the humiliations from her proud superior. But the expression flitted; and to hide a tear, perhaps, the girl looked aside to a window on the yard. Everything interested the visitor, and he perceived a man's face at the panes.

Each in this curious abode had a secret, he thought; "I hope not to be an hour here without learning Andrea's. Already I know her father's, and I guess Nicole's."

Taverney perceived his short absence of mind.

"What! are you dreaming?" he questioned. "We are all at it, here; but you might have waited for bedtime. Reverie is a catching complaint. My daughter broods; Nicole is wool-gathering; and I get puzzling about that dawdler who killed these birds—and dreams when he kills them. Gilbert is a philosopher, like Labrie. I hope you are not friendly with them? I forewarn you that philosophers do not go down with me."

"They are neither friends nor foes to me," replied the visitor; "I do not have anything to do with them."

"Very good. Zounds, they are scoundrelly vermin, more venomous than ugly. They will ruin the monarchy with their maxims, like 'People can hardly be virtuous under a monarchy;' or, 'Genuine monarchy is an institution devised to corrupt popular manners, and make slaves;' or yet, 'Royal authority may come by the grace of God, but so do plagues and miseries of mankind.' Pretty flummery, all this! What good would a virtuous people be, I beg? Things are going to the bad, since his Majesty spoke to Voltaire and read Diderot's book."

At this Balsamo fancied again to spy the pale face at the window, but it vanished as soon as he fixed his eyes upon it.

"Is your daughter a philosopher?" he asked, smiling.

"I do not know what philosophy is; I only know that I like serious matters," was Andrea's reply.

"The most serious thing is to live; stick to that," said her father.

"But the young lady cannot hate life," said the stranger.

"All depends," she said.

"Another stupid saying," interrupted Taverney. "That is just the nonsense my son talks. I have the misfortune to have a son. The Viscount of Taverney is cornet in the dauphin's horse-guards—a nice boy; another philosopher! The other day he talked to me about doing away with negro slavery. 'What are we to do for sugar?' I retorted, for I like my coffee heavily sweetened, as does Louis XV. 'We must do without sugar to benefit a suffering race.' 'Suffering monkeys!' I returned, 'and that is paying them a compliment.' Whereupon he asserted that all men were brothers! Madness must be in the air. I, brother of a blackamoor!"

"This is going too far," observed Balsamo.

"Of course. I told you I was in luck. My children are—one an angel, the other an apostle. Drink, though my wine is detestable."

"I think it exquisite," said the guest, watching Andrea.

"Then you are a philosopher! In my time we learnt pleasant things; we played cards, fought duels, though against the law; and wasted our time on duchesses and money on opera dancers. That is my story in a nutshell. Taverney went wholly into the opera-house; which is all I sorrow for, since a poor noble is nothing of a man. I look aged, do I not? Only because I am impoverished and dwell in a kennel, with a tattered wig, and gothic coat; but my friend the marshal duke, with his house in town and two hundred thousand a year—he is young, in his new clothes and brushed up perukes—he is still alert, brisk and pleasure-seeking, though ten years my senior, my dear sir, ten years."

"I am astonished that, with powerful friends like the Duke of Richelieu, you quitted the court."

"Only a temporary retreat, and I am going back one day," said the lord, darting a strange glance on his daughter, which the visitor intercepted.

"But, I suppose, the duke befriends your son?"

"He holds the son of his friend in horror, for he is a philosopher, and he execrates them."

"The feeling is reciprocal," observed Andrea with perfect calm. "Clear away, Legay!"

Startled from her vigilant watch on the window, the maid ran back to the table.

"We used to stay at the board to two A. M. We had luxuries for supper, then, that's why! and we drank when we could eat no more. But how can one drink vinegar when there is nothing to eat? Legay, let us have the Maraschino, provided there is any."

"Liqueurs," said Andrea to the maid, who took her orders from the baron thus second-hand.

Her master sank back in his armchair and sighed with grotesque melancholy while keeping his eyes closed.

"Albeit the duke may execrate your son—quite right, too, as he is a philosopher," said Balsamo, "he ought to preserve his liking for you, who are nothing of the kind. I presume you have claims on the king, whom you must have served?"

"Fifteen years in the army. I was the marshal's aid-de-camp, and we went through the Mahon campaign together. Our friendship dates from—let me see! the famous siege of Philipsburg, 1742 to 1743."

"Yes, I was there, and remember you——"

"You remember me at the siege? Why, what is your age?"

30

"Oh, I am no particular age," replied the guest, holding up his glass to be filled by Andrea's fair hand.

The host interpreted that his guest did not care to tell his years.

"My lord, allow me to say that you do not seem to have been a soldier, then, as it is twenty-eight years ago, and you are hardly over thirty."

Andrea regarded the stranger with the steadfastness of deep curiosity; he came out in a different light every instant.

"I know what I am talking about the famous siege, where the Duke of Richelieu killed in a duel his cousin the Prince of Lixen. The encounter came off on the highway, by my fay! on our return from the outposts; on the embankment, to the left, he ran him through the body. I came up as Prince Deux-ponts held the dying man in his arms. He was seated on the ditch bank, while Richelieu tranquilly wiped his steel."

"On my honor, my lord, you astound me. Things passed as you describe."

"Stay, you wore a captain's uniform then, in the Queen's Light Horse Guards, so badly cut up at Fontenoy?"

"Were you in that battle, too?" jeered the baron.

"No, I was dead at that time," replied the stranger, calmly.

The baron stared, Andrea shuddered, and Nicole made the sign of the cross.

"To resume the subject, I recall you clearly now, as you held your horse and the duke's while he fought. I went up to you for an account and you gave it. They called you the Little Chevalier. Excuse me not remembering before, but thirty years change a man. To the health of Marshal Richelieu, my dear baron!"

"But, according to this, you would be upward of fifty."

"I am of the age to have witnessed that affair."

The baron dropped back in the chair so vexed that Nicole could not help laughing. But Andrea, instead of laughing, mused with her looks on the mysterious guest. He seemed to await this chance to dart two or three flaming glances at her, which thrilled her like an electrical discharge. Her arms stiffened, her neck bent, she smiled against her will on the hypnotizer, and closed her eyes. He managed to touch her arm, and again she quivered.

"Do you think I tell a fib in asserting I was at Philipsburg?" he demanded.

"No, I believe you," she replied with a great effort.

"I am in my dotage," muttered Taverney, "unless we have a ghost here."

"Who can tell?" returned Balsamo, with so grave an accent that he subjugated the lady and made Nicole stare.

31

"But if you were living at the Siege, you were a child of four or five."

"I was over forty."

The baron laughed and Nicole echoed him.

"You do not believe me. It is plain, though, for I was not the man I am."

"This is a bit of antiquity," said the French noble. "Was there not a Greek philosopher—these vile philosophers seem to be of all ages—who would not eat beans because they contained souls, like the negress, according to my son? What the deuse was his name?"

"That is the gentleman."

"Why may I not be Pythagoras?"

"Pythagoras," prompted Andrea.

"I do not deny that, but he was not at Philipsburg; or, at any rate, I did not see him there."

"But you saw Viscount Jean Barreaux, one of the Black Horse Musketeers?"

"Rather; the musketeers and the light cavalry took turns in guarding the trenches."

"The day after the Richelieu duel, Barreaux and you were in the trenches when he asked you for a pinch of snuff, which you offered in a gold box, ornamented with the portrait of a belle, but in the act a cannon ball hit him in the throat, as happened the Duke of Berwick aforetimes, and carried away his head."

"Gad! just so! poor Barreaux!"

"This proves that we were acquainted there, for I am Barreaux," said the foreigner.

The host shrank back in fright or stupefaction.

"This is magic," he gasped; "you would have been burnt at the stake a hundred years ago, my dear guest. I seem to smell brimstone!"

"My dear baron, note that a true magician is never burnt or hanged. Only fools are led to the gibbet or pyre. But here is your daughter sent to sleep by our discussions on metaphysics and occult sciences, not calculated to interest a lady."

Indeed, Andrea nodded under irresistible force like a lily on the stalk. At these words she made an effort to repel the subtle fluid which overwhelmed her; she shook her head energetically, rose and tottered out of the room, sustained by Nicole. At the same time disappeared the face glued so often to the window glass on the outside, which Balsamo had recognized as Gilbert's.

"Eureka!" exclaimed Balsamo triumphantly, as she vanished. "I can say it like Archimedes."

"Who is he?" inquired the baron.

32

"A very good fellow for a wizard, whom I knew over two thousand years ago," replied the guest.

Whether the baron thought this boast rather too preposterous, or he did not hear it, or hearing it, wanted the more to be rid of his odd guest, he proposed lending him a horse to get to the nearest posting house.

"What, force me to ride when I am dying to stretch my legs in bed? Do not exaggerate your mediocrity so as to make me believe in a personal ill will."

"On the contrary, I treat you as a friend, knowing what you will incur here. But since you put it this way, remain. Labrie, is the Red-Room habitable?"

"Certainly, my lord, as it is Master Philip's when he is here."

"Give it to the gentleman, since he is bent on being disgusted with Taverney."

"I want to be here to-morrow to testify to my gratitude."

"You can do that easily, as you are so friendly with Old Nick that you can ask him for the stone which turns all things to gold."

"If that is what you want, apply to me direct."

"Labrie, you old rogue, get a candle and light the gentleman to bed," said the baron, beginning to find such a dialogue dangerous at the late hour.

Labrie ordered Nicole to air the Red Room while he hastened to obey. Nicole left Andrea alone, the latter eager for the solitude to nurse her thoughts. Taverney bade the guest good-night, and went to bed.

Balsamo took out his watch, for he recalled his promise to awake Althotas after two hours, and it was a half-hour more. He asked the servant if his coach was still out in the yard, and Labrie answered in the affirmative—unless it had run off of its own volition. As for Gilbert, he had been abed most likely since an hour.

Balsamo went to Althotas after studying the way to the Red Room. Labrie was tidying up the sordid apartment, after Nicole had aired it, when the guest returned.

He had paused at Andrea's room to listen at her door to her playing on the harpsichord to dispel the burden of the influence the stranger had imposed upon her. In a while he waved his hands as in throwing a magic spell, and so it was, for Andrea slowly stopped playing, let her hands drop by her sides, and turned rigidly and slowly toward the door, like one who obeys an influence foreign to will.

Balsamo smiled in the darkness as though he could see through the panels. This was all he wanted to do, for he groped for the banister rail, and went up stairs to his room.

As he departed, Andrea turned away from the door and resumed playing, so that the mesmerist heard the air again from where she had been made to leave off.

Entering the Red Room, he dismissed Labrie; but the latter lingered, feeling in the depths of his pocket till at last he managed to say:

"My lord, you made a mistake this evening, in giving me gold for the piece of silver you intended."

Balsamo looked on the old servingman with admiration, showing that he had not a high opinion of the honesty of most men.

"'And honest,'" he muttered in the words of Hamlet, as he took out a second gold coin to place it beside the other in the old man's hand.

The latter's delight at this splendid generosity may be imagined, for he had not seen so much gold in twenty years. He was retiring, bowing to the floor, when the donor checked him.

"What are the morning habits of the house?" he asked.

"My lord stays abed late, my lord; but Mademoiselle Andrea is up betimes, about six."

"Who sleeps overhead?"

"I, my lord; but nobody beneath, as the vestibule is under us."

"Oh, by the way, do not be alarmed if you see a light in my coach, as an old impotent servant inhabits it. Ask Master Gilbert to let me see him in the morning."

"Is my lord going away so soon?"

"It depends," replied Balsamo, with a smile. "I ought to be at Bar-le-Duc tomorrow evening."

Labrie sighed with resignation, and was about to set fire to some old papers to warm the room, which was damp and there was no wood, when Balsamo stayed him.

"No, let them be; I might want to read them, for I may not sleep."

Balsamo went to the door to listen to the servant's departing steps making the stairs creak till they sounded overhead; Labrie was in his own room. Then he went to the window. In the other wing was a lighted window, with half-drawn curtains, facing him. Legay was leisurely taking off her neckerchief, often peeping down into the yard.

"Striking resemblance," muttered the baron.

The light went out though the girl had not gone to rest. The watcher stood up against the wall. The harpsichord still sounded, with no other noise. He opened his door, went down stairs with caution, and opened the door of Andrea's sitting-room.

Suddenly she stopped in the melancholy strain, although she

34

had not heard the intruder. As she was trying to recall the thrill which had mastered her, it came anew. She shivered all over. In the mirror she saw movement. The shadow in the doorway could only be her father or a servant. Nothing more natural.

But she saw with spiritual eyes that it was none of these.

"My lord," she faltered, "in heaven's name, what want you?"

It was the stranger, in the black velvet riding coat, for he had discarded his silken suit, in which a mesmerist cannot well work his power.

She tried to rise, but could not; she tried to open her mouth to scream, but with a pass of both hands Balsamo froze the sound on her lips.

With no strength or will, Andrea let her head sink on her shoulder.

At this juncture Balsamo believed he heard a noise at the window. Quickly turning, he caught sight of a man's face beyond. He frowned, and, strangely enough, the same impression flitted across the medium's face.

"Sleep!" he commanded, lowering the hands he had held above her head with a smooth gesture, and persevering in filling her with the mesmeric fluid in crushing columns. "I will you to sleep."

All yielded to this mighty will. Andrea leaned her elbow on the musical-instrument case, her head on her hand, and slept.

The mesmerist retired backward, drew the door to, and went back to his room. As soon as the door closed, the face he had seen reappeared at the window; it was Gilbert's.

Excluded from the parlor by his inferior position in Taverney Castle, he had watched all the persons through the evening whose rank allowed them to figure in it. During the supper he had noticed Baron Balsamo gesticulate and smile, and his peculiar attention bestowed on the lady of the house; the master's unheard-of affability to him, and Labrie's respectful eagerness.

Later on, when they rose from table, he hid in a clump of lilacs and snowballs, for fear that Nicole, closing the blinds or in going to her room, should catch him eavesdropping.

But Gilbert had other designs this evening than spying. He waited, without clearly knowing for what. When he saw the light in the maid's window, he crossed the yard on tiptoe and crouched down in the gloom to peer in at the window at Andrea playing the harpsichord.

This was the moment when the mesmerist entered the room.

At this sight, Gilbert started and his ardent gaze covered the magician and his victim.

But he imagined that Balsamo complimented the lady on her

35

musical talent, to which she replied with her customary coldness; but he had persisted with a smile so that she suspended her practice and answered. He admired the grace with which the visitor retired.

Of all the interview which he fancied he read aright, he had understood nothing, for what really happened was in the mind, in silence.

However keen an observer he was, he could not divine a mystery, where everything had passed quite naturally.

Balsamo gone, Gilbert remained, not watching, but contemplating Andrea, lovely in her thoughtful pose, till he perceived with astonishment that she was slumbering. When convinced of this, he grasped his head between his hands like one who fears his brain will burst from the overflow of emotions.

"Oh, to kiss her hand!" he murmured, in a gush of fury. "Oh, Gilbert, let us approach her—I so long to do it."

Hardly had he entered the room than he felt the importance of his intrusion. The timid if not respectful son of a farmer to dare to raise his eyes on that proud daughter of the peers. If he should touch the hem of her dress she would blast him with a glance.

The floor boards creaked under his wary tread, but she did not move, though he was bathed in cold perspiration.

"She sleeps—oh, happiness, she sleeps!" he panted, drawing with irresistible attraction within a yard of the statue, of which he took the sleeve and kissed it.

Holding his breath, slowly he raised his eyes, seeking hers. They were wide open, but still saw not. Intoxicated by the delusion that she expected his visit and her silence was consent, her quiet a favor, he lifted her hand to his lips and impressed a long and feverish kiss.

She shuddered and repulsed him.

"I am lost!" he gasped, dropping the hand and beating the floor with his forehead.

Andrea rose as though moved by a spring under her feet, passed by Gilbert, crushed by shame and terror and with no power to crave pardon, and proceeded to the door. With high-held head and outstretched neck, as if drawn by a secret power toward an invisible goal, she opened the door and walked out on the landing.

The youth rose partly and watched her take the stairs. He crawled after her, pale, trembling and astonished.

"She is going to tell the baron and have me scourged out of the house—no, she goes up to where the guest is lodged. For she would have rung, or called, if she wanted Labrie."

He clenched his fists at the bare idea that Andrea was going

36

into the strange gentleman's room. All this seemed monstrous. And yet that was her end.

That door was ajar. She pushed it open without knocking; the lamplight streamed on her pure profile and whirled golden reflections into her wildly open eyes.

In the center of the room Gilbert saw the baron standing, with fixed gaze and wrinkled brow, and his hand extended in gesture of command, ere the door swung to.

Gilbert's forces failed him; he wheeled round on the stairs, clinging to the rail, but slid down, with his eyes fastened to the last on the cursed panel, behind which was sealed up all his vanished dream, present happiness and future hope.

CHAPTER VI

THE CLAIRVOYANT

Balsamo had gone up to the young lady, whose appearance in his chamber was not strange to him.

"I bade you sleep. Do you sleep?"

Andrea sighed and nodded with an effort.

"It is well. Sit here," and he led her by the hand the youth had kissed to a chair, which she took.

"Now, see!"

Her eyes dilated as though to collect all the luminous rays in the room.

"I did not tell you to see with your eyes," said he, "but with those of the soul."

He touched her with a steel rod which he drew from under his waistcoat. She started as though a fiery dart had transfixed her and her eyes closed instantly; her darkening face expressed the sharpest astonishment.

"Tell me where you are."

"In the Red Room, with you, and I am ashamed and afraid."

"What of? Are we not in sympathy, and do you not know that my intentions are pure, and that I respect you like a sister?"

"You may not mean evil to me, but it is not so as regards others."

"Possibly," said the magician; "but do not heed that," he added in a tone of command. "Are all asleep under this roof?"

"All, save my father who is reading one of those bad books, which he pesters me to read, but I will not."

"Good; we are safe in that quarter. Look where Nicole is."

"She is in her room, in the dark, but I need not the light to see that she is slipping out of it to go and hide behind the yard door to watch."

"To watch you?"

"No."

"Then, it matters not. When a girl is safe from her father and her attendant, she has nothing to fear, unless she is in love——"

"I, love?" she said sneeringly. And shaking her head, she added sadly: "My heart is free."

Such an expression of candor and virginal modesty embellished her features that Balsamo radiantly muttered:

"A lily—a pupil—a seer!" clasping his hands in delight. "But, without loving, you may be loved?"

"I know not; and yet, since I returned from school, a youth has watched me, and even now he is weeping at the foot of the stairs."

"See his face!"

"He hides it in his hands."

"See through them."

"Gilbert!" she uttered with an effort. "Impossible that he would presume to love me!"

Balsamo smiled at her deep disdain, like one who knew that love will leap any distance.

"What is he doing now?"

"He puts down his hands, he musters up courage to mount hither—no, he has not the courage—he flees."

She smiled with scorn.

"Cease to look that way. Speak of the Baron of Taverney. He is too poor to give you any amusements?"

"None."

"You are dying of tedium here; for you have ambition?"

"No."

"Love for your father?"

"Yes; though I bear him a grudge for squandering my mother's fortune so that poor Redcastle pines in the garrison and cannot wear our name handsomely."

"Who is Redcastle?"

"My brother Philip is called the Knight of Redcastle from a property of the eldest son, and will wear it till father's death entitles him to be 'Taverney.'"

38

"Do you love your brother?"

"Dearly, above all else; because he has a noble heart, and would give his life for me."

"More than your father would. Where is Redcastle?"

"At Strasburg in the garrison; no, he has gone—oh, dear Philip!" continued the medium with sparkling eyes in joy. "I see him riding through a town I know. It is Nancy, where I was at the convent school. The torches round him light up his darling face."

"Why torches?" asked Balsamo in amaze.

"They are around him on horseback, and a handsome gilded carriage."

Balsamo appeared to have a guess at this, for he only said:

"Who is in the coach?"

"A lovely, graceful, majestic woman, but I seem to have seen her before—how strange! no, I am wrong—she looks like our Nicole; but as the lily is like the jessamine. She leans out of the coach window and beckons Philip to draw near. He takes his hat off with respect as she orders him, with a smile, to hurry on the horses. She says that the escort must be ready at six in the morning, as she wishes to take a rest in the daytime—oh, it is at Taverney that she means to stop. She wants to see my father! So grand a princess stop at our shabby house! What shall we do without linen or plate?"

"Be of good cheer. We will provide all that."

"Oh, thank you!"

The girl, who had partly risen, fell back in the chair, uttering a profound sigh.

"Regain your strength," said the magician, drawing the excess of magnetism from the beautiful body, which bent as if broken, and the fair head heavily resting on the heaving bosom. "I shall require all your lucidity presently. O, Science! you alone never deceive man. To none other ought man sacrifice his all. This is a lovely woman, a pure angel as Thou knowest who created angels. But what is this beauty and this innocence to me now?—only worth what information they afford. I care not though this fair darling dies, as long as she tells me what I seek. Let all worldly delights perish—love, passion and ecstasy, if I may tread the path surely and well lighted. Now, maiden, that, in a few seconds, my power has given you the repose of ages, plunge once more into your mesmeric slumber. This time, speak for myself alone."

He made the passes which replaced Andrea in repose. From his bosom he drew the folded paper containing the tress of black hair, from which the perfume had made the paper transparent. He laid it in Andrea's hand, saying:

"See!"

39

"Yes, a woman!"

"Joy!" cried Balsamo. "Science is not a mere name like virtue. Mesmer has vanquished Brutus. Depict this woman, that I may recognize her."

"Tall, dark, but with blue eyes, her hair like this, her arms sinewy."

"What is she doing?"

"Racing as though carried off on a fine black horse, flecked with foam. She takes the road yonder to Chalons."

"Good! my own road," said Balsamo. "I was going to Paris, and there we shall meet. You may repose now," and he took back the lock of hair.

Andrea's arms fell motionless again along her body.

"Recover strength, and go back to your harpsichord," said the mesmerist, enveloping her, as she rose, with a fresh supply of magnetism.

Andrea acted like the racehorse which overtaxes itself to accomplish the master's will, however unfair. She walked through the doorway, where he had opened the door, and, still asleep, descended the stairs slowly.

CHAPTER VII

THE MAID AND THE MISTRESS

Gilbert had passed this time in unspeakable anguish. Balsamo was but a man, but he was a strong one, and the youth was weak: He had attempted twenty times to mount to the assault of the guest room, but his trembling limbs gave way under him and he fell on his knees.

Then the idea struck him to get the gardener's ladder and by its means climb up outside to the window, and listen and spy. But as he stooped to pick up this ladder, lying on the grass where he remembered, he heard a rustling noise by the house, and he turned.

He let the ladder fall, for he fancied he saw a shade flit across the doorway. His terror made him believe it, not a ghost—he was a budding philosopher who did not credit them—but Baron Taverney. His conscience whispered another name, and he looked up to the second floor. But Nicole had put out her light, and not another, or a sound came from all over the house—the guest's room excepted.

Seeing and hearing nothing, convinced that he had deluded himself, Gilbert took up the ladder and had set foot on it to climb where he placed it, when Andrea came down from Balsamo's room. With a lacerated heart, Gilbert forgot all to follow her into the parlor where again she sat at the instrument; her candle still burned beside it.

Gilbert tore his bosom with his nails to think that here he had kissed the hem of her robe with such reverence. Her condescension must spring from one of those fits of corruption recorded in the vile books which he had read—some freak of the senses.

But as he was going to invade the room again, a hand came out of the darkness and energetically grasped him by the arm.

"So I have caught you, base deceiver! Try to deny again that you love her and have an appointment with her!"

Gilbert had not the power to break from the clutch, though he might readily have done so, for it was only a girl's. Nicole Legay held him a prisoner.

"What do you want?" he said testily.

"Do you want me to speak out aloud?"

"No, no; be quiet," he stammered, dragging her out of the antechamber.

"Then follow me!" which was what Gilbert wanted, as this was removing Nicole from her mistress.

He could with a word have proved that while he might be guilty of loving the lady, the latter was not an accomplice; but the secret of Andrea was one that enriches a man, whether with love or lucre.

"Come to my room," she said; "who would surprise us there! Not my young lady, though she may well be jealous of her fine gallant! But folks in the secret are not to be dreaded. The honorable lady jealous of the servant,—I never expected such an honor! It is I who am jealous, for you love me no more."

In plainness, Nicole's bedroom did not differ from the others in that dwelling. She sat on the edge of the bed, and Gilbert on the dressing-case, which Andrea had given her maid.

Coming up the stairs, Nicole had calmed herself, but the youth felt anger rise as it cooled in the girl.

"So you love our young lady," began Nicole with a kindling eye. "You have love-trysts with her; or will you pretend you went only to consult the magician?"

"Perhaps so, for you know I feel ambition——"

"Greed, you mean?"

"It is the same thing, as you take it."

"Don't let us bandy words: you avoid me lately."

"I seek solitude——"

"And you want to go up into solitude by a ladder? Beg pardon, I did not know that was the way to it."

Gilbert was beaten in the first defenses.

"You had better out with it, that you love me no longer, or love us both."

"That would only be an error of society, for in some countries men have several wives."

"Savages!" exclaimed the servant, testily.

"Philosophers!" retorted Gilbert.

"But you would not like me to have two beaux on my string?"

"I do not wish tyrannically and unjustly to restrain the impulses of your heart. Liberty consists in respecting free will. So, change your affection, for fidelity is not natural—to some."

Discussion was the youth's strong point; he knew little, but more than the girl. So he began to regain coolness.

"Have you a good memory, Master Philosopher?" said Nicole. "Do you remember when I came back from the nunnery with mistress, and you consoled me, and taking me in your arms, said: 'You are an orphan like me; let us be brother and sister through similar misfortune.' Did you mean what you said?"

"Yes, then; but five months have changed me; I think otherwise at present."

"You mean you will not wed me? Yet Nicole Legay is worth a Gilbert, it seems to me."

"All men are equal; but nature or education improves or depreciates them. As their faculties or acquirements expand, they part from one another."

"I understand that we must part, and that you are a scamp. How ever could I fancy such a fellow?"

"Nicole, I am never going to marry, but be a learned man or a philosopher. Learning requires the isolation of the mind; philosophy that of the body."

"Master Gilbert, you are a scoundrel, and not worth a girl like me. But you laugh," she continued, with a dry smile more ominous than his satirical laugh; "do not make war with me; for I shall do such deeds that you will be sorry, for they will fall on your head, for having turned me astray."

"You are growing wiser; and I am convinced now that you would refuse me if I sued you."

Nicole reflected, clenching her hands and gritting her teeth.

"I believe you are right, Gilbert," she said; "I, too, see my horizon enlarge, and believe I am fated for better things than to be so mean as a philosopher's wife. Go back to your ladder, sirrah, and try not to break your neck, though I believe it would be a blessing to others, and may be for yourself."

Gilbert hesitated for a space in indecision, for Nicole, excited by love and spite, was a ravishing creature; but he had determined to break with her, as she hampered his passion and his aspirations.

"Gone," murmured Nicole in a few seconds.

She ran to the window, but all was dark. She went to her mistress' door, where she listened.

"She is asleep; but I will know all about it to-morrow."

It was broad day when Andrea de Taverney awoke.

In trying to rise, she felt such lassitude and sharp pain that she fell back on the pillow uttering a groan.

"Goodness, what is the matter?" cried Nicole, who had opened the curtains.

"I do not know. I feel lame all over; my chest seems broken in."

"It is the outbreak of the cold you caught last night," said the maid.

"Last night?" repeated the surprised lady; but she remarked the disorder of her room, and added: "Stay, I remember that I felt very tired—exhausted—it must have been the storm. I fell to sleep over my music. I recall nothing further. I went up hither half asleep, and must have thrown myself on the bed without undressing properly."

"You must have stayed very late at the music, then," observed Nicole, "for, before you retired to your bedroom I came down, having heard steps about——"

"But I did not stir from the parlor."

"Oh, of course, you know better than me," said Nicole.

"You must mistake," replied the other with the utmost sweetness: "I never left the seat; but I remember that I was cold, for I walked quite swiftly."

"When I saw you in the garden, however, you walked very freely."

"I, in the grounds?—you know I never go out after dark."

"I should think I knew my mistress by sight," said the maid, doubling her scrutiny; "I thought that you were taking a stroll with somebody."

"With whom would I be taking a stroll?" demanded Andrea, without seeing that her servant was putting her to an examination.

Nicole did not think it prudent to proceed, for the coolness of the hypocrite, as she considered her, frightened her. So she changed the subject.

"I hope you are not going to be sick, either with fatigue or

43

sorrow. Both have the same effect. Ah, well I know how sorrows undermine!"

"You do? Have you sorrows, Nicole?"

"Indeed; I was coming to tell my mistress, when I was frightened to see how queer you looked; no doubt, we both are upset."

"Really!" queried Andrea, offended at the "we both."

"I am thinking of getting married."

"Why, you are not yet seventeen——"

"But you are sixteen and——"

She was going to say something saucy, but she knew Andrea too well to risk it, and cut short the explanation.

"Indeed, I cannot know what my mistress thinks, but I am low-born and I act according to my nature. It is natural to have a sweetheart."

"Oh, you have a lover then! You seem to make good use of your time here."

"I must look forward. You are a lady and have expectations from rich kinsfolks going off; but I have no family and must get into one."

As all this seemed straightforward enough, Andrea forgot what had been offensive in tone, and said, with her kindness taking the reins:

"Is it any one I know? Speak out, as it is the duty of masters to interest themselves in the fate of their servants, and I am pleased with you."

"That is very kind. It is—Gilbert!"

To her high amaze, Andrea did not wince.

"As he loves you, marry him," she replied, easily. "He is an orphan, too, so you are both your own masters. Only, you are both rather young."

"We shall have the longer life together."

"You are penniless."

"We can work."

"What can he do, who is good for nothing?"

"He is good to catch game for master's table, anyway; you slander poor Gilbert, who is full of attention for you."

"He does his duty as a servant——"

"Nay; he is not a servant; he is never paid."

"He is son of a farmer of ours; he is kept and does nothing for it; so, he steals his support. But what are you aiming at to defend so warmly a boy whom nobody attacks?"

"I never thought you would attack him! it is just the other way about!" with a bitter smile.

44

"Something more I do not understand."

"Because you do not want to."

"Enough! I have no leisure for your riddles. You want my consent to this marriage?"

"If you please; and I hope you will bear Gilbert no ill will."

"What is it to me whether he loves you or not? You burden me, miss."

"I daresay," said Nicole, bursting out in anger at last; "you have said the same thing to Gilbert."

"I speak to your Gilbert! You are mad, girl; leave me in peace."

"If you do not speak to him now, I believe the silence will not last long."

"Lord forgive her—the silly jade is jealous!" exclaimed Andrea, covering her with a disdainful look, and laughing. "Cheer up, little Legay! I never looked at your pretty Gilbert, and I do not so much as know the color of his eyes."

Andrea was quite ready to overlook what seemed folly and not pertness; but Nicole felt offended, and did not want pardon.

"I can quite believe that—for one cannot get a good look in the nighttime."

"Take care to make yourself clear at once," said Andrea, very pale.

"Last night, I saw——"

"Andrea!" came a voice from below, in the garden.

"My lord your father," said Nicole, "with the stranger who passed the night here."

"Go down, and say that I cannot answer, as I am not well. I have a stiff neck; and return to finish this odd debate."

Nicole obeyed, as Andrea was always obeyed when commanding, without reply or wavering. Her mistress felt something unusual; though resolved not to show herself, she was constrained to go to the window left open by Legay, through a superior and resistless power.

CHAPTER VIII

THE HARBINGER

The traveler had risen early to look to his coach and learn how Althotas was faring.

All were still sleeping but Gilbert, who peeped through a window of his room over the doorway and spied all the stranger's movements.

The latter was struck by the change which day brought on the scene so gloomy overnight. The domain of Taverney did not lack dignity or grace. The old house resembled a cavern which nature embellishes with flowers, creepers and capricious rookeries, although at night it would daunt a traveler seeking shelter.

When Balsamo returned after an hour's stroll to the Red Castle ruins, he saw the lord of it all leave the house by a side door to cull roses and crush snails. His slender person was wrapped in his flowered dressing-gown.

"My lord," said Balsamo, with the more courtesy as he had been sounding his host's poverty, "allow my excuses with my respects. I ought to wait your coming down, but the aspect of Taverney tempted me, and I yearned to view the imposing ruins and pretty garden."

"The ruins are rather fine," returned the baron; "about all here worth looking at. The castle was my ancestors'; it is called the Red Castle, and we long have borne its name together with Taverney, it being the same barony. Oh, my lord, as you are a magician," continued the nobleman, "you ought with a wave of your wand uprear again the old Red Castle, as well as restore the two thousand odd acres around it. But I suppose you wanted all your art to make that beastly bed comfortable. It is my son's, and he growled enough at it."

"I protest it is excellent, and I want to prove it by doing you some service in return."

Labrie was bringing to his master a glass of spring water on a splendid china platter.

"Here's your chance," said the baron, always jeering; "turn that into wine as the greatest service of all."

Balsamo smiling, the old lord thought it was backing out and took the glass, swallowing the contents at a gulp.

"Excellent specific," said the mesmerist. "Water is the noblest of the elements, baron. Nothing resists it; it pierces stone now, and one of these days will dissolve diamonds."

"It is dissolving me. Will you drink with me. It has the advantage over wine of running freely here. Not like my liquor."

"I might make one useful to you."

"Labrie, a glass of water for the baron. How can the water which I drink daily comprise properties never suspected by me? As the fellow in the play talked prose all his life without knowing it, have I been practising magic for ten years without an idea of it?"

"I do not know about your lordship, but I do know about myself," was the other's grave reply.

Taking the glass from Labrie, who had displayed marvelous celerity, he looked at it steadily.

"What do you see in it, my dear guest?" the baron continued to mock. "I am dying with eagerness. Come, come! a windfall to me, another Red Castle to set me on my legs again."

"I see the advice here to prepare for a visit. A personage of high distinction is coming, self-invited, conducted by your son Philip, who is even now near us."

"My dear lord, my son is on military duty at Strasburg, and he will not be bringing guests at the risk of being punished as a deserter."

"He is none the less bringing a lady, a mighty dame—and, by the way, you had better keep that pretty Abigail of yours at a distance while she stays, as there is a close likeness between them."

"The promised lady guest bears a likeness to my servant Legay? What contradiction!"

"Why not? Once I bought a slave so like Cleopatra that the Romans talked of palming her off for the genuine queen in the triumph in their capital."

"So you are at your old tricks again?" laughed the baron.

"How would you like it, were you a princess, for instance, to see behind your chair a maid who looked your picture, in short petticoats and linen neckerchief."

"Well, we will protect her against that. But I am very pleased with this boy of mine who brings guests without forewarning us!"

"I am glad my forecast affords you pleasure, my dear baron; and, if you meant to properly greet the coming guest, you have not a minute to lose."

The baron shook his head like the most incredulous of beings, and as the two were near the dwelling part of the baron's daughter, he called out to her to impart the stranger's predictions.

This was the call which brought her to the window despite

47

herself, and she saw Balsamo. He bowed deeply to her while fixing his eyes upon her. She reeled and had to catch the sill not to fall.

"Good-morning, my lord," she answered.

She uttered these words at the very moment when Nicole, telling the baron that his daughter would not come, stopped stupefied and with gaping mouth at this capricious contradiction.

Instantly Andrea fell on a chair, all her powers quitting her. Balsamo had gazed on her to the last.

"This is deusedly hard to believe," remarked the baron, "and seeing is believing——"

"Then, see!" said the wonder-worker, pointing up the avenue, from the end of which came galloping at full speed a rider whose steed made the stones rattle under its hoofs.

"Oh, it is indeed——" began the baron.

"Master Philip!" screamed Nicole, standing on tiptoe, while Labrie grunted in pleasure.

"My brother!" cried out Andrea, thrusting her hands through the window.

"This is the commencement," said Balsamo.

"Decidedly you are a magician," said the baron.

A smile of triumph appeared on the mesmerist's lips.

Soon the horse approached plainly, reeking with sweat and smoking, and the rider, a young man in an officer's uniform, splashed with mud up to the countenance, animated by the speed, leaped off and hurried to embrace his father.

"It is I," said Philip of Taverney, seeing the doubt. "I bear a great honor for our house. In an hour Marie Antoinette, Archduchess of Austria and bride of the Dauphin of France, will be here."

The baron dropped his arms with as much humility as he had shown sarcasm and irony, and turned to Balsamo for his forgiveness.

"My lord," said the latter, bowing, "I leave you with your son, from whom you have been long separated and to whom you must have a great deal to say."

Saluting Andrea, who rushed to meet her brother in high delight, Balsamo drew off, beckoning Nicole and Labrie, who disappeared with him under the trees.

CHAPTER IX

THE KNIGHT OF REDCASTLE

Philip of Taverney, Knight of Redcastle, did not resemble his sister, albeit he was as handsome for a man as she was lovely for a woman.

Andrea's embrace of him was accompanied by sobs revealing all the importance of this union to her chaste heart. He took her hand and his father's, and led them into the parlor, where he sat by their sides.

"You are incredulous, father, and you, sister, surprised. But nothing can be more true than that this illustrious princess will be here shortly. You know that the Archduchess made her entry into our realm at Strasburg? As we did not know the exact hour of her arrival, the troops were under arms early, and I was sent out to scout. When I came up with the royal party, the lady herself put her head out of the coach window, and hailed me. My fatigue vanished as by enchantment. The dauphiness is young like you, dear, and beautiful as the angels."

"Tell me, you enthusiast," interrupted the baron, "does she resemble any one you have seen here before?"

"No one could resemble her—stay, come to think of it—why, Nicole has a faint likeness—but what led you to suggest that?"

"I had it from a magician, who at the same time foretold your coming."

"The guest?" timidly inquired Andrea.

"Is he the stranger who discreetly withdrew when I arrived?"

"The same; but continue your story, Philip."

"Perhaps we had better make something ready," hinted the lady.

"No," said her father, staying her; "the more we do, the more ridiculous we shall appear."

"I returned to the city with the news, and all the military marched to receive the new princess. She listened absently to the governor's speech and said suddenly: 'What is the name of this young gentleman who was sent to meet me?' And her governess wrote on her tablets my name, Chevalier Philip Taverney Redcastle. 'Sir,' she said, 'if you have no repugnance to accompany me to Paris, your superior will oblige me by relieving you of your military duties here, for I made a vow to attach to my service the first French gentleman met by me in setting foot in France; and to make him

49

happy, and his family the same, in case princes have the power to do so.'"

"What delightful words!" said Andrea, rubbing her hands.

"Hence, I rode at the princess's coach door to Nancy, through which we marched by torchlight. She called me to her to say that she meant to stop a while at Taverney, though I said our house was not fit to receive so mighty a princess.

"'The sweeter will be the welcome, then, the more plain but the more cordial,' she replied. 'Poor though Taverney may be, it can supply a bowl of milk to the friend who wishes to forget for a time that she is the Princess of Austria and the Bride of France.' Respect prevented me debating further. So I have ridden ahead."

"Impossible," said Andrea; "however kind the princess may be, she would never be content with a glass of milk and a bunch of flowers."

"And if she were," went on Taverney, "she would not tolerate my chairs which break one's back, and my ragged tapestry offending the sight. Devil take capricious women! France will be prettily governed by a featherbrain, who has such whims. Plague take such a token of a singular reign!"

"Oh, father! how can you talk so of a princess who floods our house with favors?"

"Who dishonors me!" returned the old noble. "Who was thinking about Taverney?—not a soul. My name slept under Redcastle ruins not to come forth till I arranged the fit time; and here comes the freak of a royal babe to pull us out into public, dusty, tattered and beggarly. The newspapers, always on the lookout for food for fun, will make a pretty comic talk of the brilliant princess's visit to the Taverney hovel. But, death of my life! an idea strikes me. I know history, and of the Count of Medina setting fire to his palace to win a queen's attention. I will burn down my kennel for a bonfire to the Dauphin's bride."

As nimble as though twenty once more, the old peer ran into the kitchen and plucking a brand, hurried out and over to the barn, but as he was nearing the trusses of forage, Balsamo sprang forth and clutched his arm.

"What are you about, my lord?" he asked, wrenching away the flambeau. "The Archduchess of Austria is no Constable of Bourbon, a traitor, whose presence so fouls a dwelling that it must be purified by fire."

The old noble paused, pale and trembling and not smiling as usual.

"Go and change your gown, my lord, for something more seemly," continued the mysterious guest. "When I knew the Baron of Taverney at Philipsburg Siege, he wore the Grand Cross of St. Louis. I know not of any suit that does not become rich and stylish under the ribbon of that order. Take it coolly: her highness will be kept so busy that she will not notice whether your house be new or old, dull or dazzling. Be hospitable, as a noble is bound to be. Never forestall vexations, my lord. Every dog has his day."

Taverney obeyed with the resignation he had previously shown and went to join his children, who were hunting for him, uneasy at his absence. The magician silently retired like one engaged in a piece of work.

CHAPTER X

MARIE ANTOINETTE

As Balsamo had warned them, there was no time to lose. On the high road, commonly so peaceful, resounded a great tumult of coaches, horses and voices.

Three carriages stopped at the door, held open by Gilbert, whose distended eyes and feverish tremor denoted the sharpest emotion at so much magnificence. The principal coach, loaded with gilding and mythological carvings, was no less mud-spattered and dusty than the others.

A score of brilliant young noblemen ranked themselves near this coach, out of which was assisted a girl of sixteen by a gentleman clad in black, with the grand sash of the St. Louis order under his coat. She wore no hair powder, but this plainness had not prevented the hairdresser building up her tresses a foot above her forehead.

Marie Antoinette Josepha, for it was she, brought into France a fame for beauty not always owned by princesses destined to share the throne of that realm. Without being fine, her eyes took any expression she liked; but particularly those so opposite as mildness and scorn; her nose was well shaped; her upper lip pretty; but the lower one, the aristocratic inheritance of seventeen kaisers, too thick and protruding, even drooping, did not suit the pretty visage, except when it wanted to show ire or indignation.

On this occasion, Marie Antoinette wore her womanly look and womanly smile, more, that of a happy woman. If possible, she did not mean to be the royal princess till the following day. The sweetest calm reigned on her face; the most charming kindness enlivened her eyes.

She was robed in white silk, and her handsome bare arms supported a heavy lace mantle.

She refused the arm of the gentleman in black, and freely advanced, snuffing the air, and casting glances around as though wishful to enjoy brief liberty.

"Oh, the lovely site! What fine old trees! and the pretty little house!" she ejaculated. "How happy they must dwell in this nice air and under these trees which hide us in so well."

Philip Taverney appeared, followed by Andrea, giving her arm to her father, wearing a fine royal blue velvet coat, last vestige of former splendor. Andrea wore a ruddy gray silk dress and had her hair in long plaits. Following Balsamo's hint, the baron had donned the insignia of the Knightly Order.

"Your highness," said Philip, pale with emotion and noble in his sorrow, "allow me the honor to present Baron de Taverney, Red Castle, my sire, and Mademoiselle Claire Andrea, my sister."

The old noble bowed low with the style of one who knew how queens should be saluted; his daughter displayed all the grace of elegant timidity, and the most flattering politeness of sincere respect.

Regarding the pair, and recalling what Philip had stated on their poverty, Marie Antoinette felt with them in their suffering.

"Your highness does Taverney Castle too much honor," said the baron; "so humble a place is nowise worthy to harbor such beauty and nobility."

"I know that I am at the doors of an old soldier of France," was the royal response, "and my mother, the Empress Maria Theresa, who often went to the wars, says that in your kingdom the richest in glory are oft the poorest in gold."

With ineffable grace she held out her hand to Andrea, who knelt to kiss it.

The dauphiness suddenly extricated the baron from his terror about harboring the great number of the retinue.

"My lords and gentlemen," she said, "it is not for you to bear the fatigue of my whims or enjoy the privileges of a royal princess. Pray, await me here; in half an hour I shall return. Come with me, Langenshausen," she said to the countess of that house who was her duenna. "Follow me, my lord," she added to the gentleman in black.

His plain attire was of remarkable style; he was a handsome person of thirty years and smooth manners; he stood aside to let the princess go by. She took Andrea to her side and motioned Philip to follow. The baron fell into place next the fashionable gentleman.

"So you are a Taverney of Redcastle?" queried this fop, as he preened his fine honiton lace ruffles with aristocratic impertinence.

"Am I to answer a gentleman or a nobleman?" returned the baron with equal sauciness.

"Prince will do," said the other, "or eminence."

"Well, yes, your eminence, I am a real Taverney," replied the poor nobleman, without dropping the insolent tone he usually kept.

The prince had the tact of great lords, for he readily perceived that he was not dealing with a rustic hobbledehoy.

"I suppose this is your summer residence?" he continued.

"My residence in all seasons," replied the baron, desiring to finish with this examination, but accompanying his answers with deep bows.

Philip kept turning round to his father with uneasiness; the house seemed towering up to exhibit more and more of their penury. The baron was just holding his hand toward the sill, deserted by visitors, when the dauphiness turned to him, saying:

"Excuse me not going indoors, but these shady spots are so pleasant that I could pass my life beneath them. I am rather weary of interiors. For a fortnight I have been received under roofs—and I like open air, flowers and the shade of foliage. Might I not have a drink of milk in this bower?"

"What a mean refreshment, your highness!" faltered the baron.

"I prefer it, with new-laid eggs, my lord. Such formed my feasts at Schoenbrunn."

All of a sudden, Labrie, puffed up with pride in a showy livery, and holding a damask napkin, appeared in the jessamine hung arbor which the archduchess was eyeing covetously.

"The refreshment is ready for your royal highness," he said with a neat mingling of respect and serenity.

"Am I housed by an enchanter?" exclaimed the princess, darting into the bower.

The perturbed baron forgot etiquette to leave the gentleman in black and run after his guest.

Philip and Andrea looked at each other with even more anxiety than astonishment.

Under the twining clematis, jessamine and honeysuckle an oval table was set, dazzling from the whiteness of the damask cloth and the carved bullion plate upon it. Ten sets of silver awaited as many guests. A choice but strange collation attracted the visitor's gaze. Foreign fruit preserved in sugar; cake and crackers from Aleppo and Madeira, oranges and melons of uncommon size, set in large vases.

The richest and noblest wines glittered in all hues of ruby and topaz in four cut-glass Persian decanters. The milk asked for filled a crystal cup.

"But you must have expected me, since in no ten minutes which I have been here could this sumptuous spread be placed." And the princess glanced at Labrie as much as to say: "With only one servant, too?"

"I did expect your royal highness," faltered the baron; "of your coming being apprised."

"If your son did not inform you by letter, then it must have been some fairy—I suppose, the godmother of your daughter."

"It was not so much a fairy, as a magician," said Taverney, offering a seat to the princess. "I do not know anything about how he has done this, as I do not dabble in magic, but I owe it to him that I am fitly entertaining your highness."

"Then I will have none of it. It is contrary to the faith—but his eminence is going to sin, with that liver-pie!"

"We are rather too worldly, we princes of the Church," replied the gentleman in black, "to believe the celestial wrath poisons victuals, and we are too human to visit ill on magicians who provide such good things."

"But I assure your eminence that this is a real sorcerer who conjured up this board ready spread, and who may have produced the gold of this service in the same manner."

"Does he know of the stone which changes all into gold?" questioned the churchman, with his eyes kindling with covetousness.

"This pleases the cardinal, who has passed his life seeking the philosopher's stone," said the princess.

"I own that I find nothing more interesting than supernatural things," returned the prince; "nothing more curious than what's impossible."

"So I have hit the vital spot, have I?" said the archduchess. "Every great man has a mystery, particularly when he is a diplomatist. Let me warn your eminence that I also am a witch, and that I can see into matters—if not curious and impossible—incredible."

This was an incomprehensible enigma to all but the cardinal, for he was plainly embarrassed. The gentle eye of the Austrian had flared with one of those fires denoting a storm gathering. But there was no thunderous outbreak, for she went on, restraining herself:

"Come my lord of Taverney, make the feast complete by producing your magician. Where is he? In what box have you put Old Hocus Pocus?"

"Labrie, notify Baron Joseph Balsamo that her Royal Highness the Dauphiness desires to see him."

"Balsamo?" repeated the high lady, as the valet started off. "What an odd name!"

"I fancy I have heard it before," murmured the cardinal.

Five minutes passed with none thinking of breaking the stillness, when Andrea shuddered, for she heard before any other the step beneath the foliage. The branches were parted and right in front of Marie Antoinette, Joseph Balsamo appeared.

CHAPTER XI

A MARVEL OF MAGIC

Humble was Balsamo's bow; but immediately raising his intelligent and expressive brow, he fixed his clear eye, though with respect, on the chief guest, silently waiting for her to question him.

"If you are the person Baron Taverney has mentioned, pray draw nigh that we may see what a magician is like."

Balsamo came a step nearer and bowed to Marie Antoinette.

"So you make a business of foretelling?" said the latter, sipping the milk while regarding the new comer with more curiosity than she liked to betray.

"I make no business of it, but I do foretell, please your royal highness?" was the answer.

"Educated in an enlightened faith, we place faith solely in the mysteries of our religion."

"Undoubtedly they are worthy of veneration," responded the other dialoguist with a profound congé. "But the Cardinal de Rohan here, though Prince of the Church, will tell you that they are not the only ones worthy of respect."

The cardinal started, for his title had not been announced.

Not appearing to notice this revelation, Marie Antoinette pursued:

"But you must allow that they alone cannot be controverted."

"There can be fact as well as faith," replied Balsamo, with the same respect but with the same firmness.

"You speak a trifle darkly, my lord Baron of Magic. I am at

heart a good Frenchwoman, but not in mind, and do not yet understand all the fineness of the language. They say I shall soon pick it up, even to the puns. Meanwhile, I must urge you to speak more plainly if you want my comprehension."

"I ask your highness to let me dwell obscure," said the baron, with a melancholy smile. "I should feel too much regret to reveal to so great a princess a future not equal to her hopes."

"Dear me, this is becoming serious," said Marie Antoinette, "and Abracadabra whets my curiosity in order to make me beg my fortune to be told."

"Heaven forbid my being forced into it," observed Balsamo coldly.

"Of course, for you would be put to much pains for little result," laughed the princess.

But her merriment died away without a courtier's echoing it; all suffered the influence of the mystic man who claimed the whole attention.

"Still it was you foretold my coming to Taverney?" said the mighty lady, to which Balsamo silently bowed. "How was the trick done, my lord baron?"

"Simply by looking into a glass of water, my liege lady," was the old noble's answer.

"If that be truly your magic mirror, it is guileless at any rate; may your words be as clear!"

The cardinal smiled, and the master of the place said:

"Your highness will not have to take lessons in punning."

"Nay, my dear host, do not flatter me, or flatter me better. It seems to me it was a mild quip; but, my lord," she resumed, turning toward Balsamo by that irresistible attraction drawing us to a danger, "if you can read the future in a glass for a gentleman, may you not read it for a lady in a decanter?"

"Perfectly; but the future is uncertain, and I should shrink from saddening your royal highness if a cloud veiled it, as I have already had the honor to say."

"Do you know me beforetimes? Where did you first see me?"

"I saw you as a child beside your august mother, that mighty queen."

"Empress, my lord."

"Queen by heart and mind, but such have weaknesses when they think they act for their daughters' happiness."

"I hope history will not record one single weakness in Maria Theresa," retorted the other.

"Because it does not know what is known solely to your highness, her mother and myself."

56

"Is there a secret among us three?" sneered the lady. "I must hear it."

"In Schoenbrunn Palace is the Saxony Cabinet, where the empress sits in private. One morning, about seven, the empress not being up, your highness entered this study, and perceived a letter of hers, open, on the writing-table."

The hearer blushed.

"Reading it, your highness took up a pen and struck out the three words beginning it."

"Speak them aloud!"

"'My dear Friend.'"

Marie Antoinette bit her lips as she turned pale.

"Am I to tell to whom the letter was addressed?" inquired the seer.

"No, no, but you may write it."

The soothsayer took out his memorandum book fastening with a gilt clasp, and with a kind of pencil from which flowed ink, wrote on a leaf. Detaching this page, he presented it to the princess, who read:

"The letter was addressed to the marchioness of Pompadour, mistress of King Louis XV."

The dauphiness' astounded look rose upon this clearly speaking man, with pure and steady voice, who appeared to tower over her although he bowed lowly.

"All this is quite true," she admitted, "and though I am unaware how you could learn this secret, I am bound to allow, before all, that you speak true."

"Then I may retire upon this innocent proof of my science."

"Not so, my lord baron," said the princess, nettled; "the wiser you are, the more I long for your forecast. You have only spoken of the past, and I demand the future."

Her feverish agitation could not escape the bystanders.

"Let me at least consult the oracle, to learn whether the prediction may be revealed."

"Good or bad, I must hear it!" cried Marie Antoinette with growing irritation. "I shall not believe it if good, taking it for flattery; but bad, I shall regard it as a warning, and I promise any way not to bear you ill will. Begin your witchcraft."

Balsamo took up the decanter with a broad mouth and stood it in a golden saucer. He raised it thus high up, and, after looking at it shook his head.

"I cannot speak. Some things must not be told to princes," he said.

"Because you have nothing to say?" and she smiled scornfully.

Balsamo appeared embarrassed, so that the cardinal began to laugh in his face and the baron grumbled.

"My wizard is worn out," he said. "Nothing is to follow but the gold turning into dry leaves, as in the Arabian tale."

"I would have preferred the leaves to all this show; for there is no shame in drinking from a nobleman's pewter goblet, while a dauphiness of France ought not to have to use the thimble-rigging cup of a charlatan."

Balsamo started erect as if a viper had bitten him.

"Your highness shall know your fate, since your blindness drives you to it."

These words were uttered in a voice so steady but so threatening that the hearers felt icy chills in their veins. The lady turned pale visibly.

"Do not listen to him, my daughter," whispered the old governess in German to her ward.

"Let her hear, for since she wanted to know, know she shall!" said Balsamo in the same language, which doubled the mystery over the incident. "But to you alone, lady."

"Be it so," said the latter. "Stand back!"

"I suppose this is just an artifice to get a private audience?" sneered she, turning again to the magician.

"Do not try to irritate me," said he; "I am but the instrument of a higher Power, used to enlighten you. Insult fate and it will revenge itself, well knowing how. I merely interpret its moves. Do not fling at me the wrath which will recoil on yourself, for you can not visit on me the woes of which I am the sinister herald."

"Then there are woes?" said the princess, softened by his respectfulness and disarmed by his apparent resignation.

"Very great ones."

"Tell me all. First, will my family live happy?"

"Your misfortunes will not reach those you leave at home. They are personal to you and your new family. This royal family has three members, the Duke of Berry, the Count of Provence, and the Count of Artois. They will all three reign."

"Am I to have no son?"

"Sons will be among your offspring, but you will deplore that one should live and the other die."

"Will not my husband love me?"

"Too well. But his love and your family's support will fail you."

"Those of the people will yet be mine."

"Popular love and support—the ocean in a calm. Have you seen it in a storm?"

"I will prevent it rising, or ride upon the billows."

"The higher its crest, the deeper the abyss."

"Heaven remains to me."

"Heaven does not save the heads it dooms."

"My head in danger? Shall I not reign a queen?"

"Yes—but would to God you never did."

The princess smiled disdainfully.

"Hearken, and remember," proceeded Balsamo. "Did you remark the subject on the tapestry of the first room you entered on French ground? The Massacre of the Innocents; the ominous figures must have remained in your mind. During that storm, did you see that the lightning felled a tree on your left, almost to crush your coach? Such presages are not to be interpreted but as fatal ones."

Letting her head fall upon her bosom, the princess reflected for a space before asking:

"How will those three die?"

"Your husband the king will die headless; Count Provence, legless; and Artois heartless."

"But myself? I command you to speak, or I shall hold all this as a paltry trick. Take care, my lord, for the daughter of Maria Theresa is not to be sported with—a woman who holds in hand the destinies of thirty millions of souls. You know no more, or your imagination is exhausted."

Balsamo placed the saucer and the decanter on a bench in the darkest nook of the arbor, which thus resembled a pythoness' cave; he led her within the gloom.

"Down on your knees," he said, alarming her by the action; "for you will seem to be imploring God to spare you the terrible outcome which you are to view."

Mechanically the princess obeyed, but as Balsamo touched the crystal with his magic wand, some frightful picture no doubt appeared in it, for the princess tried to rise, reeled, and screamed as she fell in a swoon.

They ran to her.

"That decanter?" she cried, when revived.

The water was limpid and stainless.

The wonder-worker had disappeared!

CHAPTER XII

TAVERNEY'S PROSPECTS BRIGHTEN

The first to perceive the archduchess's fainting fit, was Baron Taverney who was on the lookout from being most uneasy about the interview. Hearing the scream and seeing Balsamo dart out of the bower he ran up.

The first word of the dauphiness was to call for the bewitched decanter: her second to bid no harm to be done the sorcerer. It was time to say it, for Philip Taverney had rushed after the latter.

She attributed the swoon to fever from the journey. She talked of sleeping for some hours, in Andrea's room, but the Governor of Strasburg arrived in hot haste with a dispatch from Versailles, and she had to receive Lord Stainville, who was brother in-law of the prime minister.

Opening this missive, the princess read:

"The court presentation of Lady Dubarry is fixed on, if she can find a patroness, which we hope will not be. But the surest method of blocking the project is to have your royal highness here, in whose presence none will dare suggest such an offense."

"Very good. My horses must be put to. We depart at once."

Cardinal Rohan looked at Lord Stainville as if for an explanation of this abrupt change.

"The dauphin is in a hurry to see his wife," whispered the latter with such cunning that the churchman thought it had slipped his tongue and was satisfied with it.

Andrea had been trained by her father to understand royal freaks; she was not surprised at the contradiction. So the lady saw only smoothness on her face as she turned to her, saying:

"Thank you; your welcome has deeply touched me. Baron, you are aware that I made the vow to benefit the first French gentleman and his family, whom I should meet on the frontier. But I am not going to stop at this point, and Mademoiselle Andrea is not to be forgotten. Yes, I wish her to be my maid of honor. The brother will defend the king in the army, the sister will serve me; the father will instruct the first in loyalty, the other in virtue. I shall have enviable servitors, do you not agree?" she continued to Philip, who was kneeling. "I will leave one of my carriages to bring you in my train. Governor, name somebody to accompany my carriage for the Taverneys, and notify that it is of my household."

"Beausire," called out the governor, "come forward."

A sharp-eyed cavalier, some twenty-four years old, rode out from the escort and saluted.

"Set a guard over Baron Taverney's coach, and escort it."

"We shall meet soon again, then," said the princess with a smile. "Let us be off, my lords and gentlemen."

In a quarter of an hour, all remaining of the whirling cavalcade was the carriage left in the avenue and the guardsman whose horse was cropping the dandelions.

"Where is the magician?" inquired Taverney.

"Gone, too, my lord."

"I never heard of the like—leaving all that valuable plate."

"He left a note which Gilbert is fretting to deliver."

"Father," said Andrea, "I know what is tormenting you. You know I have thirty gold pieces, and the diamond-set watch Queen Maria Leczinska gave my mother."

"That is well," said the baron, "but keep it, though we must hunt up means for a handsome robe for your court presentation. Hush! here is Labrie."

"The note, my lord, which was given Gilbert by the strange gentleman."

The baron snatched it from the servant and read in an undertone:

"My Lord: Since an august hand touched this service of plate under your roof, it belongs to your lordship, and I pray you to keep it as a memento, and sometimes to remember, your grateful guest,

Balsamo."

"Labrie, is there a good goldsmith at Bar-le-Duc?"

"Yes, my lord, the one who mended our young lady's jewelry."

"Put aside the cup the princess used, and pack up the rest of the plate in our carriage. And then, haste to the cellar and serve that officer with all the liquor left. Come, come, Andrea, courage! We are going to court, a splendid place where the sun never fails. You are naturally lovely and have only to set the gem becomingly to outshine them all."

Nicole followed Andrea to her room.

"I am off to arrange my titles of nobility and proofs of service," continued the baron, trotting to his room briskly. "We shall be off from this den in an hour; do you hear, Andrea? And we leave by the golden gates, too. What a trump that magician is! Really, I have become as superstitious as the devil's own. But make haste, Labrie!" he cried to his man groping about in the cellar.

"I can't get on faster, master—we have not a candle left."

"It is plain that we are getting out in the right time," thought the baron.

CHAPTER XIII

NICOLE'S DOWER

Nicole aided her young mistress in her traveling preparations with ardor which speedily dissipated the cloud risen that morning between maid and mistress. The latter smiled as she found that she would have no need to scold her.

"She is a good, devoted girl and grateful," she mused; "only she has weaknesses, like all womankind. Let us forget."

On her part, Nicole was not the girl not to watch her mistress' face, and she saw the kindliness increasing.

"I was a fool nearly to get into a scrape with her for that rascal Gilbert, when she is going to town, where everybody makes a fortune."

"Put my lace in my box. Stop! I gave you that box, I remember; and you will want it, as you are going to set up housekeeping."

"Oh, my lady," said Nicole, reddening, and replying merrily, "my wedding garments will be easily kept in no great space."

"How so? I want you to be well off when you wed."

"Have you found me a rich match?"

"No, but a dower of twenty-five gold pieces."

"You would give me such a treasure!" Emotion followed her surprise, and tears gushed into her eyes as she kissed Andrea's hand.

Nicole began to think that Gilbert had rejected her from fear of poverty, and that now she had funds, she had better marry the ambitious spark to whom she would appear more desirable. But a germ of pride mingled with the generosity, as she wanted to humble one who had jilted her.

"It looks as though you really loved your Gilbert," observed the lady. "How incredible for something in the lad to please you. I must have a look at this lady-killer next time I see him."

Nicole eyed her with lingering doubt. Was this deep hypocrisy or perfect ignorance?

"Is Gilbert coming to Paris with us?" she inquired, to be settled on the point.

"What for? he is not a domestic and is not fitted for a Parisian establishment. The loungers about Taverney are like the birds which can pick up a living on their own ground; but in Paris a hanger-on would cost too much, and we cannot tolerate that. If you marry him, you must stay here. I give you an hour to decide between my household or your husband's. I detest these connubial details and will not have a married servant. In any case, here is the money; marry, and have it as dower; follow me, and it is your first two years' wages, in advance."

Nicole took the purse from her hand and kissed it.

The lady watched her go away and muttered: "She is happy, for she loves."

Nicole in five minutes was at the window of Gilbert's room, at the back of which he was turning over his things.

"I have come to tell you that my mistress wants me to go with her to Paris."

"Good!" said the young man.

"Unless I get married and settled here."

"Are you thinking still of that?" he asked, without any feeling.

"Particularly, since I am rich from my lady dowering me," and she showed the bright gold.

"A pretty sum," he said drily.

"That is not all. My lord is going to be rich. He will rebuild the castle, and the house will have to be guarded——"

"By the happy mate of Nicole," suggested Gilbert with irony, not sufficiently wrapped up not to wound the girl, though she contained herself. "I refuse the offer, for I am not going to bury myself here when Paris is open to me also. Paris is my stage, do you understand?"

"And mine, and I understand you. You may not regret me; but you will fear me, and blush to see to what you drive me. I longed to be an honest woman, but, when I was leaning over the verge, you repulsed me instead of pulling me back. I am slipping and I shall fall, and heaven will ask you to account for the loss. Farewell, Gilbert!"

The proud girl spun round without anger now, or impatience, having exhausted all her generosity of soul.

Gilbert quietly closed the window and resumed the mysterious business which Nicole's coming had interrupted.

She returned to her mistress with a deliberate air.

"I shall not marry," she said.

"But your great love?"

63

"It is not worth the kindness your ladyship has done me. I belong to you and shall ever so belong. I know the mistress which heaven gave me; but I might never know the master whom I give myself."

Andrea was touched by this display of emotion, which she was far from expecting in the maid. She was of course ignorant that Nicole was making her a pillow to fall back upon. She smiled to believe a human creature was better than she estimated.

"You are doing right," she said. "If bliss befalls me, you shall have your share. But did you settle with your sweetheart?"

"I told him that I would have no more to do with him."

She was restored to her former suspicions, and it was fated that the two should never understand each other—one with her diamond purity and the other with her tendency to evil.

Meanwhile, the baron had packed up his scanty valuables, and Labrie shouldered the half-empty trunk, containing them, to accompany his master out to where the corporal of guards was finishing the wine to the last drop.

This soldier gallant had remarked the fine waist and pretty limbs of Nicole, and he was prowling round the pool to see her again. He was drawn from his reverie by the baron calling for his carriage. Saluting him, he called in a ringing voice for the driver to come up the avenue. Labrie put the trunk on the rack behind with unspeakable pride and delight.

"I am going to ride in the royal coaches," he muttered.

"But up behind, my old boy," corrected Beausire, with a patronizing smile.

"Who is to keep Taverney if you take Labrie, father?" inquired Andrea.

"That lazy philosopher, Gilbert; with his gun he will have ample to eat, I warrant, for there is plenty of game at Taverney."

Andrea looked at Nicole, who laughed and added:

"He is a sly dog; he will not starve."

"Leave him a trifle," suggested Andrea.

"It will spoil him. He is bad enough now. If he wants anything we will send him help."

"He would not accept money, my lord."

"Your Gilbert must be pretty proud, then?"

"Thank heaven, he is no longer my Gilbert!"

"Deuse take Gilbert, whoever's property he is," said Taverney, to cut short what annoyed his selfishness. "The coach is stopping the way; get in, daughter."

Andrea gave the house a farewell glance and stepped into the vehicle. The baron installed himself next her; Labrie in his glorious livery and Nicole got upon the box, for the driver turned himself into a postillion and bestrode one of the horses.

"But the corporal?" queried the baron.

"I ride my charger," responded Beausire, ogling Nicole, who colored up with pleasure at having so soon replaced the rustic lad with a stylish cavalier.

Gilbert stood with his hat off at the gate, and, without seeming to see, looked on Andrea alone. She was bending out of the opposite window to watch the house to the last.

"Stop a bit," ordered Baron Taverney; "hark you, master idler," he said to Gilbert, "you ought to be a happy dog to be left by yourself, as suits a true philosopher, with nobody to bother you or upbraid you. Don't let the house catch afire while you brood, and take care of the watchdog. Go ahead, coachman!"

Gilbert slammed the gates, groaning for want of oil, and ran back to his little room, where he had his little bundle ready. It also contained his savings in a silver piece.

Mahon was howling when he came out, and straining at his chain.

"Am I not cast off like a dog? why should not a dog be cast off like a man? No, you shall at least be free to seek your livelihood like myself."

The liberated dog ran round the house, but finding all the doors closed, he bounded the ruins.

"Now we are going to see who fares the better—man or dog," said Gilbert. "Farewell, mansion where I have suffered and where all despised me! where bread was cast to me with the reproach that I was stealing it by making no return. Farewell—no, curses on you! My heart leaps with joy at no longer being jailed up in your walls. Forever be accursed, prison, hell, lair of tyrants!"

CHAPTER XIV

THE OUTCAST'S LUCK

But in his long journey to Paris he had often to regret this abode which he had cursed. Sore, wearied, famished—for he had lost his coin—he fell in the dusty highway, but with clenched fists and eyes glaring with rage.

"Out of the way, there!" yelled a hoarse voice, amid cracking of a whip.

He did not hear, for his senses left him. He remained before the hoofs of the horses, drawing a postchaise up a side road between Vauclere and Thieblemont, which he had not perceived.

A scream pealed from inside the carriage, which the horses were whirling along like a feather on the gale. The postboy made a superhuman effort and managed to keep his horses from trampling on the boy, though one of the leaders gave him a kick.

"Good God!" screamed a woman again; "you have crushed the unhappy child."

The lady traveler got out, and the postillion alighted to lift Gilbert's body from under the wheel.

"What luck!" said the man; "dashed if he be hurted—only swooned."

"With fright, I suppose."

"I'll drag him to the roadside, and let us go on, since your ladyship is in hot haste."

"I cannot possibly leave this poor boy in such a plight. So young, poor little thing! It is some truant scholar undertaking a journey beyond his powers. How pale he is—he will die. No, no! I will not abandon him. Put him inside, on the front seat."

The postboy obeyed the lady, who had already got in the berlin, as were called such carriages. Gilbert was put on a good cushion with his back supported by the padded sides.

"Away you go again," said the lady. "Ten minutes lost, for which you must make up, while I will pay you the more."

When Gilbert came to his senses he found himself in the coach, swept along by three posthorses. He was not a little surprised, too, to be almost in the lap of a young woman who attentively studied him.

She was not more than twenty-five. She had cheeks scorched by the southern sun, with a turn-up nose and gray eyes. A clear character of cunning and circumspection was given to her open and jovial countenance by the little mouth of delicate and fanciful design. Her arms, the finest in the world, were molded in violet velvet sleeves adorned with gilt buttons. Nearly the whole vehicle was filled up by the wavy folds of her large flower-patterned gray silk dress.

As the countenance was smiling and expressed interest, Gilbert stared for fear he was in a dream.

"Well, are you better, my little man?" asked she.

"Where am I?" counter-queried Gilbert, who had learned this phrase from novels, where alone it is used.

"In safety, my dear little fellow," replied the lady in a southern accent. "A while ago you ran great risk of being smashed under my carriage wheels. What happened you, to drop on the highroad right in the middle?"

"I swooned from having walked some eighteen leagues since four yesterday afternoon, or, rather, run."

"Whither are you bound?"

"To Versailles, lady. I come from Taverney, a castle between Pierrefitte and Bar-le-Duc."

"Did you not give yourself time to eat?"

"I had neither the time nor the means, for I lost a bit of money, and I soon ate the crusts I carried."

"Poor boy! but you might have asked for more bread."

"I am too proud, lady," said Gilbert, smiling loftily.

"Pride is all very well, but not when it lets one die of hunger."

"Death before disgrace!"

"Hello! where did you learn such talk?"

"Not at home, for I am an orphan. My name is Gilbert, and no more."

"Some by-blow of a country squire," thought the woman. "You are very young to roam the highway," she continued.

"I was not roaming," said the youth, who thought the truth would recommend him to a woman. "I was following a carriage."

"With your lady love in it? Dear me! there is a romance in your adventure?"

Gilbert was not enough his own master not to redden.

"What was the carriage, my little Cato?"

"One of the dauphiness' retinue."

"What, is she ahead of us?" exclaimed the woman. "Are they not making a fuss over her along the route?"

"They wanted to, but she pressed on after having talked of staying for rest at Taverney Castle, for a letter came from Versailles, they said, and she was off in three-quarters of an hour."

"A letter?"

"Brought by the Governor of Strasburg."

"Lord Stainville? Duke Choiseul's brother? The mischief! Whip on, postillion! faster, faster!"

The whip snapped and Gilbert felt the vehicle jump with more velocity.

"We may outstrip her if she stops for breakfast, or at night," meditated the woman. "Postillion, which is the next town of any account?"

"Vitry."

"Where do we change horses?"

"Vauclere."

"Go on; but tell me if you see a string of carriages on the main road. Poor child!" she continued, seeing how pale Gilbert was; "it is my fault for making him chatter when he is dying of hunger and thirst."

To make up for the lost time, she took out a traveling flask with a silver cap as stopper, into which she poured a cordial.

"Drink that and eat a cake," she said, "until you can have a substantial breakfast in an hour or two. Now, as you are a whit refreshed, tell me, if you have any trust in me, what interest you have in following the carriage belonging to the dauphiness' train?"

He related his story with much clearness.

"Cheer up," she said. "I congratulate you. But you must know that one cannot live on courage at Versailles or Paris."

"But one can by toil."

"That's so. But you have not the hands of a craftsman or laborer."

"I will work with my head."

"Yes, you appear rather knowing."

"I know I am ignorant," said Gilbert, recalling Socrates.

"You will make a good doctor, then, since a doctor is one who administers drugs of which he knows little into a body of which he knows less. In ten years I promise you my custom."

"I shall try to deserve the honor, lady," replied Gilbert.

The horses were changed without their having overtaken the royal party, which had stopped for the same and to breakfast at Vitry. The lady offered bounteously for the distance between to be covered, but the postillion dared not outstrip the princess—a crime for which he would be sent to prison for life.

"If I might suggest," observed Gilbert, "you could cut ahead by a by-road."

The vehicle therefore turned off to the right and came out on the main road at Chalons. The princess had breakfasted at Vitry, but was so tired that she was reposing, having ordered the horses to be ready to start again at three or four P. M. This so delighted the lady traveler that she paid the postboy lavishly and said to Gilbert:

"We shall have a feast at the next posting house."

But it was decreed that Gilbert should not dine there.

The change of horses was to be at Chaussee village. The most remarkable object here was a man who stood in the mid-road, as if on duty there. He looked along it and on a long-tailed barb which was hitched to a window shutter and neighed fretfully for its master to come out of the cottage.

At length the man knocked on the shutter, and called.

"I say, sir," he demanded of the man who showed his head at the window, "if you want to sell that horse, here is the customer."

"Not for sale," replied the peasant, banging the shutter to.

This did not satisfy the stranger, who was a lusty man of forty, tall and ruddy, with coarse hands in lace ruffles. He wore a laced cocked hat crosswise, like soldiers who want to scare rustics.

"You are not polite," he said, hammering on the shutter. "If you do not open, I shall smash in the blind."

The panel opened at this menace and the clown reappeared.

"Who does this Arab belong to?"

"A lady lodging here, who is very fond of it."

"Let me speak with her."

"Can't; she is sleeping."

"Ask her if she wants five hundred pistoles for the barb."

"That is a right royal price." And the rustic opened his eyes widely.

"Just, so; the king wants the creature."

"You are not the king."

"But I represent him, and he is in a hurry."

"I must not wake her."

"Then I shall!" and he swung up a cane with a gold head in his herculean fist.

But he lowered it without hitting, for at the same instant he caught sight of a carriage tearing up the slope behind three fagged horses. The skilled eye of the would-be buyer recognized the vehicle, for he rushed toward it with a speed the Arabian might have envied.

It was the post carriage of Gilbert's guardian angel, which the postboy was enchanted to stop, on seeing the man wave him to do so, for he knew the nags would never reach the post house.

"Chon, my dear Chon," said the stranger. "What joy that you turn up, at last!"

"It is I, Jean," replied the lady to whom was given this odd name; "what are you doing here?"

"A pretty question, by Jove! I was waiting for you."

The Hercules stepped on the folding-step, and kissed the lady through the window. Suddenly he caught sight of Gilbert, and turned as black as a dog from which is snatched a bone, from not knowing the terms between the pair in the berlin.

"It is a most amusing little philosopher whom I picked up," returned Chon, caring little whether she wounded the pet's feelings or not, "on the road—but never mind him."

"Another matter indeed worries us. What about the old Countess of Bearn?" asked Jean.

"I have done the job, and she will come. I said I was her lawyer's daughter, Mademoiselle Flageot, and that, passing through Verdun, I repeated from my father that her case was coming on. I added that she must appear in person, whereupon she opened her gray eyes, took a pinch of snuff, and saying Lawyer Flageot was the first of business men, she gave orders for her departure."

"Splendid, Chon! I appoint you my ambassador extraordinary. Come and have breakfast!"

"Only too glad, for this poor boy is dying of hunger. But we must make haste, for the dauphiness is only three leagues off."

"Plague! that changes the tune. Go on to the posting house, with me hanging on as I am."

In five minutes the coach was at the inn door, where Chon ordered cutlets, fowl, wine and eggs, as they had to be off forthwith.

"Excuse me, lady, but it will have to be with your own horses, for all mine are out. If you find one at the manger, I will eat it."

"You ought to have some, for the regulations require it. Let me tell you," thundered Jean with a hectoring air, "I am not the man to jest."

"If I had fifty in the stable it would be the same as none, for they are all held on the dauphiness' service."

"Fifty, and you would not let us have three?" said Jean; "I do not ask for eight, to which number royal highnesses are entitled, but three."

"You shall not have one," returned the post master, springing in between the stables and the obstinate gentleman.

"Blunderhead, do you know who I am?" cried the other, pale with rage.

"Viscount," interposed Chon, "in heaven's name, no disorder."

"You are right, my dear; no more words; only deeds." He turned to the innkeeper, saying, "I shall shield you from responsibility by taking three horses myself."

"It must not be done, I tell 'ee."

"Do not help him harness," said the posting house keeper to the grooms.

70

"Jean," said Chon, "don't get into a scrape. On an errand one must put up with anything."

"Except delay," replied Viscount Jean with the utmost ease.

And he began taking down three sets of harness, which he threw on three horses' backs.

"Mind, master," said the post master, as he followed Jean, leading the horses out to the coach, "this is high treason."

"I am not stealing the royal horses but taking them on loan."

The innkeeper rushed at the reins but the strong man sent him spinning.

"Brother, oh, brother!" screamed Chon.

"Only her brother!" muttered Gilbert.

CHAPTER XV

TAVERNEY TO THE RESCUE

At this period a window in the cottage opened and a lovely woman's face appeared, above the Arabian courser, the uproar having aroused her.

"The very person wanted," cried Jean. "Fair lady, I offer you five hundred pistoles for your horse."

"My horse?" questioned the lady in bad French.

"Yes, the barb hitched there."

"Not for sale," and the lady slammed the window.

"Come, come, I am not in luck this day," said Jean, "for folk will neither sell nor hire. Confound it all! I shall take the Arab, if not for sale, and the coach horses if not for hire, and run them to their last legs. Put the horses to," he concluded to the lady traveler's lackey, who was on the coach.

"Help me, boys?" shouted the post master to his hostlers.

"Oh, don't," cried Chon to her brother; "you will only be massacred."

"Massacred, with three to three? for I count on your philosopher," said Jean, shouting to Gilbert, who was stupefied. "Get out and pitch in with a cane, or a rock, or the fist. And don't look like a plaster image!"

Here the burlesque battle began, with the horses pulled

between Jean and their owner. The stronger man hurled the latter into the duckpond, where he floundered among the frightened ducks and geese.

"Help! murder!" he shrieked, while the viscount hastened to get the fresh horses into the traces.

"Help, in the king's name!" yelled the innkeeper, rallying his two grooms.

"Who claims help in the royal name?" challenged a horseman who suddenly galloped into the inn yard and pulled up his reeking steed amid the fighting party.

"Lieutenant Philip de Taverney!" exclaimed Gilbert, sinking back deeper than ever in the carriage corner.

Chon, who let nothing slip her, caught this name.

The young officer of the dauphin's dragoon guards leaped off his horse amid the scene, which was attracting all the villagers. The innkeeper ran up to him imploringly as the saver.

"Officer, this gentleman is trying to take away the horses kept for her Royal Highness," he faltered.

"Gentleman?" queried Philip.

"Yes, this gentleman;" retorted Jean.

"You mistake, you are mad—or no gentleman," replied the Chevalier of Redcastle.

"My dear lieutenant, you are wrong on both points," said the viscount; "I have my senses, and I am entitled to ride in the royal carriages."

"How dare you, then, lay hands on the horses for the royal princess?"

"Because there are fifty here and the Royals are entitled to but eight. Am I to go afoot when lackeys have four nags to draw them?"

"If it is the order of his Majesty, they may have what they like. So be good enough to make your fellow take back those horses."

"Yes, if you are on duty to guard them, lieutenant," replied Jean; "but I did not know that the dauphiness' dragoons were set to guard grooms. Better shut your eyes, tell your squad to do the same, and I wish you a pleasant journey!"

"You are wrong, sir; I am on duty, as the dauphiness has sent me forward to look after the relays."

"That is different. But allow the remark that you are on paltry duty, and the young Bonnibel is shamefully treating the army——"

"Of whom are you speaking in such terms?" interrupted Philip.

"Oh, only of that Austrian beauty."

Taverney turned pale as his cravat, but in his usual calm voice he said, as he caught hold of the bridle:

"Do me the pleasure to acquaint me with your name?"

72

"If you are bent upon that—I am Viscount Jean Dubarry."

"What, brother of that notorious——"

"Who will send you to rot in the Bastille prison, if you add a word to the adjective."

The viscount sprang into the coach, up to the door of which went the baron's son.

"If you do not come forth in a second I give you my word of honor that I shall run my sword through your body."

Having hold of the door with his left hand, pulling against the viscount, he drew his sword with the other.

"The idea!" said Chon; "this is murder. Give up the horses, Jean."

"Oh, you threaten me, do you?" hissed the viscount, exasperated, and snatching his sword from the cushion.

"We shall never get away at this rate," whispered Chon; "do smooth the officer down."

"Neither violence nor gentleness will stay me in my duty," observed Taverney, politely bowing to the young woman. "Advise obedience to the gentleman, or in the name of the king, whom I represent, I shall kill him if he will fight me, or arrest him if he refuses."

"Shall I lug him out, lieutenant?" asked the corporal, who had Taverney's half-dozen men as escort.

"No, this is a personal quarrel," said his superior. "You need not interfere."

There was truly no need; for, after three minutes, Jean Dubarry drew back from the conflict with Redcastle, his sleeve dyed with blood.

"Go, sir," said the victor, "and do not play such pranks any more."

"Tush, I pay for them," grumbled the viscount.

Luckily three horses came in which would do for the change, and the innkeeper was only too glad to get rid of the turbulent viscount at their price. As he mounted the carriage steps, he grumbled at Gilbert's being in the way.

"Hush, brother," said Chon; "he knows the man who wounded you. He is Philip of Taverney."

"Then we shall be even yet," said the viscount, with a gleam of gladness. "You are on the high horse at present, my little dragoon," he shouted out to Taverney; "but turn about is fair play."

"To the return, if you please," replied the officer.

"Yes, Chevalier Philip de Taverney!" called Jean, watching for the effect of the sudden declaration of his name.

Indeed, his hearer raised his head with sharp surprise, in which

73

entered some unease, but recovering himself and lifting his hat, he rejoined with the utmost grace:

"A pleasant journey, Chevalier Jean Dubarry!"

"A thousand thunders," swore the viscount, grinning horribly as the coach started. "I am in acute pain, Chon, and shall want a surgeon sooner than breakfast."

"We will get one at the first stop while this youth has his meal."

"Excuse me," said Gilbert, as the invalid expressed a desire to drink. "But strong drink is bad for you at present."

"What, are you a doctor as well as philosopher?" queried Jean.

"Not yet, my lord; though I hope to be one some day. But I read that wounded patients must not take anything heated. But if you will let me have your handkerchief, I will dip it in water at the first spring and cool the wound by bandaging it."

The carriage was stopped for Gilbert to get out and wet the cambric.

"This youngster is dreadfully in the way for us to talk business," said Dubarry.

"Pshaw! we will talk in the Southern dialect," said Chon; and it was thanks to this precaution that the two communed to the puzzlement of the youth on the rest of the journey.

But he had the consolation of thinking that he had comforted a viscount who stood in the king's favor. If Andrea only saw him now! He did not think of Nicole.

"Hello!" broke off the viscount, as he looked behind out of the window. "Here comes that Arab with the strange woman on its back. I would give a thousand pistoles for that steed, and a fortune for the beauty."

The black-eyed woman wrapped in a white cloak, with her brow shaded by a broad-brimmed felt hat with long feathers, flew by like an arrow along the roadside, crying:

"Avanti, Djerid!"

"She says 'Forward!' in Italian," said the viscount. "Oh, the lovely creature. If I were not in such pain, I would jump out and after her."

"You could not catch her, on that horse. It is the magician, and she is his wife."

"Magician?" questioned the Dubarrys together.

"Yes, Baron Joseph Balsamo."

The sister looked at the brother as much as to say: "Was I not right to keep him?" and he nodded emphatically.

CHAPTER XVI

THE KING'S FAVORITE

In the apartments of Princess Adelaide, daughter of King Louis X., he had housed the Countess Jeanne Dubarry, his favorite since a year, not without studying the effect it would have on the realm. The jolly, mirthful, devil-may-care mad-cap had transformed the silent palace into a monkey-house, where any one was tolerated who kept the fun alive.

At about nine in the morning, the hour of her reception, Jeanne Vaubernier, to give her her true name, stepped out of her couch, wrapped in an embroidered gauze gown which allowed a glimpse through the floating lace of her alabaster arms. This seductive statue, awakening more and more, drew a lace mantle over her shoulders and held out her little foot for a slipper which, with its jewels, would enrich a woodcutter in her native woods had he found it.

"Any news of Chon, or the Viscount Jean?" she asked at once of her chambermaid.

"None, and no letters, my lady."

"What a bore to be kept waiting!" pouted the royal pet, with a pretty wry face. "Will they never invent a method of corresponding a hundred miles apart? Faith, I pity anybody I visit with my vexation this day. But I suppose that, as this star the dauphiness is coming, I, the poor glowworm, will be left alone. Who is waiting, tell me?"

"Duke Daiguillon, Prince Soubise, Count Sartines and President Maupeou."

"But the Duke of Richelieu?"

"He has not yet come."

"No more than yesterday. That political weathercock has turned from me. He is afraid to be injured, Doris. You must send to his house to ask after him."

"Yes, my lady; but the king is here."

"Very well; I am ready."

The Fifteenth Louis entered the room with a smile on his lips and his head upright. He was accompanied solely by a gentleman in black, who tried by a smile to counteract the baleful effect of thin, hard lips and severe gray eyes. It was Lieutenant of Police Sartines.

The waiting maid and a little negro boy were in the room; but they were not counted.

"Good-morning, countess," hailed the monarch; "how fresh we

are looking to-day. Don't be afraid of Sartines; he is not going to talk business, I trust. Oh, how magnificent Zamore is looking!"

The blackamoor was appareled with the barbaric splendor in which Othello was attired at that period.

"Sire, he has a favor to crave of your Majesty."

"He seems to me very ambitious, after having been granted by you the greatest boon one can desire—being your slave, like myself."

Sartines bowed, smiling, but bit his lips at the same time.

"How delightful you are, sire," said the countess. "I adore you, France!" she whispered in the royal ear, and set him smiling.

"Well, what do you desire for Zamore?"

"Recompense for his long service——"

"He is only twelve years old!"

"You will be paying him in advance; that is a good way of not being treated with ingratitude."

"Capital idea! What do you think, Sartines?" asked the king.

"I support it, as all devoted subjects will gain by it."

"Well, sire, I want Zamore to be appointed governor of my summer residence, Luciennes, which shall be created a royal place."

"It would be a parody and make all the governors of the royal places protest, and with reason."

"A good thing, for they are always making a noise for nothing. Zamore, kneel down and thank his majesty for the favor. Sire, you have another royal property from this time forward. Get up, Zamore. You are appointed."

"Sartines, do you know the way to refuse this witch anything?"

"If there is one, it is not yet out into practice, sire."

"When found, I wager it will be by Chief of Police Sartines. I am expecting him to find me something—and I have been on thorns about it for three months. I want a magician."

"To have him burnt alive?" asked the sovereign, while Sartines breathed again. "It is warm weather, now; wait for winter."

"Not to burn him, but to give him a golden rod, sire."

"Oh, did he predict some ill which has not happened?"

"Nay, a blessing which came to pass."

"Tell us, countess," said Louis, settling down in an easy chair, like one who is not sure he will be pleased or oppressed but will risk it.

"I am agreeable, sire, only you must share in rewarding him."

"I must make the present entirely."

"That is right royal."

"I listen."

"It begins like a fairy tale. Once upon a time, a poor girl was walking the streets of Paris, what time she had neither pages, carriages, negro boy to hold up her train and enrage the dowagers, or parrot or monkey. Crossing the Tuileries gardens, she suddenly perceived that she was pursued."

"Deuce take it! thereupon she stopped," said the king.

"Fie! It is clear that your experience has been in following duchesses or marchionesses. She was the more alarmed as a thick fog came on, and the chaser emerged from it upon her. She screamed."

"For the rogue was ugly?"

"No, he was a bright and handsome young man; but still she sued him to spare her from harm. He smiled charmingly and called heaven as witness that he had no such intention. He only wanted her pledge to grant him a favor when—when she should be a queen. She thought she was not binding herself much with such a promise, and the man disappeared."

"Sartines is very wrong in not finding him."

"Sire, I do not refuse, but I cannot."

"Cannot ought not to be in the police dictionary," said Dubarry.

"We have a clew."

"Ha, ha! that is the old story."

"It is the truth. The fault is that your description is so slight."

"Slight? she painted him so brightly that I forbid you to find the dog."

"I only want to ask a piece of information."

"What for, when his prophecy is accomplished?"

"If I am almost a queen, I want to ask him when I shall be placed in the court."

"Presented formally?"

"It is not enough to reign in the night; I want to reign a little in the daytime."

"That is not the magician's business, but mine," said Louis, frowning at the conversation getting upon delicate ground. "Or rather yours, for all that is wanted is an introductress."

"Among the court prudes—all sold to Choiseul or Praslin?"

"Pray let us have no politics here."

"If I am not to speak, I shall act without speaking, and upset the ministers without any further notice."

At this juncture the maid Doris entered and spoke a word to her mistress.

"It is Chon, who comes from traveling and begs to present her respects to your majesty."

"Let us have Chon in, for I have missed something lately, and it may be her."

"I thank your majesty," said Chon, coming in, and hastening to whisper to her sister in kissing her:

"I have done it."

The countess could not repress an outcry of delight.

"I am so glad to see her."

"Quite so; go on and chat with her while I confer with Sartines to learn whence you come, Chon."

"Sire," said Sartines, eager to avoid the pinch, "may I have a moment for the most important matter?—about these seers, illuminati, miracle workers——"

"Quacks? make them take out licenses as conjurers at a high figure, and they will not be any cause of fear."

"Sire, the situation is more serious than most believe. New masonic lodges are being opened. This society has become a sect to which is affiliated all the foes of the monarchy, the idealists, encyclopedists and philosophers. Voltaire has been received at court."

"A dying man."

"Only his pretense. All are agitating, writing, speaking, corresponding, plotting and threatening. From some words dropped, they are expecting a leader."

"When he turns up, Sartines, we will turn him down, in the Bastille."

"These philosophers whom you despise will destroy the monarchy."

"In what space of time, my lord?"

"How can I tell?" said the chief of police, looking astonished. "Ten, fifteen or more years."

"My dear friend, in that time I shall be no more; tell this to my successor."

He turned away, and this was the opportunity that the favorite was waiting for, since she heaved a sigh, and said:

"Oh, gracious, Chon, what are you telling me? My poor brother Jean so badly wounded that his arm will have to be amputated!"

"Oh, wounded in some street affray or in a drinking-saloon quarrel?"

"No, sire! attacked on the king's highway and nearly murdered."

"Murdered?" repeated the ruler, who had no feelings, but could finely feign them. "This is in your province, Sartines."

"Can such a thing have happened?" said the chief of police, apparently less concerned than the king, but in reality more so.

"I saw a man spring on my brother," said Chon, "force him to draw his sword and cut him grievously."

"Was the ruffian alone?"

"He had half a dozen bullies with him."

"Poor viscount forced to fight," sighed the monarch, trying to regulate the amount of his grief by the countess'; but he saw that she was not pretending.

"And wounded?" he went on, in a heartbroken tone.

"But what was the scuffle about?" asked the police lieutenant, trying to see into the affair.

"Most frivolous; about posthorses, disputed for with the viscount, who was in a hurry to help me home to my sister, whom I had promised to join this morning."

"This requires retaliation, eh, Sartines?" said the king.

"It looks so, but I will inquire into it. The aggressor's name and rank?"

"I believe he is a military officer, in the dauphiness' dragoon guards, and named something like Baverne, or Faver—stop—it is Taverney."

"To-morrow he will sleep in prison," said the chief of police.

"Oh, dear, no," interrupted the countess out of deep silence; "that is not likely, for he is but an instrument and you will not punish the real instigators of the outrage. It is the work of the Duke of Choiseul. I shall leave the field free for my foes, and quit a realm where the ruler is daunted by his ministers."

"How dare you?" cried Louis, offended.

Chon understood that her sister was going too far, and she struck in.

She plucked her sister by the dress and said:

"Sire, my sister's love for our poor brother carries her away. I committed the fault and I must repair it. As the most humble subject of your majesty, I merely apply for justice."

"That is good; I only ask to deal justice. If the man has done wrong, let him be chastised."

"Am I asking anything else?" said the countess, glancing pityingly at the monarch, who was so worried elsewhere and seldom tormented in her rooms. "But I do not like my suspicions snubbed."

"Your suspicions shall be changed to certainty by a very simple course. We will have the Duke of Choiseul here. We will confront the parties at odds, as the lawyers say."

At this moment the usher opened the door and announced that the prince royal was waiting in the king's apartments to see him.

"It is written I shall have no peace," grumbled Louis. But he was not sorry to avoid the wrangle with Choiseul, and he brightened up. "I am going, countess. Farewell! you see how miserable I am with everybody pulling me about. Ah, if the philosophers only knew what a dog's life a king has—especially when he is king of France."

"But what am I say to the Duke of Choiseul?"

"Send him to me, countess."

Kissing her hand, trembling with fury, he hastened away as usual, fearing every time to lose the fruit of a battle won by palliatives and common cunning.

"Alas! he escapes us again!" wailed the courtesan, clenching her plump hands in vexation.

CHAPTER XVII

A ROYAL CLOCK-REPAIRER

In the Hall of the Clocks, in Versailles Palace, a pink-cheeked and meek-eyed young gentleman was walking about with a somewhat vulgar step. His arms were pendent and his head sunk forward. He was in his seventeenth year. He was recognizable as the king's heir by being the living image of the Bourbon race, most exaggerated. Louis Auguste, Duke of Berry and heir to the throne as the dauphin, soon wearied of his lounge and stopped to gaze with the air of one who understood horology, on the great clock in the back of the hall. It was a universal machine, which told of time to the century, with the lunar phases and the courses of the planets, and was always the prince's admiration.

Suddenly the hands on which his eyes were fastened came to a standstill. A grain of sand had checked the mechanism, and the master-piece was dead.

On seeing this misfortune, the royal one forgot what he had come to do. He opened the clock-case glazed door, and put his head inside to see what was the matter. All at once he uttered a cry of joy, for he had spied a screw loose, of which the head had worked up and caught another part of the machinery. With a tortoise shell pick in one hand, and holding the wheel with the other, he began to fix the screw, with his head in the box. Thus absorbed he never heard the usher at the door, cry out: "The king!"

Louis was some time glancing about before he spied the prince's legs as he stood half eclipsed before the clock.

"What the deuse are you doing there?" he asked, as he tapped his son on the shoulder.

The amateur clockmaker drew himself out with the proper precautions for so noble a timepiece.

"Oh, your majesty, I was just killing time while you were not present."

"By murdering my clock! Pretty amusement!"

"Oh, no, only setting it to rights. A screw was loose and——"

"Never mind mechanics! What do you want of me? I am eager to be off to Marly."

He started for the door, always trying to avoid awkward situations.

"Is it money you are after? I will send you some."

"Nay, I have savings out of my last quarter's money."

"What a miser, and yet a spendthrift was his tutor! I believe he has all the virtues missing in me."

"Sire, is not the bride near at hand yet?"

"Your bride? I should say fifty leagues off. Are you in a hurry."

The prince royal blushed.

"I am not eager for the motive you think."

"No? So much the worse. Hang it all! You are sixteen and the princess very pretty. You are warranted in being impatient."

"Cannot the ceremonies be curtailed, for at this rate she will be an age coming. I don't think the traveling arrangements are well made."

"The mischief! thirty thousand horses placed along the route, with men and carts and coaches—how can you believe there is bad management when I have made all these arrangements?"

"Sire, in spite of these, I am bound to say that I think, as in the case of your clock, there is a screw loose. The progress has been right royally arranged, but did your majesty make it fully understood that all the horses, men and vehicles were to be employed by the dauphiness?"

A vague suspicion annoyed the monarch, who looked hard at his heir; this suggestion agreed with another idea fretting him.

"Certainly," he replied. "Of course you are satisfied, then? The bride will arrive on time, and she is properly attended to. You are rich with your savings, and you can wind up my clock and set it going again. I have a good mind to appoint you Clockmaker Extraordinary to the Royal Household, do you hear?" and, laughing, he was going to snatch the opportunity to slip away, when, as he opened the door, he faced a man on the sill.

Louis drew back a step.

"Choiseul!" he exclaimed. "I had forgotten she was to send him

81

to me. Never mind, he shall pay for my son irritating me. So you have come, my lord? You heard I wanted you?"

"Yes, sire," replied the prime minister, coldly. "I was dressing to come, any way."

"Good; I have serious matters to discuss," said the sovereign, frowning to intimidate the minister, who was, unfortunately, the hardest man to browbeat in the kingdom.

"Very serious matters I have to discuss, too," he replied, with a glance for the dauphin, who was skulking behind the clock.

"Oho!" thought the king; "my son is my foe, too. I am in a triangle with woman, minister and son, and cannot escape."

"I come to say that the Viscount Jean——"

"Was nearly murdered in an ambush?"

"Nay, that he was wounded in the forearm in a duel. I know it perfectly."

"So do I, and I will tell you the true story."

"We listen," responded Choiseul. "For the prince is concerned in the affray, so far as it was on account of the dauphiness."

"The dauphiness and Jean Dubarry in some way connected?" questioned the king. "This is getting curious. Pray explain, my lord, and conceal nothing. Was it the princess who gave the swordthrust to Dubarry?"

"Not her highness, but one of the officers of her escort," replied Choiseul, as calm as ever.

"One whom you know?"

"No, sire; but your majesty ought to know him, if your majesty remembers all his old servants; for his father fought for you at Fontenoy, Philipsburg and Mahon—he is a Taverney Redcastle."

The dauphin mutely repeated the title to engrave it on his mind.

"Certainly, I know the Redcastles," returned Louis. "Why did he fight against Jean, whom I like—unless because I like him? Absurd jealousy, outbreaks of discontent, and partial sedition!"

"Does the defender of the royal princess deserve this reproach?" said the duke.

"I must say," said the prince, rising erect and folding his arms, "I am grateful to the young gentleman who risked his life for a lady who will shortly be my wife."

"What did he risk his life for?" queried the king.

"Because the Chevalier Jean in a hurry wanted to take the horses set aside by your majesty for the royal bride."

The king bit his lips and changed color, for the new way of presenting the case was again a menacing phantom.

"Yes, Chevalier Dubarry was putting the insult on the royal

house of taking the reserved royal horses, when up came the Chevalier Redcastle, sent onward by her highness, and after much civil remonstrance——"

"Oh!" protested the king. "Civil—a military man?"

"It was so," interposed the dauphin. "I have been fully informed. Dubarry whipped out his sword——"

"Was he the first to draw?" demanded the king.

The prince blushed and looked to Choiseul for support.

"The fact is, the two crossed swords," the latter hastened to say, "one having insulted the lady, the other defending her and your majesty's property."

"But who was the aggressor, for Jean is mild as a lamb," said the monarch, glad that things were getting equalized.

"The officer must have been malapert."

"Impertinent to a man who was dragging away the horses reserved for your majesty's destined daughter?" exclaimed Choiseul. "Is this possible?"

"Hasty, anyway," said the king, as the dauphin stood pale without a word.

"A zealous servitor can never do wrong," remarked the duke, receding a step.

"Come, now, how did you get the news?" asked the king of his son, without losing sight of the minister, who was troubled by this abrupt question.

"I had an advice from one who was offended by the insult to the lady of my choice."

"Secret correspondence, eh?" exclaimed the sovereign. "Plots, plots! Here you are, beginning to worry me again, as in the days of Pompadour."

"No, this is only a secondary matter. Let the culprit be punished, and that will end the affair."

At the suggestion of punishment, Louis saw Jeanne furious and Chon up in arms.

"Punish, without hearing the case?" he said. "I have signed quite enough blank committals to jail. A pretty mess you are dragging me into, duke."

"But what a scandal, if the first outrage to the princess is allowed to go unpunished, sire."

"I entreat your majesty," said the dauphin.

"What, don't you think the sword cut was enough punishment?"

"No, sire, for he might have wounded Lieutenant Taverney. In that case I should have asked for his head."

"Nay," said the dauphin, "I only ask for his banishment."

"Exile, for an alehouse scuffle," said the king. "In spite of your

83

philosophical notions, you are harsh, Louis. It is true that you are a mathematician, and such are hard as—well, they would sacrifice the world to have their ciphering come out correct."

"Sire, I am not angry with Chevalier Dubarry personally, but as he insulted the dauphiness."

"What a model husband!" sneered the king. "But I am not to be gulled in this way. I see that I am attacked under all these blinds. It is odd that you cannot let me live in my own way, but must hate all whom I like, and like all I dislike! Am I mad, or sane? Am I the master, or not!"

The prince went back to the clock. Choiseul bowed as before.

"No answer, eh? Why don't you say something? Do you want to worry me into the grave with your petty hints and strange silence, your paltry spites and minute dreads?"

"I do not hate Chevalier Dubarry," said the prince.

"I do not dread him," added Choiseul.

"You are both bad at heart," went on the sovereign, trying to be furious but only showing spite. "Do you want me to realize the fable with which my cousin of Prussia jeers me, that mine is the Court of King Petaud? No, I shall do nothing of the kind. I stand on my honor in my own style and will defend it similarly."

"Sire," said the prince with his inexhaustible meekness but eternal persistency, "your majesty's honor is not affected—it is the dignity of the royal princess which is struck at."

"Let Chevalier Jean make excuses, then, as he is free to do. But he is free to do the other thing."

"I warn your majesty that the affair will be talked of, if thus dropped," said the prime minister.

"Who cares? Do as I do. Let the public chatter, and heed them not—unless you like to laugh at them. I shall be deaf to all. The sooner they make such a noise as to deafen me, the sooner I shall cease to hear them. Think over what I say, for I am sick of this. I am going to Marly, where I can get a little quiet—if I am not followed out there. At least, I shall not meet your sister the Lady Louise there, for she has retired to the nunnery of St. Denis."

But the dauphin was not listening to this news of the breaking up of his family.

"It is going," he exclaimed in delight, real or feigned, as the clock resumed its regular tickings.

The minister frowned and bowed himself out backward from the hall, where the heir to the throne was left alone.

The king going into his study, paced it with long strides.

"I can clearly see that Choiseul is railing at me. The prince looks on himself as half the master, and believes he will be entirely so when he mounts with this Austrian on the throne. My daughter Louise loves me, but she preaches morality and she gives me the go-by to live in the nunnery. My three other girls sing songs against me and poor Jeanne. The Count of Provence is translating Lucretius. His brother of Artois is running wild about the streets. Decidedly none but this poor countess loves me. Devil take those who try to displease her!"

Sitting at the table where his father signed papers, his treaties and grandiloquent epistles, the son of the great king took up the pen.

"I understand why they are all hastening the arrival of the archduchess. But I am not going to be perturbed by her sooner than can be helped," and he wrote an order for Governor Stainville to stop three days at one city and three at another.

With the same pen he wrote:

"Dear Countess: This day we install Zamore in his new government. I am off for Marly, but I will come over to Luciennes this evening to tell you all I am thinking about at present.

France."

"Lebel," he said to his confidential valet, "away with this to the countess, and my advice is for you to keep in her good graces."

CHAPTER XVIII

THE COUNTESS OF BEARN

A hackney coach stopping at the doorway of Chancellor Maupeou, president of Parliament, induced the porter to deign to stalk out to the door of the vehicle and see why the way was thus blocked.

He saw an old lady in an antiquated costume. She was thin and bony but active, with cat's eyes rolling under gray brows. But poverty stricken though she appeared, the porter showed respect as he asked her name.

"I am the Countess of Bearn," she replied; "but I fear that I shall not have the fortune to find his lordship at home."

"My lord is receiving," answered the janitor. "That is, he will receive your ladyship."

The old lady stepped out of the carriage, wondering if she did not dream, while the porter gave two jerks to a bellrope. An usher came to the portals, where the first servant motioned that the visitor might enter.

"If your ladyship desires speech with the lord high chancellor," said the usher, "step this way, please."

"They do speak ill of this official," uttered the lady; "but he has the good trait that he is easily accessible. But it is strange that so high an officer of the law should have open doors."

Chancellor Maupeou, buried in an enormous wig and clad in black velvet, was writing in his study, where the door was open.

On entering, the old countess threw a rapid glance around, but to her surprise there was no other face than hers and that of the law lord, thin, yellow and busy, reflected in the mirrors.

He rose in one piece and placed himself with his back to the fireplace.

The lady made the three courtesies according to rule.

Her little compliment was rather unsteady; she had not expected the honor; she never could have believed that a cabinet minister would give her some time out of his business or his repose.

Maupeou replied that time was no less precious to subject than his majesty's ministers, although preference had to be given to persons with urgent affairs, consequently, he gave what leisure he had to such clients.

"My lord," said the old lady, with fresh courtesies, "I beg most humbly to speak to your excellency of a grave matter on which depends my fortune. You know that my all depends, or rather my son's, on the case sustained by me against the Saluces family. You are a friend of that family, but your lordship's equity is so well known that I have not hesitated to apply to you."

The chancellor was fondling his chin, but he could not help a smile to hear his fair play extolled.

"My lady, you are right in calling me friend of the Saluces; but I laid aside friendship when I took the seals of office up. I look into your business simply as a juris consultus. The case is soon coming on?"

"In another week I should beg your lordship to look over my papers."

"I have done so already."

"Oh! What do you think of it?"

"I beg to say that you ought to be prepared to go home and get the money together to pay the costs—for you will infallibly lose the case."

"Then my son and I are ruined!"

"Unless you have friends at court to counterbalance the influence of the Saluces brothers, who are linked with three parts of the courtiers. In fact, I know not if they have an enemy."

"I am sorry to hear your Excellency say this."

"I am sorry to say so, for I really wanted to be useful to your ladyship."

The countess shuddered at the tone of feigned kindness, for she seemed to catch a glimpse of something dark in the mind, if not the speech of the chancellor; if that obscurity could be swept away she fancied she would see something favorable to her.

"Do you know nobody at court?" he insisted.

"Only some old noblemen, probably retired, who would blush to see their old friend so poor. I have my right of entry to the palace, but what is the good? Better to have the right to enter into enjoyment of my two hundred thousand livres. Work that miracle, my lord."

"Judges cannot be led astray by private influence," he said, forgetting that he was contradicting himself. "Why not, however, apply to the new powers, eager to make recruits? You must have known the royal princesses?"

"They have grown out of remembrance."

"The prince royal?"

"I never knew him."

"Besides, he is dwelling too much on his bride, who is on the road hither, to do any one a good turn. Oh! why not address the favorites?"

"The Duke of Choiseul?"

"No, the other, the Countess——"

"Dubarry?" said the prude, opening her fan.

"Yes, she is goodhearted and she likes to do kindnesses to her friends."

"I am of too old a line for her to like me."

"That is where you are wrong; for she is trying to ally herself with the old families."

"But I have never seen her."

"What a pity! Or her sister, Chon, the other sister Bischi, her brother Jean, or her negro boy Zamore?"

"What! is her negro a power at court?"

"Indeed he is."

"A black who looks like a pug dog, for they sell his picture in the streets. How was I to meet this blackamoor, my lord?" and the dame drew herself up, offended.

"It is a pity you did not, for Zamore would win your suit for you. Ask the dukes and peers of the realm who take candies to him at Marly or Luciennes. I am the lord high chancellor, but what do you think I was about when your ladyship called? Drawing up the instructions for him as governor of Luciennes, to which Zamore has been appointed."

"The Count of Bearn was recompensed for his services of twenty years with merely the same title. What degradation! Is the monarchy indeed going to the dogs?" cried the indignant lady.

"I do not know about the government, but the crumbs are going to them, and, faith! we must scramble among them to get the tidbits away from them. If you wanted to be welcomed by Lady Dubarry, you could not do better than carry these papers for her pet to her."

"It is plain that fate is against me; for, though your lordship has kindly greeted me, the next step is out of the question. Not only am I to pay court to a Dubarry, but I must carry her negro-boy's appointment—a black whom I would not have deigned to kick out of my way on the street——"

Suddenly the usher interrupted:

"Viscount Jean Dubarry."

The chancellor dropped his hands in stupor, while the old petitioner sank back in an armchair without pulse or breath.

Our old acquaintance pranced in, with his arm in a sling:

"Oh, engaged? Pray, do not disturb yourself, my lady; I want only a couple of minutes to make a complaint, a couple of his precious minutes. They have tried to murder me! I did not mind their making fun at us, singing lewd ballads, slandering and libeling us; but it is too much of a vile thing to waylay and murder. But I am interrupting the lady."

"This is the Countess of Bearn," said the chancellor.

Dubarry drew back gracefully to make a proper bow, and the lady did the same for her courtesy, and they saluted as ceremoniously as though they had been in court.

"After you, viscount," she said; "my case is about property; yours about honor, and so takes the lead."

Profiting by her obligingness Dubarry unfolded his complaint.

"You will want witnesses on your side," observed the chancellor.

"That is awkward, for everybody there seems to be on the other side."

"Not everybody," interrupted the countess, "for if the affray was the one that happened in Chaussee village, I can be your witness. I

88

came through there a couple of hours after, and all were talking of it!"

"Have a care, my lady," said the viscount; "for if you speak in my favor, you will make an enemy of Choiseul."

"She ought to lean on your arm, then; though one is wounded, it will soon be healed, and the other is still formidable," said the law lord, while the old dame rolled from one gulf into another.

"Ah, but I know another, whose arms are perfect," said Jean, merrily; "and service for service, she will offer your ladyship hers. I am going straight to my sister, and I offer you a seat in my carriage."

"But without motive, without preparations," faltered the countess.

"Here is your excuse," whispered Maupeou, slipping Zamore's governmental instructions into her sallow, wrinkled hand.

"My lord chancellor, you are my deliverer," she gasped. "And the viscount is the flower of the chivalry."

Indeed, a splendid coach in the royal colors was waiting at the doors. The countess placed herself in it, swelling with pride. Jean entered likewise, and gave the word for the departure.

In her joy at this smooth sailing, the countess forgot that she had wanted to lay a private complaint before the chancellor as head of the legal fraternity.

It may be remembered that Chon had decoyed her into traveling to Paris by pretending to be the daughter of her lawyer Flageot.

What was her amazement, therefore, on calling on that gentleman, to learn that not only was he a bachelor without a daughter, but that he had no good news to impart to her on her suit. Burning with disappointment, she had sought a remedy against this lawyer or this woman who had hoaxed her.

CHAPTER XIX

CHON SPOILS ALL

After the king's departure from the short and unpleasant call, as he termed it to the courtiers, the Countess Dubarry remained closeted with Chon and her brother, who had kept in the background for fear that his wound would be found to be but a scratch. The outcome of this family council was that the countess, instead of going to Luciennes, went to a private house of hers in Valois Street, Paris.

Jeanne read a book while Zamore, at the window, watched for the carriage to return. When the viscount brought the old countess he left her in the anteroom while he ran to tell his sister of his success.

"Where is Chon?" he asked.

"At Versailles, where I bade her keep close."

"Then go in, my princess."

Lady Dubarry opened the boudoir door and walked into her visitor's presence.

"I have already thanked my brother," she said, "for having procured me the honor of your ladyship's visit; but I must thank you at present for making it."

"I cannot find expressions," said the delighted suitor, "to show my gratitude for the kind reception granted me."

"Allow me," said Jean, as the ladies took seats; "the countess must not seem to be applying to you for a favor. The chancellor has confided a commission for you, that is all."

The visitor gave the speaker a thankful look, and handed the letters patent from the chancellor which created Luciennes a royal castle and intrusted Zamore with the governership.

"It is I who am obliged," said the younger countess, "and I shall consider myself happy when the chance comes for me to do something in my turn."

"That will be easy," cried the other with a quickness delighting the pair of plotters. "You will not be ignorant of my name?"

"How could we? The name of the princess to whom we owe King Henry the Fourth?"

"Then you may have heard of a lawsuit which ties up my property."

"Claimed by the Saluces? Yes, the king was talking of the matter with Chancellor Maupeou, my cousin, the other evening."

"The king talked of my case? In what terms, pray?"

"Alas! he seemed to think that it ought to be the Saluces."

"Good heavens! then we would have to pay twice over a sum which morally was paid. I have not the receipt, I grant, but I can prove payment morally."

"I think moral proofs are accepted," said Jean gravely.

"The claim of two hundred thousand livres, with interest, now amounting to a capital of over a million, dated 1406. It must have been settled by Guy Gaston IV., Count of Bearn, because on his deathbed, in 1417, he wrote in his will 'Owing no debts,' and so on."

"That settles it," said Jean.

"But your adversaries hold the note?" said the countess, pretending to take an interest in the subject.

"Yes, that embroils it," said the old lady, who ought to have said, "This clears it up."

"It terribly changes the position for the Saluces."

"Oh, my lady, I would that you were one of the judges!"

"In olden times, you might have claimed a champion to do battle for you. I have such belief in your case that I would go into the lists for you. Unfortunately we have not to do with knights but a gang of robbers in black gowns, who will not understand so plain an expression as 'I die owing no debts.'"

"Stay, though; as the words were spoken three hundred years ago they would be outlawed, I think," ventured Countess Dubarry.

"But you would be convinced of the lady's rights, sister, if you were to hear her, as I have heard coming along."

"Then do me the favor of coming out to my place at Luciennes, where, by the way, the king drops in now and again."

"But I cannot rely on such a chance, for the case is called Monday, and this is Friday."

"What the deuce can be done?" grumbled the viscount, appearing to meditate profoundly.

"If I could have a royal hearing at Versailles through your introduction?" suggested the old lady.

"Not to be thought of. The king does not like me to meddle with law or politics. And at present he is worried about my presentation to the court."

"Oh!" exclaimed the aged litigant.

"The king wants it to come off before the new dauphiness arrives, so that my sister can go to the festivities at Compiegne, in spite of Choiseul's opposition, Praslin's intrigues and Lady Grammont's intervention."

"I understand. The countess has no introductress?" queried Lady Bearn, timidly.

"Beg pardon, we have Baroness Alogny, only the king would prefer somebody with a historical name."

"I cannot say that I ever heard of the Alognys," hissed the old descendant of kings with incredible envy.

"It will be a grand thing for her, for the king is tired of the jades who put on airs prouder than himself!" said Jean. "I could make Lady Alogny draw off by telling her what the king said."

"It would be unfair," said the viscount.

"What a pity! for in that case, here is a lady of ancient lineage, and regal. She would win her lawsuit, her son could have a lieutenancy in the household troops, and as Lady Bearn must have gone to much outlay in her trips to Paris, she would have compensation out of the privy purse. Such luck does not rain down twice in a lifetime."

"Alas! no," said Lady Bearn, crushed in her chair by all things being against her.

"An idea strikes me," said Jean. "All has been kept quiet, and so the king does not know that we have a lady patroness to present my sister. Suppose you were at Versailles and expressed your willingness to act as social sponsor for my sister. Why, the king would accept one who is his relative, and that would prevent the Alognys complaining. The king could do no wrong."

"The king would do right about the suit," said Jeanne. "He would be delighted and he would be sure to say to Chancellor Maupeou: 'I want you to treat Lady Bearn properly, my lord!'"

"But this may look bad, when everybody thinks my case lost," objected the old countess.

"Well, let it be lost," returned the other lady quickly: "What matter, if you are compensated?"

"Two hundred thousand livres?" said the other with sorrow.

"Pooh, what if there be a royal present of a hundred thousand livres?"

"I have a son," remarked the victim, while the two eyed her greedily.

"So much the better, as he will be another servitor for the king; he must not have less than a cornetcy in the army," said Jean. "Any other kinsmen?"

"A nephew."

"We shall find a berth for him."

"We rely on your invention," said Countess Dubarry, rising. "You will allow me to mention your ladyship to the king?"

"Do me the honor," said the old dame with a sigh.

"No later than this evening," said the royal favorite. "I trust I have won your friendship?"

"Yes, though I believe I am in a dream."

But the dream only lasted to the foot of the stairs, where Countess Bearn was conducted on Jean's hale arm, for there the irrepressible Chon came bounding out of a sedan chair. Lady Bearn recognized the pretended daughter of Lawyer Flageot.

"It is Mistress Chon," roared Zamore.

"Is that little fool Gilbert here?" asked Chon of the footmen, when she suddenly looked up and saw Jean trying to hush her.

She followed the direction of his finger and perceived Lady

Bearn. She gave a scream, lowered her cap-veil, and plunged into the vestibule.

Appearing to notice nothing, the old lady got into the carriage and gave her address to the coachman.

CHAPTER XX

ANNOYANCE AND AMUSEMENT

The king had been at Luciennes from three o'clock till dark, when, supremely wearied, he reposed on a sofa in a sitting-room, where Countess Dubarry surprised him about half-past ten.

Zamore was at the door when she woke him up.

"Have you come at last, countess?" he said.

"At last? I have been waiting for you this hour. How soundly your Majesty sleeps."

"I have slept three hours. But what do I see there?"

"That is the governor of Luciennes. The chancellor sent me the appointment, and so he donned the uniform. Swear him in quickly, and let him begin guarding us."

Zamore marched up, wearing a showy lace dress, with a sword. His huge three-cocked hat was under his arm. He went down on his knees, laid one hand on his heart, the other one was placed in the king's, and he said:

"Me swear faith and homage to my massa and missee; me will defend the castle placed under my guard to the last gasp, and me will not surrender it till the last can of jelly is eaten."

The sovereign laughed, less at the comic oath than at the black boy's gravity in taking it.

"In return for this pledge," he said with due seriousness, "I confer on you, Sir Governor, the sovereign right of dealing out justice to the extent of capital punishment over all in your hold, in earth, air, fire and water."

"Thankee, massa," said Zamore, rising.

"Now, run away into the servants hall and show your fine trappings."

As Zamore went out by one door, Chon came in by another. The king took her on his knee and kissed her.

"Good-evening, Chon. I like you because you tell me the truth. I want to know what has made your sister so late in hunting me up."

"No, Jeanne is the one to tell the truth. Still, if you will pay me for my report, I will show you that my police spies are up to the mark of Chief Sartines'."

"I have the pay ready," said the king, jingling some coins in his pocket. "No fibs."

"The Countess Dubarry went to her private residence in Valois Street, Paris, where Zamore met her about six o'clock. She went to speak with her sponsor."

"What, is she going to be baptized?"

"Her social sponsor—I do not know the right name for it."

"Say, the lady patroness. So you have fabricated one."

"Nay, she is ready made, and from away back. It is Countess Bearn, of the family of reigning princes. I guess she will not disgrace the line which is allied with the Royal Stuarts, the Dubarry-Moores."

"I never knew of any Countess Bearn but the one who lives by Verdun."

"The very one, who will call to-morrow at seven for a private audience. If the question will be allowed, she will ask when the introduction is to take place, and you will fix it shortly, eh, my Lord of France," said the countess.

The king laughed, but not frankly.

"To-morrow at eleven?"

"At our breakfast hour."

"Impossible, my darling, for I must away; I have important business with Sartines."

"Oh, if you cannot even stay supper——"

The king saw her make a sign to Chon, and suspecting a trap, he called for his horses to go. Delighted with this display of his free will, he walked to the door, but his gentlemen in waiting were not in the outer room. The castle was mute, even in its echoes to his call.

He ran and opened the window, but the courtyard was deserted. The tremulous moon shone on the river and lit up the calm night. This harmony was wasted on the king, who was far from poetic, artistic or musing, but rather material.

"Come, come, countess!" he broke forth in vexation; "put an end to this joke."

"Sire, I have no authority here," said the countess. "It is a royal residence, and the power is confided in the governor. And Governor Zamore is going the rounds with his guard of four men."

The king rather forced a smile.

"This is rather funny," he said. "But I want the horses put to my coach."

94

"The governor has locked them up in the stables for fear robbers might get at them. As for the escort, they are asleep, by orders of the governor, too."

"Then I will walk out of the castle alone."

"Hardly, for the gates are locked and the keys hang at the governor's belt."

"Pest on it! we have one castle strictly guarded!"

The countess lounged on a divan, playing with a rose, less red than her coral lips.

"But we might go in quest of him," she said, rising. "Chon, carry the light before his majesty."

The little procession of three had barely reached the end of the first hall before a whiff of delicious odor set the royal mouth watering.

"You smell supper, my lord," explained the countess. "I thought you were going to partake with me, and I had a feast prepared."

The king reflected that if he went on to Marly he would find nothing but a cold collation. Here, through a doorway open he saw a table set for two. The odor continued to scent the house.

"Bless us! you have a good cook."

"I do not know, for this is his first attempt to please us. I engaged him because he has a reputation for a choice omelet of pheasants' eggs."

"My favorite dish! I should not like to grieve your new cook, countess, and I might taste it while we wait for the governor to finish his inspection. But who will wait upon us?" he asked, entering.

"I hope to do so without upsetting any of this iced champagne— a new invention, of which I wish your opinion."

"I fear I shall never take it from your hand, for it fascinates me into solely admiring it."

"Ah, if my hired eulogists would say something so sweet as that!"

"I see that I must let you have your own way," and he settled down in an easy chair like one who was put in good humor by the prospect of a luxurious repast.

They finished it with coffee burnt in brandy, with a paper which the king held while the fair cajoler lighted.

"That is bad luck to the Choiseul party," said she; "that was one of the lampoons against us which they inspire and allow to be circulated."

"Did I call you a fay? I mistook: you are a demon."

The countess rose.

"I think I had better see if Governor Zamore is not on the return."

But the king shook his head, inflamed by the punch, the tokay and the champagne. He was conscious of still another perfume, and his nose directed him to a doorway suddenly opened. It led into a tempting chamber, hung with sky-blue satin, embroidered with flowers in their natural colors, an alcove where a mysterious soft light reigned.

"Well, sire, the governor seems to have locked us in. And unless we save ourselves out of window with the curtains——"

"No, do not let us pull them down—rather, draw them close!"

He opened his arms, laughing, and the beauty let the rose fall from her teeth and it burst all its petals open as it reached the carpet.

CHAPTER XXI

COUNTESS CUT COUNTESS

On the road to Paris from Luciennes the poor Countess Dubarry was racing along like a disembodied spirit. An advice from her brother Jean had dashed her down when she had brought the king to the point of arranging for her presentation day.

"So the old donkey has fooled us?" she cried, when she was alone with him.

"I am afraid so. But listen: I stayed in town because I am not trustful like you—and I am not wrong. An hour before the time when I ought to call for the old countess at her inn, I met my man Patrick at the door, where I had sent him to stand sentry since daybreak. He had seen nothing wrong, and I left the carriage and went up stairs quite assured. At her door a woman stopped me to say that her mistress had upset the chocolate, which she boiled herself, on her foot, and was crippled."

"Oh, heavens! you drive me to despair, Jean."

"I am not in despair. You can do what I could not; if there be any imposture you can discover it, and somehow we will punish her. I was consulting a lawyer; he says we must not thrash a person in a house; it is fine and prison, while without——"

"Beat a woman, a countess of the old stock? You mad rogue, let me rather see her and try another method."

Jean conducted her to the Chanticleer Inn, where the old lady dwelt. At the foot of the stairs she was stopped by the landlady.

"Countess Bearn is ill," she said.

"Just so; I am coming to see how she is," and Jeanne darted by her as nimble as a fawn.

"Your ladyship here!" ejaculated the old lady, on seeing the court beauty's face screwed up into the conventional expression of condolence.

"I have only just learnt of the accident. You seem to be in much pain."

"My right foot is scalded. But misfortunes will happen."

"But you know the king expected you this morning?"

"You double my despair, lady."

"His majesty was vexed at your not coming."

"My excuse is in my sufferings, and I must present my most humble excuses to his majesty."

"I am not saying this to cause you pain," said Lady Dubarry, seeing that the old noblewoman was angry, "but just to show you how set his majesty was on seeing you for the step which made him grateful. I regret the accident the more as I think it was due to your excitement from meeting a certain person abruptly at my house."

"The lady who came as I went away?"

"The same; my sister, Mademoiselle Dubarry; only she bore another name when you met her—that of Mademoiselle Flageot."

"Oh, indeed!" said the old dame, with unhidden sourness. "Did you send her to deceive me?"

"No, to do you a service at the same time as you did me one. Let us speak seriously. In spite of your wound, painful but not dangerous, could you make the effort to ride to Luciennes and stand up a short while before the king?"

"Impossible; if you could bear the sight——"

"I wish to assure myself of its extent."

To her great surprise, while writhing in agony, the lady let Jeanne undo the bandage and expose a burn, horridly raw. It spoke eloquently, for, as Lady Bearn had seen and recognized Chon, this self-inflicted hurt raised her to the height of Mutius Scaevola.

The visitor mutely admired. Come to consciousness, the old countess fully enjoyed her triumph; her wild eye gloated on the young woman kneeling at her foot. The latter replaced the bands with the tenderness of her sex to the ailing, placed the limb on the cushions as before, and said as she took a seat beside her:

"You are a grander character than I suspected. I ask your

pardon for not having gone straight to business at the start. Name your conditions."

"I want the two hundred thousand livres at stake in my lawsuit to be guaranteed me," replied the old dame, with a firmness clearly proving that one queen was speaking with another.

"But that would make double if you won your case."

"No, for I look upon the sum I am contesting with the Saluces for as mine own. The like sum is something to thank you for in addition to the honor of your acquaintance. I ask a captaincy and a company for my son, who has martial instincts inborn but would make a bad soldier because he is fit for officership alone. A captaincy now, with a promotion to a colonelcy next year."

"Who is to raise the regiment?"

"The king, for if I spent my money in so doing I should be no better off. I ask the restitution of my vineyard in Touraine; the royal engineers took six acres for the Grand Canal, and condemning it at the expert's valuation I was cheated out of half price. I went to some law expenses in the matter and my whole bill at Lawyer Flageot's is nearly ten thousand livres."

"I will pay this last bill out of my own purse," said Jeanne. "Is this all?"

"Stay, I cannot appear before our great monarch thus. Versailles and its splendors have been so long strange to me that I have no dresses."

"I foresaw that, and ordered a costume at the same maker's as mine own. It will be ready by noon to-morrow."

"I have no jewels."

"The court jewelers will loan you my set called the 'Louise,' as I bought them when the Princess Louise sold her jewels to go into the nunnery. They will charge you two hundred thousand and ten livres, but will take it back in a day or two for two hundred thousand, so that thus you will receive that sum in cash."

"Very well, countess; I have nothing to desire."

"I will write you my pledges, but first, the little letter to the king, which I beg to dictate. We will exchange the documents."

"That is fair," said the old fox, drawing the table toward her, and getting the pen and paper ready, as Lady Dubarry spoke.

"Sire: The happiness I feel at seeing your majesty's acceptance of my offer to present the Countess Dubarry at court—"

The pen stuck and spluttered.
"A bad pen; you should change it!"
"Never mind; it must be broken in."

"—emboldens me (the letter proceeded) to solicit your majesty's favorable eye when I appear at Versailles to-morrow under permission. I venture to hope for a kind welcome from my kinship to a house of which every head has shed his blood in the service of your august ancestors. Anastasie Euphramie Rodolphe, Countess of Bearn."

In return, the plotter handed over the notes and the order on her jewelry.

"Will you let me send my brother for you at three o'clock with the coach?"

"Just so."

"Mind you take care of yourself."

"Fear nothing. I am a noblewoman, and as you have my word, I will keep it to-morrow though I die for it."

So they parted, the old countess, lying down, going over her documents, and the young one lighter than she arrived, but with her heart aching at not having baffled the old litigant who easily defeated the king of France. In the main room, she perceived her brother, draining a second bottle of wine in order not to rouse suspicions on his reasons for staying in the inn. He jumped up and ran to her.

"How goes it?" he asked.

"As Marshal Saxe said to the king on showing him the field of Fontenoy: 'Sire, learn by this sight how dear and agonizing a victory is.'"

"But you have a patroness?"

"Yes, but she costs us a million! It is cruel; but I could not help myself. Mind how you handle her, or she may back out, or charge double her present price."

"What a woman! A Roman!"

"A Spartan. But bring her to Luciennes at three, for I shall not be easy till I have her under lock and key."

As the countess sprang into the coach, Jean watched her and muttered:

"By Crœsus, we cost France a nice round sum! It is highly flattering to the Dubarrys."

CHAPTER XXII

AT A LOSS FOR EVERYTHING

At eleven A. M., Lady Dubarry arrived at her house in Valois Street, determined to make Paris her starting-point for her march to Versailles. Lady Bearn was there, kept close when not under her eye, with the utmost art of the doctors trying to alleviate the pain of her burn.

From over night Jean and Chon and the waiting-woman had been at work and none who knew not the power of gold would have believed in the wonders they wrought in short time.

The hairdresser was engaged to come at six o'clock; the dress was a marvel on which twenty-six seamstresses were sewing the pearls, ribbons and trimmings, so that it would be done in time instead of taking a week as usual. At the same hour as the hairdresser, it would be on hand. As for the coach, the varnish was drying on it in a shed built to heat the air. The mob flocked to see it, a carriage superior to any the dauphiness had; with the Dubarry war-cry emblazoned on the panels: "Charge Onward!" palliated by doves billing and cooing on one side, and a heart transfixed with a dart on the other. The whole was enriched with the attributes of Cupid bows, quivers and the hymeneal torch. This coach was to be at the door at nine.

While the preparations were proceeding at the favorites' the news ran round the town.

Idle and indifferent as the Parisians pretend to be, they are fonder of novelty than any other people. Lady Dubarry in her regal coach paraded before the populace like an actress on the stage.

One is interested in those whose persons are known.

Everybody knew the beauty, as she was eager to show herself in the playhouse, on the promenade and in the stores, like all pretty, rich and young belles. Besides, she was known by her portraits, freaks, and the funny negro boy Zamore. People crowded the Palais Royal, not to see Rousseau play chess, worse luck to the philosophers! but to admire the lovely fairy in her fine dresses and gilded coach, which were so talked about.

Jean Dubarry's saying that "the Dubarrys cost the country a nice sum" was deep, and it was only fair that France who paid the bill, should see the show.

Jeanne knew that the French liked to be dazzled; she was more one of the nation than the queen, a Polander; and as she was kindly, she tried to get her money's worth in the display.

Instead of lying down for a rest as her brother suggested, she took a bath of milk for her complexion, and was ready by six for the hairdresser. A headdress for a lady to go to the court in was a building which took time, in those days. The operator had to be not only a man of art, but of patience. Alone among the craftsmen, hairdressers were allowed to wear the sword like gentlemen.

At six o'clock the court hairdresser, the great Lubin, had not arrived. Nor at a quarter past seven; the only hope was that, like all great men, Lubin was not going to be held cheap by coming punctually.

But a running-footman was sent to learn about him, and returned with the news that Lubin had left his house and would probably arrive shortly.

"There has been a block of vehicles on the way," explained the viscount.

"Plenty of time," said the countess. "I will try on my dress while awaiting him. Chon, fetch my dress."

"Your ladyship's sister went off ten minutes ago to get it," said Doris.

"Hark, to wheels!" interrupted Jean. "It is our coach."

No, it was Chon, with the news that the dressmaker, with two of her assistants, was just starting with the dress to try it on and finish fitting it. But she was a little anxious.

"Viscount," said the countess, "won't you send for the coach?"

"You are right, Jeanne. Take the new horses to Francian the coach-builder's," he ordered at the door, "and bring the new coach with them harnessed to it."

As the sound of the departing horses was still heard, Zamore trotted in with a letter.

"Buckra gemman give Zamore letter."

"What gentleman?"

"On horseback, at the door."

"Read it, dear, instead of questioning. I hope it is nothing untoward."

"Really, viscount, you are very silly to be so frightened," said the countess, but on opening the letter, she screamed and fell half dead on the lounge.

"No hairdresser! no dress! no coach!" she panted, while Chon rushed to her and Jean picked up the letter.

Thus it ran in a feminine handwriting:

"Be on your guard. You will have no hairdresser, dress or coach this evening. I hope you will get this in time. As I do not seek your gratitude, I do not name myself. If you know of a sincere friend, take that as me."

"This is the last straw," cried Jean in his rage. "By the Blue Moon, I must kill somebody! No hairdresser? I will scalp this Lubin. For it is half-past seven, and he has not turned up. Malediction!"

He was not going to court, so he did not hesitate to tear at his hair.

"The trouble is the dress," groaned Chon. "Hairdressers can be found anywhere."

The countess said nothing, but she heaved a sigh which would have melted the Choiseul party had they heard it. Then:

"Come, come," said Chon; "let us be calm. Let us hunt up another hairdresser, and see about that dress not coming."

"Then there is the coach," said Jean. "It ought to have been here by this. It is a plot. Will you not make Sartines arrest the guilty ones—Maupeou sentence them to death—and the whole gang be burned with their fellows on Execution Place? I want to rack the hairdresser, break the dressmaker on the wheel, and flay the coachbuilder alive."

The countess had come to her senses but only to see the dreadful dilemma the better.

At the height of this scene of tribulation, echoing from the boudoir to the street door, while the footmen were blundering over each other in confusion at a score of different orders, a young blade in an applegreen silk coat and vest, lilac breeches and white silk stockings, skipped out of a cab, crossed the deserted sill and the courtyard, bounded up the stairs and rapped on the dressing-room door.

Jean was wrestling with a chins stand with which his coat-tail was entangled, while steadying a huge Japanese idol which he had struck too hard with his fist, when the three knocks, wary, modest and delicate, came at the panel.

Jean opened it with a fist which would have beaten in the gates of Gaza. But the stranger eluded the shock by a leap, and falling on his feet in the third position of dancing, he said:

"My lord, I come to offer my service as hairdresser to the Countess Dubarry, who, I hear, is commanded to present herself at court."

"A hairdresser!" cried the Dubarrys, ready to hug him and dragging him into the room. "Did Lubin send you?"

"You are an angel," said the countess.

"Nobody sent me," returned the young man. "I read in the newspapers that your ladyship was going to court this evening, and I thought I might have a chance of showing that I have a new idea for a court headdress."

"What might be your name, younker?" demanded Jean, distrustfully.

"Leonard, unknown at present, but if the lady will only try me, it will be celebrated to-morrow. Only I must see her dress, that I may create the headdress in harmony."

"Oh my dress, my poor, poor dress!" moaned the countess, recalled to reality by the allusion. "What is the use of having one's hair done up, when one has no robe?" and she fell back on the lounge.

At this instant the doorbell rang. It was a dress-box which the janitor took from a porter in the street, which the butler took from him and which Jean tore out of his hands. He took off the lid, plunged his hand into the depths and yelled with glee. It enclosed a court dress of China satin, with flowers appliqué, and the lace trimming of incredible value.

"A dress!" gasped Jeanne, almost fainting with joy as she had with grief. "But how can it suit me, who was not measured for it?"

Chon tried it with the tape measure.

"It is right in length and width of the waist," said Chon. "This is fabulous."

"The material is wonderful," said Jean.

"The whole is terrifying," said the countess.

"Nonsense! This only proves that if you have bitter enemies, you have some sweet friends."

"It cannot be a mere human friend, Jean," said Chon, "for how would such know the mischief set against us? it must be a sylph."

"I don't care if it is the Old Harry, if he will help me against the Grammonts! He is not so black as those wretches," said the countess.

"Now I think of it, I wager you may entrust your hair to this hairdresser, for he must be sent by the same friend who furnishes the dress," suggested Jean. "Own up that your story was pure gammon?"

"Not at all," protested the young man, showing the newspaper. "I kept it to make the curls for the hair."

"It is no use, for I have no carriage."

"Hark, here it is rolling up to our door," exclaimed Chon.

"Quick!" shouted Jean, "do not let them get away without our knowing to whom we owe all these kindnesses."

And he rushed with janitor, steward and footmen out on the

street. It was too late. Before the door stood two magnificent bay horses, with a gilded coach, lined with white satin. Not a trace of driver or footmen. A man in the street had run up to get the job of holding the horses and those who brought them had left him in charge. A hasty hand had blotted out the coat of arms on the panels and painted a rose.

All this counter-action to the misadventures had taken place in an hour.

Jean had the horses brought into the yard, locking the gates and pocketing the key. Then he returned to the room where the hairdresser was about to give the lady the first proofs of his skill.

"Miracle!" said Chon, "the robe fits perfectly, except an inch out in front, too long; but we can take it up in a minute."

"Will the coach pass muster?" inquired the countess.

"It is in the finest taste. I got into it to try the springs," answered Jean. "It is lined with white satin, and scented with attar of roses."

"Then everything is going on swimmingly," said the countess clapping her hands. "Go on, Master Leonard; if you succeed your fortune is made."

With the first stroke of the comb, Leonard showed that he was an experienced hand. In three-quarters of an hour, Lady Dubarry came forth from his hands more seductive than Aphrodite; for she had more clothes on her, and she was quite as handsome.

"You shall be my own hairdresser," said the lady, eyeing herself in a hand glass, "and every time you do my hair up for a court occasion, you shall have fifty gold pieces. Chon, count out a hundred to the artist, for I want him to consider fifty as a retaining fee. But you must work for none but me."

"Then take your money back, my lady. I want to be free. Liberty is the primary boon of mankind."

"God bless us! It is a philosophic hairdresser!" groaned Jean, lifting his hands. "What are we coming to? Well, Master Leonard, take the hundred, and do as you deused well please. Come to your coach, countess."

These words were addressed to Countess Bearn, who limped out of the inner room.

"Four of you footmen take the lady between you," ordered Jean, "and carry her gently down the stairs. If she utters a single groan, I will have you flogged."

Leonard disappeared during this delicate task.

"Where can he have slipped away?" the young countess wanted to know.

"Where? By some rat hole or bang through the wall!" said the

104

viscount. "As the spirits cut away. Have a care, my dear, lest your headdress becomes a wasp nest, your dress a cobweb, and your carriage a pumpkin drawn by a pair of mice, on arriving at Versailles."

Enunciating this dreadful threat, Viscount Jean got into the carriage, in which was already placed Countess Bearn and the happy woman to whom she was to stand sponsor.

CHAPTER XXIII

THE PRESENTATION

Versailles is still fine to look upon; but it was splendid to view in the period of its glory.

Particularly was it resplendent when a great ceremony was performed, when the wardrobes and warehouses were ransacked to display their sumptuous treasures, and the dazzling illuminations doubled the magic of its wealth.

It had degenerated, but it still was glowing when it opened all its doors and lit up all its flambeaux to hail the court reception of Countess Dubarry. The curious populace forgot its misery and its rags before so much bewildering show, and crammed the squares and Paris road.

All the palace windows spouted flame, and the skyrockets resembled stars floating and shooting in a golden dust.

The king came out of his private rooms at ten precisely, dressed with more care than usual, his lace being richer and the jewels in his garter and shoe buckles being worth a fortune. Informed by Satines that the court ladies were plotting against his favorite, he was careworn and trembled with fury when he saw none but men in the ante-chamber. But he took heart when, in the queen's drawing-room, set aside for the reception, he saw in a cloud of powder and diamond luster, his three daughters, and all the ladies who had vowed the night before to stay away. The Duke of Richelieu ran from one to another, playfully reproaching them for giving in and complimenting them on thinking better of it.

"But what has made you come, duke?" they naturally challenged him.

"Oh, I am not here really—I am but the proxy for my daughter, Countess Egmont. If you will look around you will not see her; she alone, with Lady Grammont and Lady Guemenee has kept the pledge to keep aloof. I am sure what will happen to me for practically staying away. I shall be sent into exile for the fifth time, or to the Bastille for the fourth. That will end my plotting, and I vow to conspire never again."

The king remarked the absentees, and he went up to the Duke of Choiseul who affected the utmost calm and demanded:

"I do not see the Duchess of Grammont."

"Sire, my sister is not well, and she begs me to offer her most humble respects," said Choiseul, only succeeding in flimsy indifference.

"That is bad for her!" ominously said the sovereign, turning his back on the duke and thus facing Prince Guemenee.

"Have you brought your wife?" he questioned.

"Impossible, your majesty: when I went to bring her, she was sick abed."

"Nothing could be worse," said the king. "Good-evening, marshal," he said to Richelieu, who bowed with the suppleness of a young courtier. "You do not seem to have a touch of the complaint?"

"Sire, I am always in good health when I have the pleasure of beholding your majesty."

"But I do not see your daughter the Countess of Egmont. What is the reason of her absence?"

"Alas! sire," responded the old duke, assuming the most sorrowful mien, "my poor child is the more indisposed from the mishap depriving her of the happiness of this occasion, but——"

"Lady Egmont unwell, whose health was the most robust in the realm! this is sad for her!" and the king turned his back on the old courtier as he had on the others whom he snubbed.

Gloomy, anxious and irritated, the king went over to the window, and seizing the carved handle of the sash with one hand, he cooled his fevered brow against the pane. The courtiers could be heard chattering, like leaves rustling before the tempest, while all eyes stared at the clock; it struck the half-hour, when a great uproar of vehicles rumbling on the yard cobblestones resounded under the carriage-way vault. Suddenly the royal brow brightened and a flash shot from his eyes.

"The Right Honorable Lady the Countess of Dubarry!" roared the usher to the grand master of ceremonies. "The Right Honorable the Countess of Bearn!"

Different sensations were making all hearts leap. Invincibly drawn by curiosity, a flood of courtiers moved toward the monarch.

106

The wife of the Marshal of Mirepoix was carried close up to the king, and though she had been in the front of the anti-Dubarryists, she clasped her hands ready for adoration, and exclaimed:

"Oh, how lovely she is!"

The king turned and smiled on the speaker.

"But she is not a mere mortal," said Richelieu; "she is a fairy," which won him the end of the smile.

In truth, never had the countess been fairer, more winsome in expression, more modest in bearing, more noble in figure, more elegant in step or more cunning in showing emotion; her like had never excited admiration in the queen's drawing-room.

Charmingly beautiful, richly but not flauntingly dressed and notable for a tastefully novel headdress, she advanced held by the hand of Countess Bearn. Spite of atrocious pangs, the latter did not hobble or even wince, though the rouge fell in flakes from her face as each step wrung her to the core.

All eyes turned on the singular pair.

The old dame, with an old-fashioned low-necked robe, and her hair built up a foot high above her bright but deep-set eyes like an osprey's, her splendid attire and her skeleton-tread, seemed the image of the past giving her hand to the present. This model of cold, dry dignity guiding decent and voluptuous beauty, struck most with admiration and astonishment.

The vivid contrast made the king fancy that Countess Bearn was bringing him his favorite more youthful and brilliant than ever.

"You have a very fair novice to present, my lady," said he; "but she also has a noble introductress, than whom there is not one whom I am more pleased to see again at court."

The old lady courtesied.

"Go and bow to my daughters," whispered the monarch to Jeanne, "and show that you know how to courtesy. I hope you will not be dissatisfied with the way they reply to you."

His eyes were fixed upon his daughters and compelled them to show politeness, and as Lady Dubarry bowed more lowly than court etiquette prescribed, they were touched, and embraced her with a cordiality which pleased their father.

Henceforward, the countess' success became a triumph.

The Duke of Richelieu, as the victor of Mahon, knew how to maneuver; he went and placed himself behind the chair ready for Countess Dubarry, so that he was near her when the presentation was over, without having to battle with the crowd. Lady Mirepoix, knowing how lucky her old friend was in warfare, had imitated him, and drew her stool close to the favorite's chair.

Supported by the royal love, and the favorable welcome of the royal princesses, Jeanne looked less timidly around among the noblemen, though it was among the ladies that she expected enemies.

"Ah, my Lord of Richelieu," she said, "I had to come here to find you, for you have let a week pass without calling at Luciennes."

"I was preparing for the pleasure of seeing you here, certain here to meet!" "I wish you had imparted the certainty to me, for I was none too sure on that head—considering that I am surrounded by plots to thwart me."

She glared at the old gallant who bore the glance imperturbably.

"Plots? Goodness! what are you talking about?"

"In the first place my hairdresser was spirited away."

"Was he, indeed! what a lucky thing that I sent you a pearl of his craft whom my daughter the Countess of Egmont found somewhere—an artiste most superior to the general run, even to the royal perrukeers, my little Leonard."

"Leonard," repeated the lady.

"Yes, a little fellow who does up my Septimanie's tresses, and whom she keeps hidden from all eyes, as a miser does his cash-box. You are not complaining of him, I think, for your ladyship is turned out, as barbers say, marvelously. Curiously enough, the style reminds me of a sketch which the court painter Boucher gave my daughter, for her to be dressed in accord with it, had she not fallen ill. Poor Seppie! But you were talking of plots?"

"Yes, they kept back my dress."

"This is odious! Though you are not to be pitied when arrayed in such a choice China silk; with flower work applied; now, had you applied to me in your quandary, as I hope you will in the future, I would have sent you the dress my daughter had made for her presence here—it is so like this, that I could vow it is the same."

Countess Dubarry seized both his hands, beginning to understand who was the enchanter who had saved her from the embarrassment.

"I suppose it was in your daughter's coach that I was brought here?" she said.

"Oh, I should know hers, for it was renovated for this occasion with white satin; but there was no time to paint her blazon upon the panels——"

"Only time to paint a rose! Duke, you are a delightful nobleman."

The old peer kissed the hands, of which he made a warm and perfumed mask. Feeling them thrill, he started and asked the cause.

"Who is that man yonder, in a Prussian officer's dress, with black eyes and expressive countenance, by Prince Guemenee?"

"Some superior officer whom the king of Prussia sends to honor your presentation."

"Do not laugh, duke; but that man was in France three or four years ago, and I have been seeking for him everywhere without avail."

"You are in error, countess; the stranger is Count Fenix, who arrived but yesterday."

"How hard he looks at me!"

"Nay, how tenderly everybody is looking at you!"

"Look, he is bowing to me!"

"Everybody is doing that, if they have not done so."

A prey to extraordinary emotion, the lady did not heed the duke's compliments, and, with her sight riveted on the stranger who captivated her attention, she quitted Richelieu, in spite of herself, to move toward the foreigner. The king was watching her and perceived the movement. He thought she wanted him, and approached her, as he had quite long enough stood aloof out of regard for the social restrictions. But the countess was so engrossed that her mind would not be diverted.

"Sire, who is that Prussian officer, now turning away from Prince Guemenee to look this way?"

"The stout figure with the square face enframed in a golden collar?—accredited from my cousin of Prussia—some philosopher of his stamp. I am glad that German philosophy celebrates the triumph of King Petticoat the Third, as they nickname the Louis for their devotion to the sex of which you are the brightest gem. His title is Count Fenix," added the sovereign reflecting.

"It is he," thought Countess Dubarry, but as she kept silence the king proceeded, raising his voice:

"Ladies, the dauphiness arrives at Compiegne to-morrow, the journey having been shortened. Her royal highness will receive at midday precisely. All the ladies presented at court will be of the reception party, except those who were absent to-day. The journey is fatiguing, and her highness can have no desire to aggravate the ills of those who are indisposed."

He looked with severity at Choiseul, Guemenee and Richelieu. A silence of terror surrounded the speaker, whose words were fully understood as meaning disgrace.

"Sire, I pray the exception for the Countess of Egmont, as she is the daughter of my most faithful friend, the Duke of Richelieu."

"His Grace your friend?"

Approaching the old courtier who had comprehended from the motion of the pleader's lips, he said:

"I hope Lady Egmont will be well enough to-morrow to come?"

"Certainly, sire. She would be fit for travel this hour, if your majesty desired it." And he saluted with respect and thankfulness.

The king leaned over to the countess' ear and whispered a word.

"Sire, I am your majesty's most obedient servant." Her reverence was accompanied by a most bewitching smile.

The king waved his hand and retired to his own rooms.

Scarcely had he crossed the threshold before the countess turned more frightened than ever to the singular man who had so monopolized her. Like the others, he had bowed as the monarch withdrew, but his brow had worn a haughty, almost menacing aspect. As soon as Louis had disappeared, he came and paused within a step or two of Lady Dubarry.

Urged by invincible curiosity, she took a step toward him, so that he could say in a low voice as he bent to her:

"Am I recognized, lady?"

"Yes, as my prophet of Louis XV. Square."

"Well," queried the man with the clear, steady gaze, "Did I lie when I told you of becoming the Queen of France?"

"No; your prophecy is all but accomplished. Hence, I am ready to keep my promise. Speak your wish."

"The place is ill chosen, and the time has not come."

"I am ready to fulfill it any time."

"Can I come any time?"

"Yes; will it be as Count Fenix?"

"My title will be Count Joseph Balsamo."

"I shall not forget it, Balsamo," repeated the favorite as the mysterious stranger was merged with the crowd.

CHAPTER XXIV

THE DAUPHINESS' RECEPTION

On the following day, Compiegne was intoxicated and transported. The people had not slept through the night from getting ready to welcome the bride of the prince royal.

Latin, French, and German inscriptions adorned the evergreen arches, wound with garlands of roses and lilac.

The royal prince had come down in the night incog, with his two brothers, and they had ridden out to meet the princess from Austria. The gallant idea had not come to the dauphin of his own impulse, but from his tutor, Lord Lavauguyon, who had been instructed by the king on the proper line of conduct to be followed by the heir to the throne. Previous sovereigns had also taken this kind of preliminary view of the fated spouse, without the veil of etiquette.

The eldest prince rode out, grave, and his two brothers, smiling. At half after eight, they came back; the dauphin serious as when he started, Provence almost sulky, and Artois gayer than at the outset. The first was disquieted, the second envious, and the last delighted—for all had found the lady most lovely. Thus each betrayed his temperament.

At the meeting of the two parties, that of the king and the bride of his son, all got out of the carriages, except the king and the archduchess. Around the dauphin were all the young nobles, while the old nobility clustered round the king.

The lady's carriage door opened, and the Austrian princess sprang lightly to the ground. As she advanced toward the royal coach, Louis had the door opened, and eagerly stepped out.

The princess had so exactly calculated the steps that she threw herself on her knees just as he alighted. He stooped to lift her up, and kissed her affectionately, covering her with a look which caused her to redden.

She blushed again as the dauphin was presented to her. She had pleasant words to say to all the royal princes and princesses. But here came a hitch, till the king, glancing around, spied the Countess Dubarry, and took her hand.

Everybody stepped aloof, so that the sovereign was left alone with his favorite and the new arrival.

"I present the Countess Dubarry, my dearest friend!"

The Austrian turned pale, but the most kindly smile glittered on her blanching lips.

"Your majesty is very happy in having so lovely a friend," she said, "and I am not surprised at the attachment she inspires."

All looked on with astonishment approaching stupefaction. It was evident that the new-comer was repeating the Austrian court's instructions—perhaps her mother's own words.

While the princess entered the royal coach, passing the Duke of Choisuel without noticing him, the church bells clanged. Countess

Dubarry radiantly got into her coach, up to the door of which came Chevalier Jean.

"Do you know who that young whippersnapper is?" he asked, pointing to a horseman at the dauphiness' coach window. "That is Philip of Taverney, who gave me that sword thrust."

"Well, who is the beautiful girl with whom he is talking?"

"His sister, and to my mind you have the same need to beware of that girl as I of her brother."

"You are mad."

"I have my wits about me. I shall keep an eye on the blade anyhow."

"And I shall watch the budding beauty."

"Hush!" said Jean; "here comes your friend Richelieu."

"What is wrong, my dear duke? You look discontented," said the countess, with her sweetest smile.

"Does it not strike your ladyship that we are all very dull, not to say sad, for such a joyous affair? I can recall going out to meet another princess for the royal couch, amiable like this one, and as fair. It was the dauphin's mother. We were all jolly. Is it because we were younger?"

"No, my dear marshal, it is because the monarchy is older."

All who heard shuddered at this voice behind the duke. He turned and saw an elderly gentleman, stylish in appearance, who laid his hand on his shoulder as he smiled misanthropically.

"Gads my life! it is Baron Taverney. Countess," added the duke, "here is one of my oldest friends, for whom I beg your kindness—Baron Taverney of Redcastle."

"The father of that pair," said Jean and Jeanne to themselves, as they bowed in salutation.

"My lords and gentlemen," shouted the grand master of ceremonies, "to your places in the coaches."

The two aged nobles bowed to the favorite and her brother, and went into the same vehicle, glad to be united after long absence.

"What do you say to that? I do not like the old fellow a whit better than the cubs," said Jean Dubarry.

"What a pity that the little imp, Gilbert, ran away. As he was brought up in their house, he might furnish particulars about the family," said the countess.

The dialogue was broken off by the movement of all the carriages.

After a night at Compiegne, the united courts—the sundown of one era, the sunburst of another—swept intermingled on to Paris, that gulf which was to swallow up the whole of them.

CHAPTER XXV

GILBERT SNAPS GOLDEN CHAINS

It is time to return to Gilbert.

Our little philosopher had cooled in his admiration for Chon since at the outbreak of the collision between Chevalier Jean and Philip of Taverney he had learnt the name of his protectress.

Often, at Taverney, when he was skulking and listening to the chat of the baron and his daughter, he had heard the old noble express himself plainly about the favorite Dubarry. His interested hatred had found a sympathetic echo in the boy's bosom; and Andrea never contradicted her father's abuse, for, it must be allowed, Lady Dubarry's name was deeply scorned in the country.

What completely ranked Gilbert on the side of the old noble was that Nicole had sometimes exclaimed:

"I wish I were Dubarry."

Chon was too busy after the duel to think about Gilbert, who forgot his bad impression as he entered the court capital in his frank admiration. He was still under the spell when he slept in the attic of the royal palace. The only matter in his dreams was that he, the poor boy, was lodged like the foremost noblemen of France, without his being a courtier or a lackey.

Gilbert was in one of the thinking fits common to him when events surpassed his will or comprehension, when he was told that Mademoiselle Chon wanted to see him. She was waiting in her carriage for him to accompany her on a ride. She sat in the front seat, with a large chest and a small dog. Gilbert and a steward named Cranche were to have the other places.

To preserve his position, Gilbert sat behind Chon, and the steward, without even thinking of objecting, sat behind the dog and box.

Like all who lived in Versailles, Chon drew a free breath with pleasure in quitting the grand palace for the woods and pastures, and said as she turned half round on their leaving the town:

"How does the philosopher like Versailles?"

"It is very fine. So we are quitting it so soon?"

"We are going to our place."

"Your place, you mean," grumbled Gilbert in the tone of a bear becoming tamed.

"I mean that I am going to introduce you to my sister, whom you must try to please, for she is hand and glove with all the great

113

lords of the kingdom. By the way, Master Cranche, we must have a suit of clothes made for this young gentleman."

"The ordinary livery?" queried the man.

"Livery?" snarled Gilbert, giving the upper servant a fierce look.

"Oh, no; I will tell you the style after I communicate my notion to my sister. But it must be ready at the same time as Zamore's new clothes."

Gilbert was startled at this talk.

"Zamore is a little playfellow for you, the governor of the royal castle of Luciennes," explained Chon. "Make friends with him, as he is a good fellow, in spite of his color."

Gilbert was eager to know what color Zamore was, but he reflected that philosophers ought not to be reproved for inquisitiveness, and he contained himself.

"I will try," replied the youth with a smile which he thought full of dignity.

Luciennes was what had been described to him.

"So this is the pleasure house which has cost the country so dearly!" he mused.

Joyous dogs and eager servants came to greet the mistress' sister. Jeanne had not come, and Chon was glad to see her first of all.

"Sylvie," she said to a pretty girl who came to take the lap dog and the chest, "give Misapoof and the box to Cranche, and take my little philosopher to Zamore!"

The chambermaid did not know what kind of animal a philosopher was, but Chon's glance directed her to Gilbert, and she beckoned him to follow her. But for the tone of command which Chon had used, the youth would have taken Sylvie for other than a servant. She was dressed more like Andrea than Nicole. She gave Gilbert a smile, for the recommendation denoted that Chon had a fancy, if not affection for the new-comer.

Gilbert was rather daunted by the idea of appearing before so grand an official as a royal governor, but the words that Zamore was a good fellow reassured him. Friend of a viscount and a court lady already, he might face a governor.

"How the court is slandered!" he thought; "for it is easy to make friends among the courtiers. They are kind and hospitable."

In a noble Roman room, on cushions, with crossed legs, squatted Zamore, eating candies out a satin bag.

"Oh!" exclaimed the incipient philosopher, "what do you call this thing?"

"Me no ting—me gubbernor," blubbered Zamore.

Gilbert had never before seen a negro. The uneasy glance which

114

he turned up to Sylvie caused that lively girl to burst into a peal of laughter.

Grave and motionless as an idol, Zamore kept on diving with his paw in the bag of sweetmeats and munching away.

At this moment the door opened to give admission to Steward Cranche and a tailor to take the measures of Gilbert.

"Do not pull him about too much," said the steward.

"Oh, I am done," said the knight of the thimble; "the costume of Sganarelle is a loose one, and we never bother about a fit."

"Oh, he will look fine as Sganarelle," said Sylvie. "And is he to have the high hat like Mother Goose's?"

Gilbert did not hear the reply, as he pushed aside the tailor and would not help any more preparations. He did not know that Sganarelle was a comic character in a popular play, but he saw that it was a ludicrous one, and he was enlightened further by Sylvie's laughter. She departed with tailor and steward, leaving him alone with the black boy, who continued to roll his eyes and devour the bonbons.

What riddles for the country boy! what dreads and pangs for the philosopher who guessed that his manly dignity was in as much danger in Luciennes as at Taverney.

Still he tried to talk to Zamore, but that interesting African, sitting astride of a chair on casters, made it run him round the room a dozen times with a celerity which ought to have shown by anticipation that the velocipede was a practical machine.

Suddenly a bell tinkled and Zamore darted out of the room with as much rapidity as he had shown on the novel quadricycle.

Gilbert would have followed, but on looking through the doorway, he saw the passage so crowded with servants guarding noblemen in gay clothes, that he shivered and slunk back.

An hour passed, without the return of Zamore or Sylvie. Gilbert was longing for human company, when a footman came to take him to Mademoiselle Chon.

Free, after having informed her sister how she had conducted the mission to Lady Bearn, Chon was breakfasting with a hearty appetite, in a loose dressing-gown, in a morning room. She cast a glance on Gilbert without offering him a seat.

"How have you hit off with Zamore?" she inquired, after tossing off a glass of wine like liquid topaz.

"How could I make the acquaintance of a black boy who does not speak, but stares and gulps down candies?"

"I thought you said all were equal?"

"He may be my equal, but I do not think him so," answered Gilbert.

115

"What fun he is!" muttered Chon: "you seem not to give away your heart in a hurry?"

"With slowness, lady."

"I hoped you held me in affection?"

"I have considerable liking for you personally, but——"

"Thanks for so much! You overpower me. How long does it take for one to win the good graces of so disdainful a fellow?"

"Much time; some would never win them."

"Ah, this explains why you could suddenly leave Taverney Castle after staying there eighteen years. It appears that its masters could not obtain your friendship and confidence?"

"Not all."

"What did they do? Who displeased you?"

"I am not complaining."

"Oh, very well! if you do not want to give your confidence. I might help you to come out even with these Taverneys if you told me what they are like."

"I take no revenge, or I take it with my own hand," said Gilbert proudly.

"Still as you bear a grudge against them, or several, and we have one, we ought to be allies."

"You are wrong, lady. I feel very different toward different members of the family."

"Is Lord Philip one whom you paint black or rosy?"

"I bear no ill to Master Philip, who has done nothing to me one way or another."

"Then you would not be a witness against him in favor of my brother about that duel?"

"I should be bound to speak the truth, and that would be unfavorable toward Chevalier Dubarry."

"Do you make him out wrong?"

"He was so, to insult the dauphiness."

"Are you upholding the dauphiness?"

"I stand for justice."

"You are mad, boy; never talk of justice in a royal residence. When one serves a master, he takes the responsibility."

"Not so; every man should obey his conscience. Any way, I have no master. I did not ask to come here, and now I will go away, freely as I came."

"Oh, no, you don't," cried Chon, amazed at this rebellion and getting angered.

Gilbert frowned.

"No, no, let us have peace. Here you will have but three persons to please. The king, my sister and myself."

116

"How am I to please you?"

"Well, you have seen Zamore? He gets already so much a year out of the royal private purse; he is governor of Luciennes, and though he may be laughed at for his blubber lips and complexion, he is courted and called my lord."

"I shall not do that."

"What, when you assert that all men are brothers?"

"That is the reason why I will not acknowledge him my lord."

Chon was beaten with her own weapons; she bit her lips.

"You do not seem to be ambitious?"

"Yes, I am," and his eyes sparkled.

"To be a doctor? You shall be a doctor. That was the costume you were measured for. Royal physician, too."

"I? who know not the A B C of medical science. You are mocking at me, lady."

"Does Zamore know anything about governing a castle?"

"I see: you want me to be a sham doctor, a buffoon? The king wants another merry-maker?"

"Why not? Don't you know that the Duke of Tresmes begs my sister to appoint him her monkey. But don't hang your head. Keep that lumpish air for your doctoral uniform. Meanwhile, as you must live on something better than your pills, go and have breakfast with the governor."

"With Zamore? I am not hungry."

"You will be before evening; if we must give you an appetite, we will call in the whipper to the royal pages."

The youth trembled and turned pale.

"Go back to my Lord Zamore," continued Chon, taking the silence for consent, or at least submission. "You will find he is fed daintily. Mind not to be an ingrate, or you will be taught what gratitude is."

A lackey conducted Gilbert to the mock governor's dining-room, but he would not eat anything. Nevertheless, when the costume of the doctor in Molière's comedy was brought, he submitted to being shown how he was to wear it.

"I thought that the doctors of that time carried an inkhorn and a quill to write out their prescriptions," suggested Gilbert.

"By Jove they did!" exclaimed the steward. "Let us have the **** complete while we are about it."

The foreman charged to get the articles, also acquainted Chon, who was going to join her sister in Paris, with the astonishing willingness of her pet. She was so pleased that she sent a little purse with some silver in it, to be added to the doctor's girdle along with the inkhorn.

117

Gilbert sent his thanks, and expressed a wish to be left alone to put on the costume.

"Make haste," said the steward, "that the young lady may see you before she is off to Paris."

Gilbert looked out of the window to see how the gardens were arranged. Returning to the table, he tore the long black doctoral gown into three strips, which he made a rope of by tying the ends together. On the table he laid the hat and the purse and the following declaration which he wrote:

"Lady: The foremost of boons is Liberty. The holiest of duties is topreserve it. As you do violence to my feelings, I set myself free.
Gilbert."

He addressed this epistle to Chon, tied his twelve feet of serge rope to the window sill, glided down like a serpent, and dropped on the terrace at risk of breaking his neck. Though stunned a little by the fall, he ran to some trees, scrambled up among the boughs, slipped downward till he was on a lower level and could reach the ground where he ran away with all his might.

When they came for him half an hour after, he was far beyond their reach.

CHAPTER XXVI

THE OLD BOTANIST

On the trunk of a tree overthrown by a storm in Meudon Woods a man was seated.

Under his grizzled wig he showed a mild and shrewd visage. His brown coat was of good cloth, as were his breeches; and his gray waistcoat was worked on the flaps. His gray cotton stockings imprisoned well-made and muscular legs; his buckled shoes, though dusty in patches, had been washed at the top by the morning dews.

Near him, on the trunk, was a green box, open and stuffed with freshly gathered plants. Between his legs he held a cane with a crutch handle, ending in a sort of pick.

He was eating a piece of bread, and tossing crumbs to the wild birds, which flew down on the pieces and took them off to their nooks with joyful peeps.

Suddenly he heard hurried steps, and seeing on looking up, a young man with disquieting aspect, he rose. He buttoned up his coat and closed his overcoat above it.

His air was so calming that the intruder on his peace came to a stop and doffed his hat.

It was Gilbert. Gilbert, much the worse for his roaming the woods through the night since he had fled from Luciennes in order not to lose his freedom.

Remarking this sudden timidity, the old man appeared to be put at ease by it.

"Do you want to speak to me, my friend?" he asked, smiling, and laying the piece of bread on the tree.

"Yes, for I see that you are throwing away bread on the birds as though it were not written that the Lord provides for the sparrows."

"The Lord provides," returned the old gentleman, "no doubt, young man; but the hand of man is one of the means. You are wrong if you said that as a reproach, for never is cast-away bread—in the desert or on the crowded street—lost to living creatures. Here, the birds get it; there, the beggars."

"Though this be the wilds, I know of a man who wants to dispute that bread with the birds," said Gilbert, though struck by the soft and penetrating voice of the stranger.

"Are you the man—and are you hungered?"

"Sharply so, and if you would allow——"

With eager compassion the gentleman took up the crust, but, suddenly reflecting, he scrutinized Gilbert with a quick yet profound glance.

Gilbert was not so like a starving man that the meditation was warranted. His dress was decent, though earth-stained in places. His linen was white, for he had at Versailles, on the previous evening, changed his shirt out of his parcel; but from its dampness, it was visible that he had slept in the woods. In all this and his white and taper hands, the man of vague reverie was revealed rather than the hard worker.

Not wanting for tact, Gilbert understood the distrust and hesitation of the stranger in respect to him, and hastened to annul conjectures which might be unfavorable.

"After twelve hours, hunger begins, and I have eaten nothing for four-and-twenty," he observed.

The truth of the words was supported by his emotion, the quaver of his voice and the pallor of his face. The old gentleman

119

therefore ceased to waver, or rather to fear. He held out not only the bread, but a handkerchief in which he was carrying cherries.

"I thank you," said Gilbert, repulsing the fruit gently; "only the bread, which is ample."

Breaking the crust in two, he took one portion and pushed back the other. Then he sat on the grass, a yard or two away from the old gentlemen, who viewed him with increasing wonder. The meal did not last long, as the bread was scant and Gilbert hungry. With no words did the observer trouble him, but continued his mute and furtive examination while apparently only attending to his plants and flowers in the box.

But seeing that Gilbert was going to drink at a pool, he quickly called out:

"Do not drink that water, young man. It is infected by the detritus of the plants dead last year and by the frog-spawn swimming on the surface. You had better take some cherries, as they will quench thirst better than water. I invite you to partake as I see you are not an importunate guest."

"It is true, sir; importunity is the opposite of my nature. I fear nothing so much as being importunate, as I have just been proving at Versailles."

"Oh! so you come from Versailles?" queried the stranger, looking hard at him. "A rich place, where only the proud or the poor die of want."

"I am both, sir."

"Have you quarreled with your master?"

"I have no master."

"That is a very lofty answer," said the other, putting away the plants in the box, while regarding the young man.

"Still it is exact."

"No, young man, for everybody has a master here, as we all suffer the domination of a higher power. Some are ruled by men, some by principles: and the sternest masters are not always those who order or strike with the human voice or hand."

"I confess I am ruled by principles," replied Gilbert. "They are the only masters which the mind may acknowledge without shame."

"Oh, those are your principles, are they? You seem very young to have any settled principles."

"I am young but I have studied, or rather read a little in such works as 'On the Inequality of Classes,' and 'The Social Contract;' out of them comes all my knowledge, and perhaps all my dreams."

These words kindled a flame in the hearer's eyes; he so started that he broke a flower rebellious to being packed away.

"These may not be your principles, but they are Rousseau's."

"Dry stuff for a youth," said the other; "sad matter for contemplation at twenty years of age; a dry and scentless flower for imagination in the springtide of life."

"Misfortune ripens a man unseasonably, sir."

"As you study the philosopher of Geneva, do you make a personal allusion there?"

"I do not know anything about him," rejoined Gilbert, candidly.

"Know, young man, that he is an unhappy creature." With a sigh he said it.

"Impossible! Jean Jacques Rousseau unhappy? Is there no justice above more than on earth? The man unhappy who has consecrated his life to the welfare of the race."

"I plainly see that you do not know him; so let us rather speak of yourself. Whither are you going?"

"To Paris. Do you belong there?"

"So far as I am living there, but I was not born in it. Why the question?"

"It is attached to the subject we were talking of; if you live in Paris, you may have seen the Philosopher Rousseau."

"Oh, yes, I have seen him."

"He is looked at as he passes along—they point to him as the benefactor of humanity?"

"No; the children follow him, and, encouraged by their parents, throw stones at him."

"Gracious! still he has the consolation of being rich," said Gilbert, with painful stupefaction.

"Like yourself, he often wonders where the next meal is coming from."

"But, though poor, he is powerful, respected and well considered?"

"He does not know of a night, in lying down, that he will not wake in the Bastille."

"How he must hate men!"

"He neither loves not hates them: they fill him with disgust, that is all."

"I do not understand how he can not hate those who ill use him," exclaimed Gilbert.

"Rousseau has always been free, and strong enough to rely on himself. Strength and liberty make men meek and good; it is only weakness and slavery which create the wicked."

"I guessed this as you explain it; and that is why I wished to be free." I see that we agree on one point, our liking for Rousseau.

"Speak for yourself, young man: youth is the season for illusions."

"Nay; one may be deceived upon things, but not on men."

"Alas, you will learn by and by, that it is men particularly about whom deception is easiest. Perhaps Rousseau is a little fairer than other men; but he has his faults, and great ones."

Gilbert shook his head, but the stranger continued to treat him with the same favor, though he was so uncivil.

"You said you had no master?"

"None, though it dwelt with me to have a most illustrious one; but I refused on the condition that I should make the amusement of noble idlers. Being young, able to study and make my way, I ought not to lose the precious time of youth and compromise in my person the dignity of man."

"This was right," said the stranger gravely; "but have you determined on a career?"

"I should like to be a physician."

"A grand and noble career, where one may decide between true science, modest and martyr-like, and quackery, impudent, rich and bloated. If you love truth, young man, be a doctor. If you love popular applause, be a doctor."

"I am afraid it will cost a lot of money to study, although Rousseau learned for nothing."

"Nothing? oh, young man," said the plant-collector, with a mournful smile, "do you call nothing the most precious of heavenly blessings—candor, health and sleep? That was the price the Genevian seeker of wisdom paid for the little he knows."

"Little! when he is a great musical composer!"

"Pooh, because the king sings 'I have lost my servant,' that does not prove 'The Village Sorcerer' to be a good opera."

"He is a noted botanist!"

"An herb-gatherer, very humble and ignorant amid the marvels known as plants and flowers."

"He is a Latin scholar, for I read that he had translated Tacitus."

"Bah, because in his conceit he wanted to be master of all crafts. But Tacitus, who is a rough antagonist to wrestle with, tired him. No, no, my good young man, in spite of your admiration, there are no more Admirable Crichtons, and what man gains in breadth he loses in depth. Rousseau is a superficial man whose surface is a trifle wider than most men's, that is all."

"Many would like to attain his mark," said the youth.

"Do you slur at me?" asked the stranger with a good nature disarming Gilbert.

"God forbid, for it is too much pleasure to chat for me to disoblige you. You draw me out and I am amazed at the language I

122

am using, for I only picked it out of books, which I did not clearly follow. I have read too much, but I will read again with care. But I forget that while your talk is valuable to me, mine only wastes your time, for you are herb-gathering."

"No," said the botanist, fixing his gray eyes on the youth, who made a move to go but wanted to be detained. "My box is clearly full and I only want certain mosses; I heard that capillary grows round here."

"Stay, I saw some yonder."

"How do you know capillarys?"

"I was born on the woodland; the daughter of the nobleman on whose estate I was reared, liked botany; she had a collection and the objects had their names on labels attached. I noticed that what she called capillary was called by us rustics maidenhair fern."

"So you took a taste for botany?"

"It was this way. I sometimes heard Nicole—she is the maid to Mademoiselle Andrea de Taverney—say that her mistress wanted such and such a plant for her herbarium, so I asked her to get a sketch of them, and I searched in the woods till I raked them up. Then I transplanted them where she must find them, and used to hear the lady, in taking her walk, cry out: 'How odd! here is the very thing I was looking for!'"

The old gentleman looked with more heed and it made Gilbert lower his eyes blushing, for the interest had tenderness in it.

"Continue to study botany, which leads as a flowery path to medicine. Paris has free schools, and I suppose your folks will supply your maintenance."

"I have no relations, but I can earn my living at some trade."

"Yes, Rousseau says in his 'Emile,' that every one should learn a trade even though he were a prince's son."

"I have not read that book, but I have heard Baron Taverney mock at the maxim, and pretend grief at not having made his son a joiner. Instead, he made him a soldier, so that he will dismember instead of joining."

"Yes, these nobles bring their sons up to kill and not to nourish. When revolution comes, they will be forced to beg their bread abroad or sell their sword to the foreigners, which is more shameful. But you are not noble, and you have a craft?"

"No, I have a horror for rough toil; but give me a study and see how I will wear out night and day in my tasks."

"You have been to school, if not to college?"

"I know but to read and write," said Gilbert, shaking his head. "My mother taught me to read, for seeing me slight in physique, she said, 'You will never be a good workman, but must try to be priest or scholar. Learn to read, Gilbert, and you will not have to split wood, guide the plow or hew stone.' Unhappily my mother died before I could more than read, so I taught myself writing. First I traced letters on sand with a sharp stick till I found that the letters used in writing were not those of print, which I was copying. Hence I hope to meet some one who will need my pen, a blind man who will need my eyes, or a dumby who needs my tongue."

"You appear to have willingness and courage; but do you know what it will cost you to live in town?—at least three times what it did in the country."

"Well, suppose I have shelter and for rest after toil, I can shift on six cents a day."

"That is the right talk. I like this kind of man," said the plant collector. "Come with me to Paris and I will find you an independent profession by which you may live."

"Oh, my friend," exclaimed Gilbert, intoxicated with delight. "I accept your offer and I am grateful. But what will I have to do in your company?"

"Nothing but toil. But you will mete out the amount of your work. You will exercise your right of youth, freedom, happiness and even of idleness after you earn the right to be at leisure," added the unnamed benefactor, smiling as though in spite of his will.

Then, raising his eyes to heaven, he ejaculated: "Oh, youth, vigor and liberty!" with an inexpressibly poetical melancholy spreading over his fine, pure lineaments.

"Now, lead me to the spot where the maidenhair is to be found," he said.

Gilbert stepped out before the old gentleman and the pair disappeared in the underwood.

CHAPTER XXVII

MASTER JACQUES

Before the day was over the pair could enter the capital. The young man's heart beat as he perceived Notre Dame Cathedral towers and the ocean of housetops.

"Oh, Paris!" he cried with rapture.

"Yes, Paris, a mass of buildings, a gulf of evils," said the old gentleman. "On each stone yonder you would see a drop of blood or a tear, if the miseries within those abodes could show themselves without."

Gilbert repressed his enthusiasm, which cooled of itself.

They entered by a poor district and the sights were hideous.

"It is going on eight," said the conductor, "let us be quick, young man, for goodness' sake."

Gilbert hurried on.

"I forget to say that I am a married man," said the stranger, after a cold silence which began to worry the youth. "And my wife, who is a genuine Parisian, will probably grumble at our coming home late. Besides, she does not like strangers. Still, I have invited you; so, come along. Or, rather, here we are."

By the last sunbeams, Gilbert, looking up, saw the name-plate of Plastrière Street at a corner.

The other paused before an alley door with iron bars to the upper portion. He pulled a leather thong hanging out of a hole, and this opened the door.

"Come quickly," he called to the youth, who hesitated on the threshold, and he closed the alley door after them.

At the end of a few steps up the dark passage, Gilbert stumbled on the lower step of a black, steep flight of stairs. Used to the locality, the old gentleman had gone up a dozen steps. Gilbert rejoined him and stopped only when he did, on a landing worn by feet, on which opened two doors. The stranger pulled a hare's foot hanging at one, and a shrill bell tinkled inside the room.

A woman some fifty years of age appeared, and she and the man spoke together:

"Is it very late, Therese?" asked the latter timidly.

"A nice hour to come to supper, Jacques!" snarled the woman.

"Come, come, we will make up for the delay," said the one called Jacques, shutting the door and taking the collecting case from Gilbert's hands.

"Have we a messenger boy here?" exclaimed the old woman: "We only wanted him to complete the merry company. So you can no longer do so much as carry your heap of weeds and grass? Master Jacques does the grand with a boy to carry his trash—I beg his pardon, he is becoming quite a great nobleman."

"Be a little quiet, Therese."

"Pay the boy and get rid of him; we want no spies here."

Pale as death, Gilbert sprang toward the door, but Jacques stopped him, saying with some firmness:

125

"This is not a messenger-boy or a spy. He is a guest whom I bring home."

"A guest?" and the hag let her hands drop along her hips. "This is the last straw."

"Light up, Therese," said the host, still kindly, but showing more will; "I am warm, and we are hungry."

The vixen's grumbling diminished in loudness. She drew fire with flint and steel, while Gilbert stood still by the sill which he regretted he had crossed. Jacques perceived what he suffered, and begged him to come forward.

Gilbert saw the hag's yellow and morose face by the first glimmer of the thin candle stuck in a brass candlestick. It inspired him with dislike. On her part the virago was far from liking the pale, fine countenance, circumspect silence and rigidity of the youth.

"I do not wonder at your being heated and hungry," she growled. "It must be tiresome to go browsing in the woods, and it is awful hard work to stoop from time to time to pick up a root. For I suppose this person gathers leaves and buds, too, for herb-collecting is the trade for those who do not any work."

"This is a good and honest young man," said Jacques, in a still firmer voice, "who has honored me with his company all day, and whom my good Therese will greet as a friend, I am sure."

"Enough for two is scant for three," she grumbled.

"We are both frugal."

"I know your kind of frugality. I declare that there is not enough bread in the house for such abstemiousness, and that I am not going down three flights of stairs for more. Anyway, the baker's is shut up."

"Then, I will go," said Jacques, frowning. "Open the door, for I mean it."

"Oh, in that case, I suppose I must do it," said the scold.

"What am I for but to carry out your freaks? Come and have supper."

A table was set in the next room, small and square, with cherry wood chairs, having straw bottoms, and a bureau full of darned hose.

Gilbert took a chair; the old woman placed a plate and the appurtenances, all worn with hard use, before him, with a pewter goblet.

"I thought you were going after bread?" said Jacques.

"Never mind; I found a roll in the cupboard, and you ought to manage on a pound and a half of bread, eh?"

So saying, she put the soup on the board. All three had good appetites, but Gilbert held in his, but he was the first to get through.

126

"Who has called to-day?" inquired the host, to change the termagant's ideas.

"The whole world, as usual. You promised Lady Boufflers four quires of music, Lady Escars two arias, and Lady Penthievre a quartet with accompaniment. They came or sent. But the ladies must go without their music because our lord was out plucking dandelions."

Jacques did not show anger, though Gilbert expected him to do so, for he was used to this manner. The soup was followed by a chunk of boiled beef, on a delft plate grooved with knife points. The host served Gilbert scantily, as Therese was watching, took the same sized piece and passed the plate to his Xantippe.

She handed a slice of bread to the guest. It was so small that Jacques blushed, but he waited until she had helped him and herself, when he took the loaf from her. He handed it to Gilbert and bade him cut off according to his wants.

"Thank you," said Gilbert, as some beans in butter were served, "but I have no longer any hunger. I never eat but one dish. And I drink only water."

Jacques had a little wine for himself.

"You must see about the young man's bed," said the latter, putting down the bottle. "He must be tired."

Therese dropped her fork and stared at the speaker.

"Sleep here? you must be mad. Bring people home to sleep—I expect you want to give up your own bed to them. You must be off your head. Is it keeping a lodging-house you are about? If this is so, don't look to me! get a cook and servants. It is bad enough to be yours, without waiting on Tom, Dick and Harry."

"Therese, listen to me," replied Jacques, with his grave, even voice; "it is for one night only. This young man has never set foot in Paris, and comes under my safe-conduct. I am not going to have him go to an inn, though he has to have my own bed, look you."

Therese understood that struggle was out of the question for the present and she changed her tactics by fighting for Gilbert, but as an ally who would stab him in the back at the first chance.

"I daresay you know all about him, or you would not have brought him home, and he ought to stay here. I will shake up some kind of a bed in your study among the papers."

"No, no, a study is not fit for a sleeping-room; a light might set fire to the writings."

"Which would be no loss," sneered Therese.

"There is the garret; the room with a fine outlook over such gardens as are scarce in Paris. Have no anxiety, Therese; the young man will not be a burden; he will earn his own living. Take a candle and follow me."

Therese sighed, but she was mastered. Gilbert gravely rose and followed his benefactor. On the landing Gilbert saw drinking water in a tank.

"Is water dear in town?" he inquired.

"They charge for it; but any way, bread and water are two things which man has no right to refuse to his fellow-man."

"But at Taverney, water ran freely, and the luxury of the poor is cleanliness."

"Take as much as you like, my friend," said Master Jacques.

Gilbert filled a crock and followed the host, who was astonished at so young a man allying the firmness of the people with the instinct of the aristocratic.

CHAPTER XXVIII

IN THE LOFT

To tell the truth, the loft where Jacques stowed his guest was not fit for habitation. The mattress was on the floor and the chief article of furniture. Rats had pulled about and gnawed a heap of yellowed papers. On clotheslines across the attic were paper bags in which were drying beans, herbs and household linen.

"It is not nice to look upon," apologized the host, "but sleep and darkness make the sumptuous palace and the meanest cottage much alike. Sleep as youth can do, and nothing will prevent you thinking you slept in the royal palace. But mind you do not set the house afire. We will talk over matters in the morning."

"Good-night and hearty thanks," said Gilbert, left alone in the garret.

With all the precaution recommended, he took up the light and made the rounds of the room. As the newspapers and pamphlets were tied in bales he did not open them; but the bean bags were made of printed pages of a book, which caught his eye with the lines. One sack, knocked off the line by his head, burst on the floor, and in trying to replace the beans, he fell to reading the wrappers. It was a page from the love of a poor youth for a lovely and fashionable lady named Lady Warrens. Gilbert was congratulating himself on having the whole night to read this love story on the wrappers when the candle went out and left him in gloom. He was ready to weep with rage. He dropped the papers on the heap of beans and flung himself on his couch where he slept deeply in spite of his disappointment.

He was roused only by the grating of the lock. It was bright day; Gilbert saw his host gently enter.

"Good-morning," he muttered, with the red of shame on his cheeks as he saw Jacques staring at the beans and emptied bags.

"Did you sleep soundly?"

"Ye-es."

"Nay, are you not a sleep-walker?"

"Alas, I see why you say that. I sat up reading till the candle was burnt out, from the first sheet on which my eyes fell so greatly interesting me. Do you, who know so much, know to what lovely novel those pages belong?"

"I do not know, but as I notice the word 'Confessions' on the headline, I should think it was Memoirs."

"Oh, no, the man so speaking is not doing so of himself; the avowals are too frank—the opinions too impartial."

"I think you are wrong," said the old gentleman quickly. "The author wanted to set an example of showing himself to his fellows as heaven created him."

"Do you know the author?"

"The writer is Jean Jacques Rousseau. These are stray pages out of his 'Confessions.'"

"So this unknown, poor, obscure youth, almost begging his way afoot on the highroads, was the man who was to write 'Emile' and the 'Social Contract?'"

"Yes—or, rather no!" said the other with unspeakable sadness. "This author is the man disenchanted with life, glory, society and almost with heaven; but the other Rousseau, Lady Warrens', was the youth entering life by the same door as Aurora comes into the world; youth with his joys and hopes. An abyss divides the two Rousseaus thirty years wide."

The old gentleman shook his head, let his arms sadly droop, and appeared to sink into deep musing.

"So," went on Gilbert, "it is possible for the meanly born like Rousseau to win the love of a mighty and beautiful lady? This is calculated to drive those mad who have lifted their eyes to those above their sphere."

"Are you in love and do you see some likeness between your case and Rousseau's?" asked the old gentleman.

Gilbert blushed without answering the question.

"But he won, because he was Rousseau," he observed. "Yet, were I to feel a spark of his flame of genius, I should aspire to the star, and seek to wear it even though——"

"You had to commit a crime?"

Jacques started and cut short the interview by saying:

"I think my wife must be up. We will go down stairs. Besides, a working day never begins too soon. Come, young man, come."

On going forth, Jacques secured the garret door with a padlock.

This time he guided his ward into what Therese called the study. The furniture of this little room was composed of glazed cases of butterflies, herbs and minerals, framed in ebonized wood; books in a walnut case, a long, narrow table, covered with a worn and blackened cloth; with manuscripts orderly arranged on it, and four wooden chairs covered in horsehair. All was glossy, lustrous, irreproachable in order and cleanness, but cold to sight and heart, from the light through the gauze curtains being gray and weak, and luxury, or comfort itself, being far from this cold, ashy and black fireside.

A small rosewood piano stood on four legs, and a clock on the mantel-piece alone showed any life in this domestic tomb.

Gilbert walked in respectfully, for it was grand in his eyes; almost as rich as Taverney, and the waxed floor imposed on him.

"I am going to show you the nature of your work," said the old gentleman. "This is music paper. When I copy a page I earn ten cents, the price I myself fix. Do you know music?"

"I know the names of the notes but not their value, as well as these signs. In the house where I lived was a young lady who played the harpsichord——" and Gilbert hung his head, coloring.

"Oh, the same who studied botany," queried Jacques.

"Precisely; and she played very well."

"This does not account for your learning music."

"Rousseau says that the man is incomplete who enjoys a result without seeking the cause."

"Yes; but, also, that man in perfecting himself by the discovery, loses his happiness, freshness and instincts."

"What matter if what he gains compensates him for the losses?"

"Gad! you are not only a botanist and a musician, but a logician. At present we only require a copyist. While copying, you will train your hand to write more easily when you compose for yourself. Meanwhile, with a couple of hours' copy work at night, you may earn the wherewithal to follow the courses in the colleges of medicine, surgery and botany."

"I understand you," exclaimed Gilbert, "and I thank you from the bottom of my heart."

He settled himself to begin work on the sheet of paper held out by the kind gentleman.

CHAPTER XXIX

WHO MASTER JACQUES WAS

While the novice was covering the paper with his first attempts, the old gentleman set to reading printer's proofs—long leaves blank on one side like the paper of which was made the bean bags.

At nine Therese rushed in.

"Quick, quick!" she cried to Jacques, who raised his head. "Come out. It is a prince who calls. Goodness me! when will this procession of high-cockalorums cease? I hope this one will not take it into his head to have breakfast with us, like the Duke of Chartres the other day."

"Which prince is this one?" asked Jacques in an undertone.

"His Highness the Prince of Conti."

Gilbert let a blob of ink fall on the paper much more resembling a blot than a full note.

Jacques went out, smiling behind Therese, who shut the door after them.

"Princes here!" thought Gilbert. "Dukes calling on a copier of music!"

With his heart singularly beating, he went up to the door to listen.

"I want to take you with me," said a strange voice.

"For what purpose, prince?" inquired Jacques.

"To present you to the dauphiness. A new era opens for philosophers in her coming reign."

"I am a thousand times thankful to your highness; but my infirmities keep me indoors."

"And your misanthropy?"

"Suppose it were that? Is it so curious a thing that I should put myself out for it?"

"Come, and I will spare you the grand reception at the

celebration at St. Denis, and take you on to Muette, where her royal highness will pass the night in a couple of days."

"Does she get to St. Denis the day after to-morrow?"

"With her whole retinue. Come! the princess is a pupil of Gluck and an excellent musician."

Gilbert did not listen to any more after hearing that the dauphiness' retinue would be at St. Denis, only a few miles out, in a day or two. He might soon be within view of Andrea. This idea dazzled him like a flash from a looking-glass in his face. When he opened his eyes after this giddiness they fell on a book which happened to be open on the sideboard; it was Rousseau's Confessions, "adorned with a portrait of the author."

"The very thing I was looking for. I had never seen what he was like."

He quickly turned over the tissue paper on the steel plate and as he looked, the door opened and the living original of the portrait returned. With extended hands, dropping the volume, and trembling all over, he muttered:

"Oh! I am under the roof of Jean Jacques Rousseau!"

The old gentleman smiled with more happiness at this unstudied ovation than at the thousand triumphs of his glorious life.

"Yes, my friend, you are in Rousseau's house."

"Pray forgive me for the nonsense I have talked," said the hero-worshiper, clasping his hands and about to fall on his knees.

"Did it require a prince's call for you to recognize the persecuted philosopher of Geneva? poor child—but lucky one—who is ignorant of persecution."

"Oh, I am happy to see you, to know you, to dwell by you."

"Yes, yes, that is all very well; but we must earn our living. When you shall have copied this piece—for you have practiced enough to make a start—you will have earned your keep to-day. I charge nothing for the lodging—only do not sit up late and burn up the candles, for Therese will scold. What was left over from supper last night will be our breakfast; but this will be the last meal we take together, unless I invite you. In the street is a cheap dining-house for artisans, where you will fare nicely. I recommend it. In the mean time, let us breakfast."

Gilbert followed without a word, for he was conquered, for the first time; but then this was a man superior to others.

After the first mouthfuls he left table; the shock had spoilt his appetite. At eight in the evening he had copied a piece of music, not artistically but legibly, and Rousseau paid him the six cents.

"We have plenty of bread," remarked Therese, on whom the

132

young man's gentleness, application and discretion had produced good effect.

"I shall never forget your kindness, madame," he said, about to excuse himself, when he caught the host's eye and guessed that it would offend him.

"I accept," he said.

He went up to his loft, with the bread and money.

"At last I am my own master," he said to himself, "or should be but for this bread, which is from charity."

Although hungry, he placed it on the window sill and did not touch it during the night, though famine made him remember it.

He woke up at daylight, but still he did not eat the bread. He took it up, though, and at five o'clock, went down and outdoors.

From suspicion, or merely to study his guest, Rousseau was on the lookout, and he followed the youth up the street.

A beggar coming up to Gilbert, he gave him the hunk of bread. Entering the baker's, he bought another roll.

"He is going into the eating-house," thought the watcher, "where the money will soon fly."

But Gilbert munched part of the roll while strolling; he washed down the rest at the public fountain, washed his hands and sauntered home.

"By my faith, I believe that I am happier than Diogenes and have found an honest man," thought Rousseau.

The day passed in uninterrupted labor. At even Gilbert had turned out seven pages of copy—if not elegant, faultless. He tested in his hand the money received for it with ardent satisfaction.

"You are my master," he said, "since I find work in your place and you give me lodgings gratis. I should therefore lay myself open to be badly thought of by you if I acted without consulting you."

"What," said Rousseau, frightened; "what are you going to do? Going off elsewhere to work?"

"No, only I want a holiday, with your leave, to-morrow."

"To idle?"

"No, to go to St. Denis to see the dauphiness arrive."

"I thought you scorned the pomps of this worldly show," said Rousseau. "I, though an obscure citizen, despised the invitation of these great people to be of the reception party."

Gilbert nodded approval.

"I am not philosophic," said he, "but I am discreet."

This word struck the tutor, who saw there was some mystery in this behavior, and he looked at the speaker with admiration.

"I am glad to see you have a motive."

"Yes, and one which does not resemble the curiosity of a man at a show."

"It is for the better, or for the worse, for your look is deep, young man, and I seek in it in vain for youthful calm and candor."

"I told you I was unfortunate," returned Gilbert; "and such have no youth."

"But at the hour when you are seeing all the pomps of society glitter before you, I shall open one of my herbariums and review the magnificence of nature."

"But would you not have turned your back on herbariums if you were going to see your sweetheart—the one to whom you tossed a bunch of cherries?"

"Quite true! And you are young. Go to the show, my boy. It is not ambition in him, but love," he commented when Gilbert had gone out gleefully.

CHAPTER XXX

OLD PATRICIANS AND NEW

When the news spread of the royal splendor over the reception of the bride from Austria, the dreadful curiosity of the Parisians was sharpened, and they were to be seen flocking out to St. Denis by scores, hundreds and thousands.

Gilbert was lost in the multitude, but, seeing some urchins climb up in the trees, and the exercise being child's play to him, he clambered into a linn tree and perched on a bough to wait.

Half an hour after, drums beat, cannon thundered, and the majestic cathedral bell began to boom.

In the distance a shrill cry arose, but became full and more deep as it drew near. It made Gilbert prick up the ear and his whole body quiver.

"Long life to the king!"

It was the customary cheer.

A herd of horses, neighing under housings of gold and purple, swarmed on the highway; they were the royal household troops, guards, Swiss dragoons, musketeers and gendarmes.

Then a massive and magnificent coach loomed up.

134

Gilbert perceived a stately head under a hat, when all were uncovered, and a blue sash. He saw the royal glance, cold and penetrative, before which all bowed and heads were bared. Fascinated, intoxicated, panting and frozen, he forgot to lift his hat. A violent blow drew him from his ecstasy; his hat had been knocked off with the stroke of a soldier's halberd.

"I beg pardon," he stammered. "I am fresh from the country."

"Then learn that you must salute all the royal carriages, whoever may be in them," said the halberdier gruffly. "If you do not know the emblem of the lilyflower, I will teach you."

"You need not. I know," said Gilbert.

The royal equipages passed in a prolonged line. Gilbert gazed on them so intently that he seemed stupefied.

At the Royal Abbey doors they stopped successively to let the noblemen and ladies alight. These setting-down movements caused halts of a few minutes.

In one of them Gilbert felt a burning dart rush through his heart.

He was dazzled so that all was effaced in his sight, and so violent a shivering overwhelmed him that he was forced to catch at the branch not to tumble off.

Right in front of him, not ten paces off, in one of the vehicles with the lily brand which he had been advised to salute, he perceived the splendidly luminous face of Andrea Taverney; she was clad in white, like an angel or a ghost.

He uttered a faint outcry; but then, triumphing over the emotions which had mastered him together, he commanded his heart to cease to beat that he might look at the star.

Such was the young man's power over himself that he succeeded.

Wishful to learn why the horses had been reined in, Andrea leaned out, and, as her bright blue eyes traveled round, she caught sight of Gilbert and recognized him.

Gilbert suspected that she would be surprised and would inform her father of the discovery, as he sat next her.

He was not wrong, for Andrea called the baron's attention to the youth.

"Gilbert," said the nobleman, who was puffing himself up at the coach window, in his handsome red sash of the order of knighthood. "He, here? Who is taking care of my hound, then?"

Hearing the words, the young man respectfully bowed to Andrea and her father. But it took him all his powers to make the effort.

"It is so. It is the rascal in person," said the baron.

135

On Andrea's face, observed by Gilbert with sustained attention, was perfect calm under slight surprise.

Leaning out of the carriage, the baron beckoned to his ex-retainer. But the soldier who had given the youth a lesson in etiquette stopped him.

"Let the lad come to me," said the lord; "I have a couple of words to say to him."

"You may go half a dozen, my lord," said the sergeant, flattered by the nobleman addressing him; "plenty of time, for they are speechifying under the porch. Pass, younker."

"Come hither, rogue," said the baron on Gilbert affecting not to hurry himself out of his usual walk. "Tell me by what chance you are out here at St. Denis when you ought to be at Taverney?"

"It is no chance," replied Gilbert, saluting lord and lady for the second time, "but the act of my free will."

"What do you mean by your will, varlet? Have you such a thing as a will of your own?"

"Why not? Every free man has his own."

"Free man? Do you fancy yourself free, you unhappy dog?"

"Of course, since I parted with my freedom to no one."

"On my word, here's a pretty knave," said the baron, taken aback by the coolness of the speaker. "How dare you be in town, and how did you manage to get here?"

"I walked it," said Gilbert shortly.

"Walked!" repeated Andrea with some pity.

"But I ask what you have come here for?" continued the baron.

"To get an education, which is assured me, and make my fortune, which I hope for."

"What are you doing meanwhile—begging?"

"Begging?" reiterated Gilbert, with superb scorn.

"Thieving, then?"

"I never stole anything from Taverney," retorted Gilbert, with such proud and wild firmness that it riveted the girl's attention on him for a space.

"What mischief does your idle hand find to do, then?"

"What a genius is doing, whom I seek to resemble if only by perseverance; I copy music," replied the rebel.

"You copy music?" queried Andrea, turning round. "Then you know it?" in the tone of one saying, "You are a liar."

"I know the notes, and that is enough for copying. I like music dearly, and I used to listen to the lady playing at the harpsichord."

"You eavesdropper!"

"I got the airs by heart to begin with; and next, as I saw they were written in a book, I saw a method in it and I learnt it."

136

"You dared to touch my book?" said Andrea, at the height of indignation.

"I had no need to touch it; it lay open. I looked, and there is no soiling a printed page by a look."

"Let me tell you," sneered the baron, "that we shall have this imp declare that he can play the piano like Haydn."

"I might have learnt that if I had presumed to touch the keys," said the youth, confidently.

Against her inclination, Andrea cast a second look on the face animated by a feeling like a martyr's in fanaticism. But the lord, who had not his daughter's calmness and clear head, felt his wrath kindle at the youth being right and their being inhumane in leaving him with the watchdog at Taverney. It is hard to forgive an inferior for the wrong which he may convict us with; hence he grew heated as his daughter cooled.

"You rapscallion!" he said. "You desert and play the vagabond and spout such tomfoolery as we hear when you are brought to task. But as I do not wish the king's highway to be infested with gipsy tramps and thieves——"

Andrea held up her hand to appease the patrician, whose exaggeration annulled his superiority. But he put her aside and continued:

"I shall tell Chief of Police Sartines about you, and have you locked up in the House of Correction, you fledgeling philosopher."

"Lord Baron," returned Gilbert, drawing back but slapping his hat down on his head with the ire which made him white, "I have found patrons in town at whose door your Sartines dances attendance!"

"The deuse you say so?" questioned the baron. "You shall taste the stirrup leather anyway. Andrea, call your brother, who is close to hand."

Andrea stooped out toward the offender and bade him begone in an imperious voice.

"Philip," called the old noble.

Gilbert stood on the spot, mute and unmoving, as in ecstatic worship. Up rode a cavalier at the call; it was the Knight of Redcastle, joyous and brilliant in a captain's uniform.

"Why, it is Gilbert," he exclaimed. "The idea of his being here! Good-day, Gilbert. What do you want, father?"

"I want you to whip this malapert with your sword-scabbard," roared the old patrician, pale with anger.

"What has he done?" inquired Philip, looking with growing astonishment from his father in age to the youth who had tranquilly returned his greeting.

137

"Never mind what he has done, but lash him, Philip, as you would a dog!"

"What has he done?" asked the chevalier, turning to his sister. "Has he insulted you?"

"I insult her?" repeated Gilbert.

"Not at all," answered Andrea. "He has done nothing. Father let his passion get the upper hand of him. Gilbert is no longer in our service and has the right to go wherever he likes. Father does not understand this and flew into a rage."

"Is that all?" asked Captain Philip.

"All, brother, and I do not understand father's wrath about such stuff and for the trash who do not deserve a look. Just see if we are not to go on again, Philip."

Subdued by his daughter's serenity, the baron was quiet. Crushed by such scorn, Gilbert lowered his head. Something ran through his heart much like hatred. He would have preferred Philip Taverney's sword or even a cut of his whip. He came near swooning.

Luckily the speechmaking was over and the procession moved forward once more. Andrea was carried on, and faded as in a dream.

Gilbert thought he was alone in his grief, believing that he could never support the weight of such misfortune. But a hand was laid on his shoulder.

Turning, he saw Philip, who came smiling toward him, having dismounted and given his steed to his orderly to hold.

"I should like to hear what has happened," he said, "and how my poor Gilbert has come to Paris?"

This frank and cordial greeting touched the young man.

"What was I to do on the old place?" he asked, with a sigh, torn from his wild stoicism. "I should have died of hunger, ignorance and despair."

Philip started, for his impartial mind, like Andrea's, was struck by the painful loneliness in which the youth was left.

"But do you imagine that you can succeed in Paris, a poor boy, without resources and protectors?"

"I do. The man who can work rarely dies of want, where so many want to live without working."

The hearer started at this reply; previously he had regarded him as a dependent of no importance.

"I earn my daily bread, Captain Philip, and that is a great gain for one who was blamed for eating bread which he did nothing for."

"I hope you are not referring to what you had at Taverney, for your father and mother were good tenants and you were often useful."

"I only did my duty."

"Mark me, Gilbert," continued the young gentleman. "You know I always liked you. I looked upon you differently to others. The future will show whether I was right or wrong. To me your standing aloof was fastidiousness; your plainspokenness I called straightforward."

"Thanks," said the young man, breathing delightedly.

"It follows that I wish you well. Young like you and unhappy as I was situated, I thus understood you. Fortune has smiled upon me. Let me help you in anticipation of the lady on the wheel smiling on you likewise."

"I thank you."

"Do you blush to take my help, when all men are brothers?"

Gilbert fastened his intelligent eyes on the speaker's noble features, astonished at hearing the language from those lips.

"Such is the talk of the new generation," said he; "opinions shared by the dauphin himself. Do not be proud with me, but take what you may return me another day. Who knows but that you may be a great financier or statesman——"

"Or doctor-surgeon," said Gilbert.

"Just as you please. Here is my purse; take half."

"I thank you, but I need nothing," replied the unconquerable young man, softened by Philip's admirable brotherly love; "but be sure that I am more grateful to you than if I had accepted your offer."

He mingled with the mob, leaving Philip stupefied for several seconds, unable to credit sight and hearing. Seeing Gilbert did not reappear, he mounted his horse and regained his place.

CHAPTER XXXI

THE MAGICIAN'S WIFE

All the rumbling of the coaches, the booming of the bells swinging to the full extent, the rolling of the drums, all the majesty of the society the Princess Louise had discarded in order to live in the nunnery, glided over her soul and died away at the base of her cell wall, like the useless tide. She had refused to return to the court, and while her sisterhood were still agitated by the royal visit, she alone did not quiver when the heavy door banged and shut out the world from her solitude.

She summoned her treasurer to her.

"During these two days of frivolous uproar," she inquired, "have the poor been visited, the sick attended, and those soldiers on guard given bread and wine!"

"Nobody has wanted in this house."

Suddenly the kick of a horse was heard against the woodwork of the stables.

"What is that? Has any courtier remained?"

"Only his eminence the Cardinal de Rohan; that is the horse of the Italian lady who came here yesterday to crave hospitality of your highness."

"True; I remember. Where is she?"

"In her room, or in the church. She refuses all food save bread, and prayed in the chapel all through the night."

"Some very guilty person, no doubt," said the lady superior, frowning.

"I know not, for she speaks to no one."

"What is she like?"

"Handsome, but proud, along with tenderness."

"How did she act during the royal ceremony?"

"She peeped out of her window, hiding in the curtains, and examined everybody as though she feared to see an enemy."

"Some member of the class which I have reigned over. What is her name?"

"Lorenza Feliciani."

"I know of no person of that name, but show her in."

Princess Louise sat in an ancient oak chair, carved in the reign of Henri II. and used by nine Carmelite abbesses. Before this seat of justice many poor novices had quailed between spiritual and temporal power.

A moment following the treasurer returned, ushering in the foreigner whom we know; she wore a long veil. With the piercing eye of her race, Princess Louise studied Lorenza on her entering the closet; but her hostile feelings became sisterly and benevolent on seeing so much grace and humility in the visitor, so much sublime beauty, and, in short, so much innocence in the large black eyes wet with tears.

The princess prevented her dropping on her knees.

"Draw near and speak," said she. "Are you called Lorenza Feliciani?"

"Yes, lady."

"You want to confide a secret to me?"

140

"I am dying with the desire."

"But why do you not go to the penitential chamber? I have no power but to console; a priest can comfort and forgive." She spoke the last word hesitatingly.

"I need comfort alone; and to a woman alone can I entrust my confession. Will you listen patiently to my most strange story, to be told to you alone, for you are mighty, and I require the hand of heaven to defend me."

"Defend? Are you pursued and attacked?"

"Yes, indeed, my lady," said the fugitive, with unutterable fright.

"Reflect, madame, that this is a nunnery and not a castle," said the princess; "what agitates mankind enters here but to be extinguished; weapons to use against man are not here; it is the abode of God, not of might, repression and justice."

"The very thing I seek," answered Lorenza; "in the abode of God alone can I find a life of rest."

"But not of vengeance. If you want reprisal on your foes, apply to the magistrates."

"They can do nothing against the man whom I dread."

"Who can he be?" asked the lady superior, with secret and involuntary fright.

"Who?" said the Italian, approaching the princess-abbess under the sway of mysterious exaltation. "I am certain that he is one of those devils who war against mankind, endowed by their Prince Satan with superhuman power."

"What are you telling me?" said the other, regarding the woman to make sure that she was not mad.

"What a wretch am I to have fallen across the path of this demon," groaned Lorenza, writhing her lovely arms, seemingly reft from a flawless ancient statue. "I am possessed of a fiend," she gasped, going up to the lady and speaking in a low voice, as if afraid to hear her own tones.

"Possessed! Speak out, if you are in your senses."

"I am not mad, though I may become so, if you drive me away."

"But allow me to say that I see you like a creature favored by heaven; you seem rich and are beauteous; you express yourself correctly, and your face does not wear traces of the terrible and mysterious complaint called demoniac possession."

"In my life, madame, and its adventures resides the sinister secret which I wish I could keep from myself. Lady, I am a Roman, where my father came of the old patricians, but like most Roman nobles, he is poor. I have also a mother and elder brother. In France, when an aristocratic family has a son and a daughter, she is put into a nunnery that the money which should have been her marriage portion shall buy the son a military commission. Among us, the daughter is sacrificed to help the son rise in holy orders. I was given no education, while my brother was trained to be a cardinal, as my mother simply said. I was destined to take the veil among the Subiaco Carmelites. Such a future had been held out to me from youth as a necessity. I had no will or strength in the matter. I was not consulted but ordered, and had to obey. We Roman girls love society without knowing anything about it, as the suffering souls in paradise love heaven. I was surrounded by examples which would have doomed me, had the idea of resistance come to me, but none such came. But my mother fondled me a little more than usual when the fatal day dawned.

"My father gathered five hundred Roman crowns to pay my entrance fee into the convent, and we set out for Subiaco. It is some nine leagues from Rome; but the mountain roads were so bad that we were five hours getting over three of them. But the journey pleased me, though it might be fatiguing. I smiled on it as my last pleasure, and along the road bade farewell to the trees, bushes, stones and the dried grass itself. I feared that in the nunnery would be not even grass and flowers.

"Suddenly, amid my dreams, and as we were passing between a grove and a pile of rocks, the carriage stopped. I heard my mother scream, and my father jumped to get his pistols. My eyes and mind dropped from the skies to the earth, for we were stopped by highwaymen."

"Poor girl!" exclaimed Princess Louise, interested in the tale.

"I was not frightened, for the brigands waylaid us for money, and what they took was to pay my way into the nunnery; hence there would be a delay until it was made up again, and I knew that it would take time and trouble. But when, after sharing this plunder, the bandits, instead of letting us go our way, sprang upon me, and I saw my father's efforts to defend me and my mother's tears in entreaty, then I comprehended that a great though unknown misfortune threatened me, and I began to call for mercy. It was natural, though I knew that it was useless calling and that nobody would hear in this wild spot. Hence, without heeding my father's struggles, my mother's weeping, or my appeals, the banditti tied my hands behind my back, and began throwing dice on one of their handkerchiefs spread on the ground, while burning me with hideous glances, which I understood from terror giving me clearness of sight.

"What most frightened me was not to see any stake on the

board. I shuddered as the dice cup passed from hand to hand, at the thought that I was the stake.

"All of a sudden, one of them, with a yell of triumph, jumped up, while the others ground their teeth and swore. He ran up to me, took me in his arms and pressed his lips to mine. The contact of redhot iron could not have drawn a more heartrending scream from me.

"'Rather death, O God!' I shrieked.

"My mother writhed on the ground where my father lay, in a dead swoon. My only hope was that one of the losing villains would kill me out of spite with the dagger he held in his clenched fist. I waited for this stroke—longed, prayed for it.

"Suddenly a horseman rode up the path. He spoke to one of the sentinels, who let him pass, exchanging a sign with him. He was of medium stature, imposing in mien and resolute in gaze. He came on at the walking pace of his horse, calm and tranquil. He stopped in front of me. The bandit who had clutched me turned round sharply at the first blow of the whistle which the stranger carried in the handle of his riding whip. He let me drop to the ground.

"'Come here,' said the horseman, and as the bandit hesitated, he formed a triangle with his arms, crossing his forefingers upon his breast.

"As though this were the token of a mighty master, the robber went up to the stranger, who stooped down to his ear, and said:

"'Mak.'

"I am sure he uttered but this single word, for I looked at him as one looks at the knife about to slay oneself, and listened as one does for the sentence of life or death.

"'Benak,' answered the highwayman.

"Subdued like a lion, with growling, he returned to me, untied the rope round my wrists, and did the same release for my parents. As the coin had been shared, every man went and put his portion on a flat rock. Not a piece was missing. Meanwhile I felt myself coming to life again in the hands of my father and mother.

"'Be off,' said the deliverer to the robbers, who obeyed and dived into the wood to the last man.

"'Lorenza Feliciani,' said the stranger, covering me with a superhuman gaze, 'you are free to go your way.'

"My father and mother thanked the stranger who knew me and yet was unknown to us. They stepped into the carriage where I followed them with regret, for some unknown power irresistibly attracted me toward my savior. He remained unstirring in the same spot, as if to continue between us and harm. I looked at him as long as I could and the oppression on my bosom did not go off until he was lost to view. In a couple of hours we reached Subiaco."

"But who was this extraordinary man?" cried Princess Louise, moved by the simplicity of the story.

"Kindly let me finish. Alas! this is not the whole of it.

"On the road, we three did nothing but talk about the singular liberator who had come mysteriously and powerfully like an agent of heaven. Less credulous than me, my father suspected him to be one of those heads of the robber leagues infesting the suburbs of Rome, who have absolute authority to reward, punish and share. Though I could not argue against my father's experience, I obeyed instinct and the effect of my gratitude, and did not believe him a robber. In my prayers to the Madonna, I set aside a special one for her to bless my savior.

"That same day I entered the convent. As the money was ready, nothing prevented my reception. I was sad but more resigned than ever. A superstitious Italian, I believed that heaven had protected me from the devils to hand me over pure to the religious haven. So I yielded with eagerness to the wishes of my parents and the lady superior. A petition to be made a nun without having to go through the novitiate in the white veil was placed before me, and I signed it. My father had written it in such fervent strains that the pope must have thought the request was the ardent aspiration of a soul disgusted with the world and turning to solitude. The plea was granted and I only had to be a novice for one month. The news caused me neither joy nor displeasure. I seemed already to be dead to the world, and a corpse with simply the impassible spirit outliving it.

"They kept me immured a fortnight for fear the worldly craving would seize me, and on the fifteenth morning ordered me to go down into the chapel with the other sisters.

"In Italy, the convent chapels are public churches, the pope not believing that priests should make a private house of any place set aside for the worshippers of the Divine.

"I went into the choir and took my place. Between the green screens supposed to veil the choir in was a space through which the nave could be viewed. By this peep-crack out on the world I saw a man standing by himself among the kneeling crowd. The previous feeling of uneasiness came over me once more—the superhuman attraction to my soul to draw it forth, as I have seen my brother move iron filings on a sheet of paper by waving a magnet underneath it.

"Alas! vanquished and subjugated, with no power to withstand this attraction, I bent toward him, clasping my hands as in worship,

144

and with lips and heart I sent him my thanks. My sisters stared at me with surprise, for they had not comprehended my words nor my movement. To follow the direction of my gesture and glance, they rose on tiptoe to peer over into the nave, and I trembled; but the stranger had disappeared. They questioned me, but I only blushed and faltered, as next I turned pale.

"From that time, madame," said Lorenza, in despair, "I have lived in the control of the devil!"

"I cannot say I see anything supernatural in this," observed the princess, with a smile. "Pray be calm, and proceed."

"You do not know what I feel. The demon possesses me entirely—body and soul. Love would not make me suffer so much; would not shake me like a tree by the storm, and would not give me the wicked thoughts coming to me. I ought to confess these to the priest, and the demon bids me not to think of such a thing.

"One day a pious friend, a neighbor and a Roman lady, came to see me. She passed most of the time praying before the image of the Virgin. That night in undressing I found a note in the lining of my robe. It contained these lines:

"'It is death here in Rome for a nun to love a man. But will you not risk death for him who saved your life?'

"That made his possession of me complete, lady; for I should lie if I said that I thought about anybody more than I do about that man."

Frightened at her own words, Lorenza stopped to study the abbess' sweet and intelligent countenance.

"This is not demoniac possession," said Louise of France with firmness. "It is but an unfortunate passion, and unless in the state of regret, human passions have no business here."

"Regret? you see me in tears, on my knees, entreating you to deliver me from the power of this infernal wretch, and you talk of my regret? More than that, I feel remorse!

"My misery could not escape my companions' eyes. The superior was notified, and she acquainted my mother. Only three days after I had taken the vows, I saw the three persons enter my cell who were my only kin—my mother, father and brother. They came to embrace me for the last time, they said, but I saw that they had another aim. Left alone with me, my mother questioned me. The influence of the demon was plain once more, for I was stubbornly silent.

"The day when I was to take the black veil came amid a terrible struggle with myself, for I feared that then the fiend would work his

145

worst. Yet I trusted that heaven would save me as it had when the robbers seized me, forgetting that heaven had sent that man to rescue me.

"The hour of the ceremonial arrived. Pale, uneasy, but not apparently more agitated than usual, I went down into the church. I hurriedly assented to everything, for was I not in the holy edifice and was I not my own mistress while that demon was out of the way? All at once I felt that his step was on the sill; irresistible attraction as before caused me to turn my eyes away from the altar, whatever my efforts.

"All my strength fled me, even while the scissors were thrust forward to cut my hair off—my soul seemed to leap out of my throat to go and meet him, and I fell prostrate on the stone slabs. Not like a woman swooning but like one in a trance. I only heard a murmur, when the ceremony was interrupted by a dreadful tumult."

The princess clasped her hands in compassion.

"Was not this a dreadful event," said the Roman, "in which it was easy to recognize the intervention of the enemy of mankind?"

"Poor woman!" said the abbess, with tender pity; "take care! I am afraid that you are apt to attribute to the wonderful what was but natural weakness. I suppose you saw this man, and you fainted away. There was nothing more. Continue."

"Madame, when I came to my senses," said Lorenza, "it was night. I expected to find myself in the chapel or in my cell. But I saw rocks and trees around me; clouds; I was in a grotto and beside me was a man, that persecutor! I touched myself to make sure if I were alive and not dreaming. I screamed, for I was clad in bridal white. On my brow was a wreath or white roses—such as the bride of man—or in religion—wears."

The princess uttered an exclamation.

"Next day," resumed the Italian, sobbing, and hiding her head in her hands, "I reckoned the time which had elapsed, I had been three days in the trance, ignorant of what transpired."

CHAPTER XXXII

THE NUN'S HUSBAND

A deep silence long surrounded the two women, one in painful meditation, the other in astonishment readily understood.

"If you were removed out of the nunnery," said Lady Louise, to break this silence, "you are unaware of how it was done? Yet a convent is well enclosed and guarded, with bars to the windows, walls of height and a warder who keeps the keys. In Italy it is particularly so, where the regulations are stricter than in France."

"What can I tell your ladyship, when I puzzle my brains without finding a clue?"

"But if you saw this man, did you not blame him for the abduction?"

"I did, but he excused himself on the plea that he loved me. I told him that he frightened me, and that I was sure that I did not like him. The strange feeling is another kind. I am not myself when he is by, but his; whatever he wills, I must do; one look fascinates me and subdues me. You see, lady, this must be magic."

"At least, it is strange, if not supernatural," said the princess. "But you are in the company of this man?"

"Yes; but I do not love him."

"Then why not appeal to the authorities, your parents, the ecclesiastical powers?"

"He so watched me that I could not move."

"But you could have written."

"On the road, he stopped at houses where everything is owned by him and he is master of everybody. When I asked the people about for writing materials, they gave no answer; they were his bondwomen."

"But how did you travel?"

"At first in a postchaise; but at Milan, he had a kind of house on wheels to continue the journey in."

"Still, he must have left you alone sometimes?"

"Yes; but then he bade me sleep, and sleep I did, only waking up when he returned."

"You could not have strongly wanted to get away," observed Princess Louise, shaking her head, "or else you would have managed it."

"Alas! I was so fascinated."

"By his loving speech and endearments?"

"Seldom did he speak of love, and I remember me of no caresses save a kiss night and morning."

"Really, this is very strange?" muttered the abbess; but as a suspicion struck her, she resumed: "Repeat to me that you do not love him, and that as no worldly tie unites you, he would have no claim on you if he came."

"He has none."

"But tell me how you came here through all; for I am in a fog," said the princess.

"I took advantage of a violent thunderstorm, which broke on us near a town called Nancy, I believe. He left me to go into a part of his travelling house which is inhabited by an old man; I leaped upon his horse and fled. My resolution was to hide in Paris, or some great city where I could be lost to all eyes, especially to his. When I arrived here, all were talking of your highness' retirement into the Carmelite convent. All extolled your piety, solicitude for the unhappy, and compassion for the afflicted. This was a ray of heavenly light, showing me that you alone were generous enough to receive me and powerful enough to defend me."

"You continually appeal to power, my child, as though he were powerful?"

"I am ignorant what he is. I only know that no king inspires more respect—no idol commands more adoration—than he from those to whom he deigns to reveal himself."

"But his name—how is he entitled?"

"I have heard him called by many names. But only two remain in my memory. One is used by the old man who is his traveling companion from Milan to where I left him; the other that he gives himself. The aged man calls him Acharat, and that sounds anti-Christian, does it not, lady? He calls himself Joseph Balsamo."

"What does he say of himself?"

"He knows everything and divines what he knew not. He is the contemporary of all time. He has lived through all ages. He speaks— the Lord forgive me! and forgive him for such blasphemy! not only of Alexander the Great, Cæsar and Charlemagne, as though he had known them, albeit I believe they were dead ever so long ago, but also of the high priest Caiaphas, Pontius Pilate and Our Lord Himself, whose martyrdom he claims to have witnessed."

"He is some quack," said the Princess Louise.

"I do not clearly understand the word, madame; but he is a dangerous man, terrible too, before whom everything bends, snaps and crumbles away. When he is taken to be defenseless he is armed at all points; when believed alone, he stamps his foot and an army springs up; or at a beck of the finger—smiling the while."

"Very well," soothed the daughter of France; "take cheer, my child; you will be protected against him. So long as you desire the protection, of course. But do not believe any longer in these supernatural visions born of a sick brain. In any case the walls of St. Denis Abbey are a sure rampart against infernal power, and what is more to be dreaded, mark you! against human power. Now, what do you propose doing?"

"With this property of mine, in jewels, I mean to pay for my repose in a convent—if possible, in this one."

Lorenza placed on the table some twenty thousand crowns' worth of bracelets, rings and earrings of price.

"These jewels are mine, as Balsamo gave them to me, and I shall turn them over to Heaven's use. I have nothing of his but his steed Djerid, which was the instrument of my deliverance, but I should like him to have it. So I solicit the favor of staying here, on my knees."

"Rest easy, my child," said the lady superior; "from this time forth you may dwell among us; and when you shall have shown by your exemplary conduct that you deserve the favor, you may again be the bride of the Lord; and I will answer for it that you will not be removed out of St. Denis without knowledge of the superior."

Lorenza fell at the princess feet and poured forth the most affectionate and sincere thanks.

But suddenly she rose on one knee, and listened with trembling and pallor.

"Oh, God, how I shake! he is coming! he means to be my destroyer—that man is at hand. Do you not see how my limbs quiver?"

"I see this, indeed."

"Now I feel the stab in the heart," continued the Italian: "he comes nearer and nearer."

"You are mistaken."

"No, no. In spite of myself, he draws me to him. Hold me back from him."

Princess Louise seized the speaker in her arms.

"Recover your senses, child," she said. "Even if any one came, even he, you would be in safety here."

"He approaches—I tell you, he approaches," screamed Lorenza, terrified into inertia, but with her hands and her eyes directed toward the room door.

"Madness!" said the abbess. "Do you think that anybody can intrude on the Royal Lady of France? None but the bearer of an order from the king."

"I do not know how he entered," stammered the fugitive,

recoiling, "but I am certain that he is coming up the stairs—he is not ten steps off—there he is!"

The door flew open, so that the princess receded, frightened in spite of herself by the odd coincidence. But it was a nun who appeared.

"What do you want—who is there?" cried her superior.

"Madame, it is a nobleman who presents himself to have speech with your royal highness."

"His title?"

"Count Fenix, please your highness."

"Do you know the name as his?" inquired the princess of the fugitive.

"I do not know the name, but it is he," she replied.

"Charged with a mission to the king of France from the king of Prussia," said the nun, "he wishes the honor of a hearing by your highness."

Princess Louise reflected an instant; then turning to Lorenza and bidding her go into her inner room, she ordered the sister to show in the visitor. She went and took her chair, waiting, not without emotion, for the sequel of the incident.

Almost instantly reappearing, the Carmelite ushered in a man whom we have seen under the title of Fenix, at the presentation of Jeanne Dubarry at court. He was garbed in the same Prussian uniform, of severe cut; he wore the military wig and the black stock; his expressive black eyes lowered in presence of Princess Louise, but only with the respect of any man for a princess of the royal house, whatever his rank. He raised them rapidly, as though he feared showing too much timidity.

"I thank your royal highness for the favor kindly done me," he said, "though I reckoned upon it from knowing that your highness always upholds the unfortunate."

"I endeavor so to do, my lord," replied the lady with dignity, for she hoped in ten minutes to defeat the man who impudently came to claim outside help to oppress where he had abused his powers.

The count bowed as if he did not see any hidden meaning in the rejoinder.

"What can I do for your lordship?" continued the lady in the same tone of irony.

"Everything. I should like your highness to believe that I would not without grave motives vex you in the solitude she has chosen, but you have sheltered a person in whom I am interested in all points."

"What is the name of this person?"

"Lorenza Feliciani."

"What is this person to you—a relative, sister?"

"She is my wife."

"Lorenza Feliciani, wife of Count Fenix!" said the abbess, raising her voice so as to be heard in the inner room. "No Countess Fenix is in St. Denis Abbey," she dryly added.

"It may be," said the count, who was not yet acknowledging his defeat, "that your highness is not persuaded that Lorenza and Countess Fenix are the same person. Kindly give the order that Lorenza shall be brought before you, and all doubt will cease. I ask pardon for being so persistent, but I am tenderly attached to this wife of mine, and I believe she is sorry we are separated, poor as is my merit."

"Ah!" thought the princess, "Lorenza spoke the truth, for this man is highly dangerous."

The count stood with a calm bearing, strictly according to court etiquette.

"I must prevaricate," thought Princess Louise, before she said: "My lord, I am not in the position to restore a wife who is not here. I understand your seeking her with such persistency, if you love her as dearly as you say; but you will have to seek elsewhere if you want success."

On entering, the count had glanced round the closet, and his gaze had caught a reflection, however slight, of the jewels placed by Lorenza on the little table in the darkest corner. By the sparkling Fenix recognized them.

"If your royal highness would kindly collect your memory, though I have to ask her to do such violence—it will be recalled that Lorenza Feliciani was here, for she laid those jewels on yonder table before she retired into the next room."

The princess colored up as the count continued:

"So that I wait solely for your highness' leave for me to order her to come forth, for I cannot doubt that she will immediately obey."

The abbess remembered that Lorenza had locked the door behind her, and consequently that she could not be prevailed upon except by her own will to come out. No longer trying to dissimulate her vexation at having been lying uselessly to this man, from whom nothing could be concealed, she said:

"Were she to enter, what would be done to her?"

"Nothing, your highness; she will merely tell you that she wishes to go with her husband."

This encouraged the princess, recalling the Italian woman's protests.

"It would seem that your highness does not believe me," said

151

the count, in answer to her apparent indignation. "Is there anything incredible in Count Fenix marrying Lorenza Feliciani, and claiming his wife. I can easily lay before your royal highness's eyes the marriage certificate, properly signed by the priest who performed the ceremony."

The princess started, for such calmness shook her conviction. He opened a portfolio and took out a twice-folded paper.

"This is the proof of my claim on my wife," he said; "the signature ought to carry belief. It is that of the curate of St. John's in Strasburg, well-known to Prince Louis of Rohan for one, and were his eminence the cardinal here——"

"He is here at this very time," exclaimed the abbess, fastening fiery looks on the count. "His eminence has not left the abbey, where he is with the cathedral canons; so nothing is more easy than the verification you challenge."

"This is a great boon to me," said the count, coolly replacing the document in the pocket-book. "I hope this verification will dispel your royal highness' unjust suspicions against me."

"Indeed, impudence does disgust me," said the princess, ringing her hand bell quickly.

The nun in waiting entered hastily.

"Send my courier to carry this note to Cardinal Rohan, who is in the cathedral Chapter. Let his eminence come hither, as I await him."

While speaking she scribbled a couple of lines on paper which she handed the nun, whispering:

"Post two archers of the rural guard in the corridor, and let not a soul issue without my leave. Go!"

The count had watched all the princess' preparations to fight out the battle with him. While she was writing, he approached the inner room, and he muttered some words while extending and working his hands in a movement more methodical than nervous, with his eyes fastened on the door. The princess, turning, caught him in the act.

"Madame," said the count, "I am adjuring Lorenza Feliciani to come personally and confirm by her own words and by her free will whether I am or not a forger and an impostor, without prejudice to the other proofs your highness may exact. Lorenza," called out the count, rising above all—even to the princess' will, "come forth!"

The key grated in the lock and the princess beheld with unspeakable apprehension the coming of the Italian beauty. Her eyes were fixed on the count, with no show of hatred or anger.

"What are you doing, child," faltered the Lady Louise, "and why

152

do you come to the man whom you shunned? I told you that you were in safety there."

"She is also in safety in my house, my lady," replied the nobleman. "Are you not in safety there, Lorenza," he demanded of the refugee.

"Yes," was the other's answer.

At the height of amazement the princess clasped her hands and dropped into her chair.

"Lorenza," went on the count, in a soft voice but one with the accent of command, "I am accused of doing you violence. Tell me if I have ever acted so toward you?"

"Never," replied the woman, in a clear and precise voice but without any gesture accompanying the denial.

"Then what did the story about the abduction mean?" questioned the princess.

Lorenza remained dumb, but looking at the count as though all her life, and speech—which is its expression—must come from him.

"Her highness doubtless wishes to know how you came to leave your nunnery. Relate what happened from your fainting in the choir until you awoke in our postchaise."

"I remember," said Lorenza in the same monotonous voice.

"Speak, for I wish it."

"When I fainted, as the scissors touched my hair, I was carried into my cell, and placed in bed. My mother stayed with me until evening, when the village doctor declared that I was dead."

"How did you know this?" inquired the princess.

"Her highness wishes to know how you were aware of what went on," said the count.

"Strange thing!" said Lorenza, "I could see and hear but without having my eyes open. I was in a trance."

"In fact," said the abbess, "I have heard Doctor Tronchin speak of patients in catalepsy who were buried alive."

"Proceed Lorenza."

"My mother was in despair and would not believe in my death. She passed six-and thirty hours beside me, without my making a move or uttering a sigh. The priest came three times and told my mother that she was wrong to dispute the interment as her daughter had passed away just as she was speaking the vow, and that my soul had gone straight from the altar to heaven. But my mother insisted on watching all Monday night.

"Tuesday morning I was in the same insensibility, and my mother retired, vanquished. The nuns hooted her for the sacrilege.

"The death-candles were lighted in the chapel, where the custom was for the exposure of the body to repose a day and a night.

"I was shrouded, dressed in white, as I had not taken the vow; my hands crossed on my bosom, and a wreath of white blossoms placed on my brow.

"When the coffin was brought in, I felt a shiver pass over my body; for, I repeat, I saw all that happened as though I were my second self standing invisibly beside my counter-part.

"I was placed in the coffin, and after my time of lying in state, left with only the hospital sister to watch me.

"A dreadful thought tormented me in this lethargy—that I should be buried living on the morrow unless some interposition came.

"Each stroke of the time bell echoed in my heart, for I was listening—doleful idea! to my own death-knell.

"Heaven alone knows what efforts I made to break the iron bonds which held me down on the bier; but it had pity on me in my frozen sleep, since here I am.

"Midnight rang.

"At the first stroke, I felt that convulsion experienced whenever Acharat approached me; a shock came to my heart; I saw him appear in the chapel doorway."

"Was it fright that you felt?" asked Count Fenix.

"No, no; it was joy, bliss, ecstasy, for I knew that he came to tear me from the desperate death which I so abhorred. Slowly he came up to my coffin; he smiled on me as he gazed for a moment, and he said:

"'Are you glad to live? Then come with me.'

"All the bonds snapped at his call; I rose, extricated myself from the bier as from the grave clothes, and passed by the slumbering nun. I followed him who for the second time had snatched me from death.

"Out in the courtyard I beheld the sky spangled with stars which never more had I expected to see. I felt that cool night air which blesses not the dead, but which is so refreshing to the living.

"'Now,' said my liberator, 'before quitting the convent, choose between it and me. Will you be a nun, or will you be my wife?' I wanted to be his wife, and I followed him.

"The tower gate was closed and locked. He asked where were the keys, and as I said in the pocket of the wardress, who slept within, he sent me there to get them.

"Five minutes after we were in the street. I took his arm and we ran to the end of Subiaco village. A hundred paces beyond the last house a postchaise was waiting, all ready. We got in, and off it went at a gallop."

154

"And no violence was done you? No threat was proffered? You followed the man willingly?"

Lorenza remained mute.

"Her royal highness asks you, Lorenza, if by threat or act I forced you to follow me."

"No; I went because I loved you, darling."

With a triumphant smile, Count Fenix turned round to the royal princess.

CHAPTER XXXIII

COUNT AND CARDINAL

What took place under the princess-abbess' sight was so extraordinary that her mind, strong and yet tender, questioned if she did not face a true magician who disposed of sentiments and wills as he liked. But Count Fenix was not going to leave things thus.

"As your royal highness has heard only part of the story from my wife's lips, doubts might linger if the rest was not spoken by them. Dear Lorenza," he said, turning again to the Italian, "after leaving your country we went on a tour to the Alps and to the Rhine, the magnificent Tiber of the North——"

"Yes, Lorenza has seen these sights," said the woman.

"Lured by this man—led by a power resistless of which you spoke, my child?" suggested the princess.

"Why should your highness believe this when all you hear is to the contrary? I have a palpable proof in the letter my wife wrote me when I was obliged to leave her at Maintz. She sorrowed and longed for me, so that she wrote this note, which your highness may read."

She looked at the letter which the count took out of the letter case.

"Return, Acharat; for all goes when you leave me. When shall I have you for eternity?

Lorenza."

With the flame of choler on her brow the princess went up to the fugitive, holding out this letter. The other allowed her to

155

approach, without seeming to see or hear any but the count. "I understand," said the latter, decided to clear up matters completely. "Your highness doubts, and wishes to be sure the writing is Lorenza's. She herself shall enlighten you. Lorenza, answer; who wrote this note?"

On his putting the paper in her hand, she pressed it to her heart.

"It was Lorenza," she said.

"Lorenza knows what is in it?"

"Of course."

"Well, then, tell the princess what it says, that she may not believe that I deceive her in asserting that you love me. I want you to tell her."

Appearing to make an effort, but without looking at the note, unfolding it or bringing it to her eyes, she read, word for word, what the princess had seen without speaking it aloud.

"This is hard to believe," said the superior. "And I do not believe you, from what is supernatural and inexplicable in what happens."

"It was this very letter which determined me to hurry on our wedding," said Count Fenix, without heeding the interruption. "I love Lorenza as much as she loves me. In our roaming life, accidents might happen. If I died, I wanted my property to be my dear one's; so we were united when we reached Strasburg."

"But she told me that she was not your wife."

"Lorenza," said the count, without replying to the abbess, and turning to the Italian, "do you remember where and when we were married?"

"Yes; in the St. John's Chapel of Strasburg Cathedral, on the third of May."

"Did you oppose any resistance to the marriage?"

"No; I was only too happy."

"The fact is, Lorenza," continued the count, taking her hand, "the princess thinks you were constrained to it."

"I hate you?" she said, shivering all over with delight. "Oh, no; I love you. You are good, generous and mighty."

Seized with affright, the princess recoiled to where an ivory crucifix gleamed on a black velvet background.

"Is this all your highness wishes to know?" asked Fenix, letting Lorenza's hand fall.

"Keep away!" gasped the abbess; "and she, too!"

A carriage was heard to stop before the nunnery door.

"The cardinal?" exclaimed the lady superior; "we shall see how things stand at last."

Fenix bowed, said a few words to the Italian woman, and waited with the calmness of one who directs events.

In another instant the door opened and Cardinal Rohan was announced.

"Show him in," said the abbess, encouraged by the new addition to the party being a churchman.

The prince had no sooner saluted the princess than he exclaimed with surprise on seeing Balsamo:

"Are you here, my lord?"

"Are you acquaintances?" cried the princess, more and more astonished. "Then you can tell me who this is."

"Nothing is easier; the gentleman is a magician."

"His eminence will make this clear presently, and to everybody's satisfaction," said the count.

"Has the gentleman been telling your highness' fortune, that I see you so affected?" questioned the cardinal.

"The marriage certificate at once!" cried the princess, to the astonishment of the newcomer, ignorant of the allusion.

"What is this?"

"My lord, the question is, whether this paper is real and the signature valid?" said the princess, as Balsamo held out the document.

Rohan read the paper as presented by the abbess and nodded.

"It is in proper form, and the signature is Curate Saint-Remy's, of St. John's, Strasburg, one of my appointees. But what does this matter to your highness?"

"Considerable; but——"

"The signature might have been extorted."

"True, that is possible," said the princess.

"How about Lorenza's consent, then?" said the count, sarcastically.

"By what means could a priest have been induced——"

"By the magic in the gentleman's powers."

"Your eminence is jesting."

"Not at all, and the proof is that I want to have a serious explanation from this gentleman. Do not forget, my lord, that I shall do all the questioning," added the cardinal, with haughtiness.

"And remember that I was quite willing to answer aloud, even before her royal highness—if your eminence desired so; but I am certain you will not desire it."

The cardinal had to smile.

"My lord," said he, "it is hard to play the wizard nowadays. I have seen you perform, and with great success; but everybody has not the patience, and still less the generosity, of the dauphiness."

157

"The dauphiness?" queried Princess Louise.

"Yes, your highness, I had the honor of presentation to her," said the count.

"But how did you repay the honor? Answer that, my lord."

"Alas, with more evil than I liked," said Fenix, "for I have no personal hate to men, and less to women. My misfortune was that I was compelled to tell your august niece the truth she craved."

"A piece of truthfulness which caused her to faint."

"Is it fault of mine," retorted the mesmerist, in that voice which he could sometimes make thunderous, "that truth is so awful as to produce such effects? Did I seek out the princess, and beg to be presented to her? No, I was avoiding her, when they almost dragged me before her, and she ordered me to answer her interrogation."

"But what was the dreadful truth you told her, my lord?" inquired the princess.

"She saw it in the gap which I tore in the veil over the future," rejoined the mysterious man. "That future which has appeared so awful to your royal highness that you have fled into a cloister to wrestle against it at the altar with tears and prayers. Is it fault of mine, I say, if this future, revealed to you as a holy woman, should be shown to me as a precursor; and if the dauphiness, alarmed at the fate personally threatening her, swooned when it loomed upon her?"

"Do you hear this?" said the cardinal.

"Woe is me!" moaned the Carmelite superior.

"For her reign is doomed as the most fatal and unfortunate of the entire monarchy," continued the count.

"My lord!" cried the abbess.

"Perchance your prayers will earn your grace," proceeded the prophet, "but then you will see nothing of what comes to pass, as you will rest in the arms of the angels. Pray, lady; continue to pray!"

Overcome by this prophetic voice, which harmonized so well with the terrors in her soul, the princess dropped kneeling before the crucifix and began indeed to pray, and with fervor.

"Now, our turn, cardinal," said the count turning to the prince, and leading him into a window recess. "Speak as to your want of me."

"I want to know what you are?"

"You do know—you say that I am a magician."

"I mean that you are called Joseph Balsamo in the south; and here, Count Fenix."

"That merely proves that I change my name."

"Yes; but I would have you know that such changes on the part of such a man will set Chief of Police Sartines to thinking."

"This is petty warfare for a Rohan," said the other, smiling.

"Your eminence stoops to wrangle over words. Verba et voces, says the Latin. Is there nothing worse to fling at me?"

"You are railing, my lord."

"Always; it is my style."

"Then I shall make you change your note; which will help me in the good graces of the dauphiness, whom you have offended."

"Do so, as it will not be a useless act, considering the delicate ground on which you stand as regards her," returned Balsamo phlegmatically.

"What will you say if I have you arrested straightway, my lord the horoscopist?"

"You would do yourself injury, my lord cardinal."

"Really! How do you make that out?" demanded the proud peer with crushing scorn.

"You would unmake yourself."

"At least, we shall know who really is Baron Joseph Balsamo, alias Count Fenix, a sprig of a family tree of which I have never seen the picture in any heraldic work in Europe."

"You should have asked to see it in the portfolio of the Duke of Breteuil, your friend——"

"His grace is no friend of mine."

"He was, and an intimate one, or your eminence would never have written him that letter—but draw closer, my lord, lest we are overheard in what may compromise you!—that letter written from Vienna to Paris to dissuade the dauphin from making his marriage."

"That letter!" gasped the prince, starting with fright.

"I know it by heart."

"Breteuil has betrayed? because he said it was—burned when I asked it back, when the marriage was settled."

"He did not like to admit that he had lost it. A lost letter may be found; and, indeed, I found it in the Marble Court at Versailles. I took good care not to restore it to the duke, for I knew your eminence was ill-disposed toward me. If you were going through the woods and expected highwaymen to attack you, and you found a loaded pistol, would you not pick it up to use it? A man would be an idiot not to do so."

The cardinal felt giddy and leaned on the window-sill. After hesitation, during which the count watched the play of his features, he said:

"Granted thus. But it shall never be said that a prince of my line yielded to the threats of a mountebank. Though this letter may have been lost, and found, and will be shown to the dauphiness herself, and may ruin me as a politician, I will stand to it that I am still a loyal subject and a faithful ambassador. I will speak the truth—that I thought the alliance injurious to the interests of my country, and let it defend me or blame me."

"But what will be the answer of this faithful subject and loyal envoy if somebody asserts that this gallant young beau of an ambassador, never doubting his winning all before him with his title of prince and name of Rohan, did not say this from any opinion that the alliance would be hurtful to his country, but because—being graciously welcomed by Marie Antoinette—this coxcomb of an envoy had the vanity to think the feast was fitter for Jack than his master?"

"He would deny; for of this feeling which you pretend to have existed, no proof can be exhibited."

"You are wrong; the token is in the dauphiness' coldness toward you."

The cardinal wavered.

"Believe me, prince," went on the count, "instead of quarreling, as we should have done, only for my having more prudence than you, we had better be friends—good ones, for such do one another service."

"Have I ever asked aught of your lordship?"

"Just there you are wrong; for you might have called on me during the two days you spent in town. You cannot conceal from a sorcerer what you have been about. You left the Austrian princess at Soissons, whence you rushed posthaste to Paris, where you dunned your friends for help, which they all refused you. This left you desperate."

"What kind of help could I expect from you, had I applied?" asked the Rohan, confounded.

"Such as a man gives who can make gold. And you ought to want gold when you have to pay five hundred thousand francs in forty-eight hours. You want to know what good a man is who makes gold? Why, he is the very one where you will find the cash demanded. You could easily tell my house in Saint Claude Street in the swamp, as the knocker is a brass griffin."

"When could I call?"

"Six, to-morrow afternoon, please your eminence, and whenever after you like. But we have finished our chat in time, for the princess has concluded her devotions."

The cardinal was conquered.

"Your highness," he said, "I am forced to acknowledge that Count Fenix is quite right; the document he produces is most reliable, and the explanations he has furnished have completely satisfied me."

"Your highness' orders?" asked the count, bowing.

"Let me put one last question to this young lady."

Again the count bowed in assent.

"Is it of your own free will that you quit the abbey of St. Denis, where you came to seek refuge?"

"Her highness," repeated Fenix, quickly, "asks you whether you are leaving this place of your own free will. Speak out Lorenza."

"I go of my own free will," replied the Italian.

"In order to accompany Count Fenix, your husband?" prompted the magician.

"To accompany my husband."

"In this case I retain neither of you," said the princess, "for it would be running counter to my feelings. But, if there be anything in all this out of the natural order of things, may the divine punishment fall on whomsoever disturbs the harmony of nature for his profit or interests. Go, my Lord Count Fenix; and you, Lorenza Feliciani—I detain you no more. But take back your jewels."

"They are for the poor," replied Balsamo; "distributed by your hands, the alms will be doubly agreeable to God. All I ask is to have my horse Djerid."

"Take him as you go forth. Begone!"

Bowing to the speaker, the count presented his arm to Lorenza, who leaned upon it and walked out without a word.

"Alas, my lord cardinal," sighed the abbess, sadly shaking her head, "in the very air we breathe are fatal and incomprehensible things!"

CHAPTER XXXIV

NEAR NEIGHBORS

On parting from young Taverney, Gilbert had plunged into the crowd. But not with a heart bounding with glee and expectation—rather with the soul ulcerated by grief which the noble's kind welcome and obliging offers of assistance could not mollify.

Andrea never suspected that she had been cruel to the youth. The fair and serene maiden was completely unaware that there could be any link between her and her foster-brother, for joy or sorrow. She soared over earthly spheres, casting on them shine or shadow according to her being smiling or gloomy. This time it chanced that her shade of disdain had chilled Gilbert; as she had merely followed the impulse of her temper, she was ignorant that she had been scornful.

But Gilbert, like a disarmed gladiator, had received the proud speech and the scorning looks straight in the heart. He was not enough of a philosopher yet not to console himself with despair while the wound was bleeding.

Hence he did not notice men or horses in the press. Gathering up his strength, he rushed into it, at the risk of being crushed, like a wild boar cutting through the pack of hounds.

At length breathing more freely, he reached the green sward, water side and loneliness. He had run to the river Seine, and came out opposite St. Denis island. Exhausted, not by bodily fatigue but by spiritual anguish, he rolled on the grass, and roared like a lion transfixed by a spear, as if the animal's voice better expressed his woes than human tongue.

Was not all the vague and undecided hope which had flung a little light on the mad ideas, not to be accounted for to himself, now extinguished at a blow? To whatever step on the social ladder Gilbert might rise by dint of genius, science and study, he would always be a man or a thing—according to her own words, for which her father was wrong in paying any attention, and not worth her lowering her eyes upon.

He had briefly fancied that, on seeing him in the capital, and learning his resolution to struggle till he came up through the darkness, Andrea would applaud the effort. Not only had the cheer failed the brave boy, but he had met the haughty indifference always had for the dependent by the young lady of the manor.

Furthermore she had shown anger that he should have looked at her music book; had he touched it, he did not doubt that he would be thought fit to be burned at the stake.

As he writhed on the turf, he knew not whether he loved or hated his torturer; he suffered, that was all. But as he was not capable of long patience, he sprang out of his prostration, decided to invent some energetic course.

"Granted that she does not love me," he reasoned, "I must not hope that she never will. I had the right to expect from her the mild interest attached to those who wrestle with their misfortune. She did not understand what her brother saw. He thought that I might become a celebrity; should it happen so, he would act fairly and let me have his sister, in reward of my earned glory, as he would have exchanged her for my native aristocracy, had I been born his equal.

162

"But I shall always be plain Gilbert in her eyes, for she looks down in me upon what nothing can efface, gild or cover—my low birth. As though, supposing I attain my mark, it would not be greater of me than if I had started on her high level! Oh, mad creature! senseless being! oh, woman, woman—your other name is Imperfection.

"Do not be deluded by the splendid gaze, intelligent smile, and queenly port of Andrea de Taverney, whose beauty makes her fit to rule society—she is but a rustic dame, straitlaced, limited, swathed in aristocratic prejudices. Equals for her are those empty-headed fops, with effete minds, who had the means to learn everything and know nothing; they are the men to whom she pays heed. Gilbert is but a dog, less than a dog, for I believe she asked after Mahon, and not about my welfare.

"Ah, she is ignorant that I am fit to cope with them; when I wear the like coats, I shall look as well; and that, with my inflexible determination, I shall grasp——"

A dreadful smile was defined on his lips where the sentence died away unfinished. Frowning, he slowly lowered his head.

What passed in that obscure soul? What terrible plan bent the pale forehead, already sallow with sleepless nights, and furrowed by thinking? Who shall tell?

At the close of half an hour's profound meditation, Gilbert rose, coldly determined. He went to the river, drank a long draft, and looking round, saw the distant waves of the people in a sea coming out of St. Denis.

They so crowded in upon the first coaches that the horses had to go at a walk, on the road to St. Ouen.

The dauphin wanted the ceremony to be a national family festival. So the French family abused the privilege; a number of Parisians climbed on the footboards and hung there without being disturbed.

Very soon Gilbert recognized the Taverney carriage, with Philip holding in his capering horse by the side.

"I must know where she goes," thought the lover; "and so shall follow them."

It was intended that the dauphiness should sup with the royal family in private at Muette, but Louis XV. had broken the etiquette so far as to make up a larger party. He handed a list of guests to the dauphiness, with a pencil, and suggested she should strike out the names of any not liked to come. When she came to the last name, Countess Dubarry's, she felt her lips quiver and lose blood; but sustained by her mother's instructions, she summoned up her powers to her aid, and with a charming smile returned the paper and pencil to the king, saying that she was very happy to be let into the bosom of all his family at the very first.

Gilbert knew nothing about this, and it was only when he got to Muette that he recognized the coach of Dubarry, with Zamore mounted on a high white horse. Luckily it was dark, and Gilbert threw himself on the ground in a grove and waited.

The king, then, shared supper between mistress and daughter-in-law, and was merry especially on seeing that the newcomer treated the usurper more kindly even than at Compiegne.

But the dauphin, gloomy and careworn, spoke of having the headache, and retired before they sat at table.

The supper was prolonged to eleven o'clock.

The king sent a band of music to play to the repast for the gentry of the retinue—of which our proud Andrea had to admit she was a member; as the accommodation was limited, fifty masters had to picnic on the lawn, served by men in royal livery. In the thicket, Gilbert lost nothing of this scene. Taking out a piece of bread, he ate along with the guests, while watching that those he attended to did not slip away.

After the meal, the dauphiness came out on the balcony to take leave of her hosts. Near her stood the king. Countess Dubarry kept out of sight in the back of the room, with that exquisite tact which even her enemies allowed she had.

The courtiers passed under the balcony to salute the king, who named such of them to the dauphiness as she did not already know. From time to time some happy allusion or pleasant saying dropped from his lips, to delight those who received it. Seeing this servility, Gilbert muttered to himself:

"I am a touch above these slaves, for I would not crouch like that for all the gold in the world."

He rose on one knee when the turn came for the Taverneys to pass.

"Captain Taverney," said the dauphiness, "I grant you leave to conduct your father and sister to Paris."

In the nightly silence and amid the attention of those drinking in the august words, Gilbert caught the sound coming in his direction.

"My lord baron," continued the princess, "I have no accommodation yet for you among my household; so guard your daughter in town until I set up my establishment at Versailles. Keep me in mind, my dear young lady."

The baron passed on with son and daughter. Others came up for whom the princess had pretty stuff to say, but that little mattered to Gilbert. Gliding out of the covert, he followed the baron among the two hundred footmen shouting out their master's names, fifty coachmen roaring out in answer to the lackeys, while sixty coaches rolled over the pavement like thunder.

As Taverney had a royal carriage, it waited for him aside from the common herd. He stepped in, with Andrea and Philip, and the door closed after them.

"Get on the box with the driver," said Philip to the footman. "He has been on his feet all day, and must be worn out."

The baron grumbled some remonstrance not heard by Gilbert, but the lackey mounted beside the driver. Gilbert went nearer. At the time of starting a trace got loose and the driver had to alight to set it right.

"It is very late," said the baron.

"I am dreadfully tired," sighed Andrea. "I hope we shall find a sleeping place somewhere."

"I expect so," replied her brother. "I sent Labrie and Nicole straight to Paris from Soissons. I gave him a letter to a friend for him to let us have a little house in the rear of his, where his mother and sister live when they come up from the country. It is not luxury, but it is comfortable. You do not want to make a show while you are waiting for the coming out in the suitable style."

"Anything will easily beat Taverney," said the old lord.

"Unfortunately, yes," added the captain.

"Any garden?" asked Andrea.

"Quite a little park, for town, with fine trees. However, you will not long enjoy it, as you will be presented as soon as the wedding is over."

"We are in a bright dream—do not waken us. Did you give the coachman the address?"

"Yes, father," replied the young noble, while Gilbert greedily listened.

He had hoped to catch the address.

"Never mind," he muttered; "it is only a league to town. I will follow them."

But the royal horses could go at a rattling gait when not kept in line with others. The trace being mended, the man mounted his box and drove off rapidly—so rapidly that this reminded poor Gilbert of how he had fallen on the road under the hoofs of Chon's post-horses.

Making a spurt, he reached the untenanted footboard, and hung on behind for an instant. But the thought struck him that he was in the menial's place behind Andrea's carriage, and he muttered:

"No! it shall not be said that I did not fight it out to the last. My legs are tired, but not my arms."

Seizing the edge of the footboard with both hands, the inflexible youth swung his feet up under the body of the coach so as to get them on the foresprings; thus suspended, he was carried on, spite of the jerking, over the wretched rutty road. He stuck to the desperate situation by strength of arm, rather than capitulate with his conscience.

"I shall learn her address," he thought. "It will be another wakeful night; but to-morrow I shall have repose, seated while I am copying music. I have a trifle of money, too, and I will take a little rest."

He reflected that Paris was very large and that he might be lost after seeing the baron to his house. Happily it was near midnight, and dawn came at half after three.

As he was pondering he remarked that they crossed an open place where stood an equestrian statue in the midst.

"Victories Place," he thought gleefully; "I know it."

The vehicle turning partly round and Andrea put her head out to see the statue.

"The late king," explained her brother. "We are pretty nearly there now."

They went down so steep a hill that Gilbert was nearly scraped off.

"Here we are," cried the dragoon captain.

Gilbert dropped and slipped out from beneath to hide behind a horseblock on the other side.

Young Taverney got out first, rang at a house doorbell, and returned to receive Andrea in his arms. The baron was the last out.

"Are those rascals going to keep us out all night?" he snarled.

At this the voices of Labrie and Nicole were heard, and a door opened. The three Taverneys were engulfed in a dark courtyard where the door closed upon them. The vehicle and attendants went their way to the royal stables.

Nothing remarkable was apparent on the house; but the carriage lamps had flashed on the next doorway, which had a label: "This is the mansion of the Armenonvilles." Gilbert did not know what street it was as yet, but going to the far end, the same the carriage had gone out of, he was startled to see the public fountain at which he drank in the mornings. Going ten paces up the street he saw the baker's shop where he supplied himself. Still doubting, he returned to the corner. By the gleam of a swinging lamp, he could read on a white stone the name read three days before when coming from Meudon Wood with Rousseau:

166

"Plastrière Street."

It followed that Andrea was lodged a hundred steps apart, nearer than she was to him at Taverney.

So he went to his own door, hoping that the latchet might not be drawn altogether within. It was pulled in, but it was frayed and a few threads stuck out. He drew one and then another so that the thong itself came forth at last. He lifted the latch, and entered, for it was one of his lucky days.

He groped up the stairs one by one, without making any noise, and finally touched the padlock on his own bedroom door, in which Rousseau had thoughtfully left the key.

CHAPTER XXXV

THE GARDEN HOUSE

From coming home so late, and dropping off to sleep so soon and heavily, Gilbert forgot to hang up the linen cloth which served as curtain to the garret window. The unintercepted sunbeam struck his eyes at five and speedily woke him. He rose, vexed at having overslept.

Brought up in the country, he could exactly tell the time by the sun's inclination and the amount of heat it emitted. He hastened to consult this clock. The pallor of the dawn, scarcely clearing the high trees, set him at ease; he was rising too early, not too late.

He made his ablutions at the skylight, thinking over what had happened over night, and gladly baring his burning and burdened forehead to the fresh morning breeze. Then it came to his mind that Andrea was housed next door to Armenonville House, in an adjoining street. He wanted to distinguish this residence.

The sight of shade-trees reminded him of her question to her brother,—Was there a garden where they were going?

"Why may it not be just such a house in the back garden as we have yonder?" he asked himself.

By a strange coincidence with his thought, a sound and a movement quite unusual drew his attention where it was turning; one of the long fastened up windows of a house built at the rear of the one on the other street shook under a rough or clumsy hand.

167

The frame gave way at the top; but it stuck probably with damp swelling it at the bottom. A still rougher push started the two folds of the sash, which opened like a door, and the gap showed a girl, red with the exertion she had to make and shaking her dusty hands.

Gilbert uttered an outcry in astonishment and quickly drew back, for this sleepy and yawning girl was Nicole.

He could harbor no doubt now. Philip Taverney had told his father that he had sent on Labrie and their maid servant to get a lodging ready in Paris. Hence this was the one. The house in Coq-Heron Street, where the travelers had disappeared—was this with the extra building in the rear.

Gilbert's withdrawal had been so marked that Nicole must have noticed it only for her being absorbed in that idle fit seizing one just arisen. But he had retired swiftly, not to be caught by her while looking out of a garret window. Perhaps if he had lived on the first floor, and his window had given a view within of a richly furnished apartment, he would have called her attention on it. But the fifth flat still classed him among social inferiors, so that he wanted to keep in the background.

Besides, it is always an advantage to see without being seen.

Again, if Andrea saw him, might she not consider that enough to induce her to move away, or at least not to stroll about the garden?

Alas, for Gilbert's conceit! it enlarged him in his own eyes; but what mattered Gilbert to the patrician, and what would make her move a step nearer or further from him? Was she not of the class of women who would come out from a bath with a peasant or a footman by, and not regard them as men?

But Nicole was not of this degree, and she had to be avoided.

But Gilbert did not keep away from the window. He returned to peep out at the corner.

A second window, exactly beneath the other, opened also, and the white figure appearing there was Andrea's. In a morning gown, she was stooping to look after her slipper fallen under a chair.

In vain did Gilbert, every time he saw his beloved, make a vow to resist his passion within a rampart of hate; the same effect followed the cause. He was obliged to lean on the wall, with his heart throbbing as if to burst and the blood boiling all over his body.

As the arteries cooled gradually, he reflected. The main point was to spy without being seen. He took one of Madame Rousseau's old dresses off the clothesline, and fastened it with a pin on a string across his window so that he might watch Andrea under the improvised screen.

Andrea imitated Nicole in stretching her lovely arms, which, by

168

this extension, parted the gown an instant; then she leaned out to examine the neighboring grounds at her leisure. Her face expressed rare satisfaction, for while she seldom smiled on men, she made up for it by often smiling on things.

On all sides the rear house was shaded by fine trees.

Rousseau's house attracted her gaze like all the other buildings, but no more. From her point, the upper part alone could be espied, but what concern had she in the servants' quarters in a house?

Andrea therefore came to the conclusion that she was unseen and alone, with no curious or joking face of Parisians on the edge of this tranquil retreat, so dreaded by country ladies.

Leaving her window wide open for the sunshine to flush the remotest corners, the young lady went to pull the bellrope at the fire-place side and began to dress in the twilight. Nicole ran in and opening the straps of a shagreen dressing-case dating from a previous reign, took a tortoise-shell comb and disentangled her mistress' tresses.

Gilbert smothered a sigh. He could hardly be said to recognize the hair, for Andrea followed the fashion in powdering it, but he knew her a hundred times fairer without the frippery than in the most pompous decorations. His mouth dried up, his fingers scorched with fever, and his eye ceased to see from his staring too hard.

Chance ruled that Andrea's gaze, idle as it was from her sitting still to have her hair brushed, fell on Rousseau's attic.

"Yes, yes, keep on staring," uttered the youth, "but you will see nothing and I shall see all."

But he was wrong, for she descried the novel screen of the old dress which floated round the man's head as a kind of turban. She pointed out this odd curtain to her maid. Nicole stopped and pointed with the comb to the object to ask whether that were the reason for her mistress' amusement.

Without his suspecting it, this had a fourth spectator.

He suddenly felt a hasty hand snatch Madame Rousseau's dress from his brow, and he fell back thunderstricken at recognizing the master.

"What the deuse are you up to?" queried the philosopher, with a frowning brow and a sour grin as he examined the gown.

"Nothing," stammered the other, trying to divert the intruder's sight from the window.

"Then why hide up in this dress?"

"The sun was too bright for me."

"The sun is at the back of us, and I think it is you who are too bright for me. You have very weak eyes, young man."

169

Rousseau walked straight up to the window. By a very natural feeling to be a veil to his beauty, Gilbert, who had shrunk away, now rushed in between.

"Bless me, the rear house is lived in now!" The tone froze the blood in Gilbert's veins, and he could not get out a word. "And by people who know my house, for they are pointing up to it," added the suspicious author.

Gilbert, fearful now that he was too forward, retreated. Neither the movement nor its cause escaped Rousseau, who saw that his employee trembled to be seen.

"No, you don't, young man!" he said, grasping him by the wrist; "there is some plot afoot, for they are pointing out your garret. Stand here, pray."

He placed him before the window, in the uncovered glare.

Gilbert would have had to struggle with his idol, and respect restrained him from thus being free.

"You know those women, and they know you," continued Rosseau, "or, why do you shrink from showing yourself?"

"Monsieur Rousseau, you have had secrets in your life. Pity for mine!"

"Traitor!" cried the writer; "I know your sort of secret. You are the tool of my enemies, the Grimms and Holbachs. They taught you a part to captivate my benevolence, and, sneaking into my house, you are betraying me. Threefold fool that I am, stupid lover of nature, to think I was helping one of my kind, and to nourish a spy!"

"A spy?" repeated the other in revolt.

"When are you to deliver me to my murderers, O Judas?" demanded Rousseau, draping himself in Therese's dress, which he had mechanically kept in hand, and looking droll when he fancied he was sublime with sorrow.

"You calumniate me, sir," said Gilbert.

"Calumniate this little viper!" said the philosopher, "when I catch you corresponding in dumb show with my enemies—I daresay acquainting them in signs with my latest work."

"Had I come to steal your story, sir, I should better have made a copy of the manuscript, lying on your desk, than to convey it in signs."

This was true, and Rousseau felt that he had made one of those blunders which escaped him in his moments of fear, and he became angry.

"I am sorry for you, but experience makes me stern," he said. "My life has passed amid deceit. I have been betrayed by everybody, denied, sold and martyrized. You know I am one of those illustrious unfortunates whom governments outlaw. Under such circumstances, I may be allowed to be suspicious. As you are a suspicious character, you must take yourself out of this house."

Gilbert had not expected this conclusion. He was to be driven forth! He clenched his fists, and a flash in his eyes made Rousseau start. Gilbert reflected that in going he would lose the mild pleasure of seeing his loved one during the day, and lose Rousseau's affection—it was shame as well as misfortune.

Dropping from his fierce pride, he clasped his hands and implored:

"Listen to me, if only one word!"

"I am merciless," replied the author: "man's injustice has made me more ferocious than a tiger. Go and join my enemies with whom you correspond. League yourself with them, which I do not hinder, but do all this beyond my domicile."

"Those young women are no enemies of yours—they are Mademoiselle Andrea of Taverney, the young lady I told you of, on whose estate I was born, and her maid Nicole. Excuse me troubling you with such matters, but you drive me to it. This is the lady whom I love more than you ever loved all your flames. It is she whom I followed afoot, penniless and wanting bread, until I fell exhausted on the highway and racked with pain. It is she whom I saw once more yesterday at St. Denis, and behind whose coach I came till I housed her in the place yonder. In short, it is she for whom I wish one of these days to be a great man—a Rousseau!"

His hearer knew the human heart, and the gamut of its exclamations. The best actor could hardly have Gilbert's tearful voice and the feverish gesture accompanying the effusion.

"So this is your lady love?"

"My foster-sister, yes."

"Then you lied a while ago when you said you knew her not, and you are a liar, if not a traitor."

"You are racking my heart and you would hurt me less were you to slay me on the spot."

"Pooh! that is a mere piece of fustian out of the Diderot or Marmontel books. You are a liar, sir."

"Have it so, and the worse for you that you do not understand such white lies!" retorted Gilbert. "I shall go, heartbroken, and you will have my despair on your conscience."

Rousseau smoothed his chin and regarded the youth whose case had so much analogy with his own.

"He is either a great rogue or a lad with a big heart," he mused; "but after all, if he is in a plot against me, it will be best to have the wires of the puppets in my hand."

Gilbert strode to the door, but he paused with his hand on the knob, waiting for the last word to recall or banish him.

"Enough on this head, my son," said the man of letters. "It is hard enough for you to be in love, to this degree. But it is getting on, and we have thirty pages of music to copy this day. Look alive, Gilbert, look alive!"

Gilbert grasped the speaker's hand and pressed it to his lips as he would not a king's. While Gilbert leaned up against the doorjamb with emotion, Rousseau took a last peep out of the window. This was the moment when Andrea stood up to put on her dress, but seeing a person up at the attic window, she darted back and bade Nicole shut the sashes.

"My old head frightened her," mumbled the philosopher; "his youthful one would not have done that. Oh, youth, lovely youth!" he broke forth, sighing, "'Spring is the love-time of the year! love is the springtime of life!'"

Hanging up the dress, he melancholically descended the stairs at the heels of Gilbert, for whose youth he would at that time have bartered his reputation, at that juncture counterbalancing Voltaire's and with it sharing the admiration of the entire world.

CHAPTER XXXVI

BALSAMO AT HOME

The house in St. Claude Street, to which Joseph Balsamo invited the Cardinal Prince of Rohan did not look strange in his day, but it resembled a fortress to such an extent that it would be remarkable at present. Strongly built, and with barred windows and grated doors, to say nothing of the ditch in front and high balconies, it was in keeping with this part of the town, pretty unsafe at this epoch after dark.

There were scarcely a dozen houses on the quarter of a league to the Bastille, and the municipal authorities did not think it worth while to supply lamps. Along this deserted and unlighted highway a carriage was driven after nine one evening, which stopped at the low, deep doorway where gleamed the brazen griffin for a knocker which Count Fenix had described.

The arms of the nobleman were on the carriage panels. He preceded it by some yards, riding Djerid, who whisked his long tail till it whistled in the dust of the dirty pavement.

Behind the closed blinds slumbered Lorenza on the cushions.

At the rolling of the wheels, the door opened as by enchantment, and the carriage vanished in the black gulf of the mansion courtyard.

There was no need of any mystery, for nobody was about to see the count come home or mark what he brought, even if it were the treasure-chest of St. Denis Abbey.

A skillful calculator, given the size of the building lot and that of the house on street, would be surprised how so small a one covered so much ground. The fact of the matter was that there stood a house behind the outer house, known only to the tenant.

A German servant, aged about thirty; closed the coachway door and bolted it. Opening the coach door while the emotionless driver unharnessed the team, he drew from within the senseless Lorenza, whom he carried indoors to an antechamber. He laid her on a table and discreetly wrapped her in her long veil to the feet.

He went out to light at the coach lamps a seven-candle chandelier, with which he came back.

During that short space, Lorenza had disappeared.

In fact Count Fenix had entered after the valet went out. He had taken up the girl in his arms, and carried her out by a secret passage into a room furnished with trophies of outlandish weapons.

With his foot he pressed the spring of the backplate of the high fireplace, which turned on well-oiled hinges, so that the count could go forth, as he did, while the secret panel slid to behind him.

On the other side of the chimney was another flight of steps. Mounting a dozen, covered with Utrecht velvet carpet, he reached the sill of a room elegantly tapestried with satin, so wonderfully embroidered in high relief with flowers in their natural colors that they seemed real.

The extremely rich furniture was of a boudoir and toilet chamber leading to a parlor.

Curtains hid two windows, but as it was night, they were not wanted to give light. Lamps burning perfumed oil burnt here night and day, for the room had no external openings. They were drawn up through apertures in the ceiling by unseen hands when they needed replenishing.

Not a sound penetrated here, and one might feel as a thousand miles out of the world. But gilding flashed on all sides and Bohemian glass mirrors sparkled as, dissatisfied with the light, after having placed Lorenza on a sofa, the count struck a fire with the silver phosphorus matchbox so startling to Gilbert, and kindled two pink candled chandeliers on the mantel-piece.

Returning to Lorenza, and kneeling with one knee on a pile of cushions beside her, he called her by name. Though her eyes remained closed, she rose on one elbow, but without replying.

"Are you sleeping naturally or through the magnetic spell?"

"Lorenza sleeps in the magnetic sleep," she replied.

"Then you can answer my questions. Look into the room of the Princess Louise which we have just quitted, and tell me if the Cardinal of Rohan is there."

"No; the abbess is praying before going to rest."

"Look through the house for the cardinal. Is his carriage at the door? Is it on the road? Come along nearer to Paris, as we drove. Nearer!"

"Ah, I see it! It has stopped at the tollbar. A footman gets down to speak with his master."

"List to him, Lorenza, for it is important that I should know what the cardinal says to this man."

"You did not order me to listen in time, for he has done speaking to the man. But the man speaks to the coachman, who is told to drive to St. Claude Street, in the swamp, by the rampart road."

"Thank you, Lorenza."

The count went to the wall, pulled aside an ornament which disclosed an ivory mouthpiece and spoke some words in a tube of unknown length and direction; it was his way of corresponding here with his man of trust, Fritz.

"Are you content with me?" asked the medium.

"Yes, dear Lorenza, and here is your reward," he said, giving her a fond caress.

"Oh, Joseph, how I love you!" she said with an almost painful sigh.

Her arms opened to enfold Balsamo on her heart.

CHAPTER XXXVII

THE DOUBLE EXISTENCE

But he recoiled swiftly, and the arms came together ere falling folded on her bosom.

"Would you like to speak with your friend?" he asked.

"Yes, speak to me often. I like to hear your voice."

"You have often told me, dearest, that you would be very happy if we could dwell together afar from the world."

"That would indeed be bliss."

"Well, I have realized your wish, darling. We are by ourselves in this parlor, where none can hear and none intrude."

"I am glad to hear it."

"Tell me how you like the place."

"Order me to see it."

"Does it please you?" asked the count, after a pause.

"Yes; here are my favorite flowers. Thank you, my kind Joseph. How good you are!"

"I do all I can to please you."

"Oh, you are a hundred times kinder to me than I deserve."

"You confess that you have been wicked?"

"Very badly so, but you will overlook that?"

"After you explain the enigma which I have struggled against ever since I knew you."

"Hearken, Balsamo. In me are two Lorenzas, quite distinct. One loves you and the other detests you, as if I lived two existences. One during which I enjoy the delights of paradise, the other when I suffer the opposite."

"These two existences are your waking mood and your magnetic sleep?"

"Yes."

"Why do you hate me when in your waking senses and love me when in the charmed sleep?"

"Because Lorenza is the superstitious Italian girl who believes that science is a crime and love a sin. Then she is afraid of the sage Balsamo and the loving Joseph. She has been told that to love would destroy her soul; and so she flees from the lover to the confines of the earth."

"But when Lorenza sleeps?"

"It is another matter. She is no longer a Roman girl and superstitious, but a woman. She sees that the genius of Balsamo

175

dreams of sublime themes. She understands how petty an object she is compared with him. She longs to live by him and die at his side, in order that the future shall breathe her name while it trumpets the glory of—Cagliostro."

"Is that the name I am to be celebrated under?"

"The name."

"Dear Lorenza! so you like our new home?"

"It is richer than any you have found for me; but that is not why I like it more—but because you say you will be oftener with me here."

"So, when you sleep, you know how fondly I adore you?"

"Yes," she said with a faint smile, "I see that passion, then, and yet there is something you love above Lorenza," she sighed. "Your dream."

"Rather say, my task."

"Well, your ambition!"

"Say, my glory."

"Oh, heaven!" and her heart was laboring; her closed lids allowed tears to struggle out.

"What is it you see?" inquired Balsamo, astounded at the lucidity which frightened even him.

"I see phantoms gliding about among the shadows. Some hold in their own hands their severed crowned heads, like St. Denis in that Abbey; and you stand in the heart of the battle like a general in command. You seem to rule, and you are obeyed."

"Does that not make you proud of me?" inquired the other joyfully.

"You are good enough not to care to be great. Besides, in looking for myself in this scene, I see nothing of me. Oh, I shall not be there," she sighed. "I shall be in the grave."

"You dead, my dearest Lorenza!" said Balsamo, frowning. "No, we shall live and love together."

"No, you love me no more, or not enough," crowding upon his forehead, held between her hands, a multitude of glowing kisses. "I have to reproach you for your coldness. Look now how you draw away from me as though you fled my fondlings. Oh, restore to me my maiden quietude, in my nunnery of Subiaco—when the night was so calm in my cell. Return me those kisses which you sent on the wings of the wind coming to me in my solitude like golden-pinioned sylph, which melted on me in delight. Do not retreat from me. Give me your hand, that I may press it; let me kiss your dear eyes—let me be your wife, in short."

"Lorenza, sweetest, you are my well-beloved wife."

"Yet you pass by the chaste and solitary flower and scorn the perfume? I am sure that I am nothing to you."

"On the contrary, you are everything—my Lorenza. For it is you who give me strength, power and genius—without you I should be nothing. Cease, then, to love me with this insensate fever which wrecks the nights of your people, and love me as I love you. Thus I am happy."

"You call that happiness?" scornfully said the Italian.

"Yes, for to be great is happiness."

She heaved a long sigh.

"Oh, if you only knew the gladness in being able to read the hearts of man and manipulate them with the strings of their own dominant passions."

"Yes, I know that in this I serve your purpose."

"It is not all. Your eyes read the sealed book of the future. You, sweet dove, pure and guideless, you have taught me what I could not ascertain in twenty years' application. You enlighten my steps, before which my enemies multiply traps and snares; on my mind depend my life, fortune and liberty—you dilate it like the lynx's eye which sees in the dark. As your lovely orbs close on this world, they open in superhuman clarity. They watch for me. It is you who make me rich, free and powerful."

"And in return, you make me unhappy," replied Lorenza, wrapped up in her frenzy.

More fiery than ever, she enfolded him in her arms, so that he was impregnated with a flame which he feebly resisted. But he made such an effort that he broke the living bondage.

"Have pity, Lorenza!" he sued.

"Was it to pity you that I left my native land, my name, my family, my faith!" she said, almost threatening with her lovely arms, rising white and yet muscular amid the waves of her long black tresses coming down. "Why have you laid on me this absolute empire, so that if I am your slave and have to give you my life and breath? Was it to mock me ever with the name of the virgin Lorenza?"

Balsamo sighed, himself crushed by the weight of her immense despair.

"Alas, is it your fault, or that of the Creator. Why were you made the angel with the infallible gaze, by whose aid I should make the universe submit? Why is it that you are the one to read a soul through its bodily envelope as one may read a book through a glass! Because you are an angel of purity, Lorenza, and nothing throws a shadow upon your soul. In your radiant and immaculate bosom the divine spark may be enshrined, a place without sullying where it may fitly nestle. You are a seer because you are blameless, Lorenza; as a woman, you would be but so much substance."

"And you prefer this to my love," continued the Italian, clapping her hands with such rage that they became impurpled; "you set my love beneath these whims that you pursue and fables that you invent? You snatch me out of the cold cloister, but, in the bustling, ardent world you condemn me to the conventional chastity? Joseph, you commit a crime, I tell you."

"Do not blaspheme," said Balsamo, "for I suffer, too. Read in my heart, and never again say that I love you not. I resist you because I want to raise you on the throne of the world."

"Ugh, your ambition!" sneered the young Roman; "will your ambition ever give you what you might have in my love?"

He yielded to her and his head rested in her arms.

"Ah, yes," she cried, "I see at last that you love me more than your ambition, than power, than your aspiration! Oh, you love me as I love you!"

But at the touch of their lips, reason came to him who would be master of Europe. With his hands he beat aside the air charged with magnetic vapor.

"Lorenza, awake, I bid you!"

Thereupon the chain which he could not break was relaxed, and the opening arms were dropped, while the kiss died away on the paling lips of Lorenza, languishing in her last sigh. Her closed eyes parted their lids; the dilated pupils resumed their normal size. She shook herself with an effort, and sank in lassitude, but awake, on the sofa.

Seated three paces from her, the mesmerist sighed deeply.

"Good-bye to the dream!" he said; "good-bye to happiness!"

CHAPTER XXXVIII

THE WAKEFUL STATE

As soon as Lorenza's sight had recovered its power, she glanced rapidly around her. After examining everything without one of the many knick-knacks which delight woman brightening her brow, she stopped with her look upon Balsamo, and nervously shuddered.

"You again?" she said, receding.

On her physiognomy appeared all the tokens of alarm; her lips became white and perspiration came as pearls at the root of her hair.

"Where am I?" she asked as he said nothing.

"As you know where you came from, you can readily guess where you are," he responded.

"You are right in reminding me; I do, indeed, remember. I know that I have been pursued by you, and torn from the arms of the royal intermediary whom I chose between heaven and you."

"Then you ought to know that this princess has been unable to defend you, however powerful she may be."

"You have overruled her by some witching violence," said Lorenza, wringing her hands, "Oh, saints of mercy, deliver me from this demon!"

"Where do you see anything demoniacal in me," returned Balsamo, shrugging his shoulders. "Once for all I beg you to lay aside this pack of puerile beliefs brought from Rome, and all the rubbish of absurd superstitions which you have carted about with you since you ran away from the nunnery."

"Oh, my dear nunnery—who will restore me to my dear nunnery?" cried the Italian, bursting into tears.

"Indeed, a nunnery is much to be deplored," said Balsamo.

Lorenza ran to one of the windows, opened the curtains and then the sash, but came against iron bars, which were there unmistakably—however many flowers were masking them.

"If I must live in a prison," she said, "I prefer that whence one goes to heaven to that which has a trap door into hades." And she began trying the bars with her dainty hands.

"Were you more reasonable, Lorenza, you would find only flowers at your window, and not bars."

"Was I not reasonable when you confined me in that other prison, the one on wheels, with the vampire you call Althotas? But still you kept your eye on me when by, and never left me till you had breathed into me that spirit which possesses me and I cannot shake it off. Where is that horrid old man who frightens me to death? In some corner, I suppose. Let us hush and listen till his ghostly voice be heard."

"You let your fancy sway you, like a child," said Balsamo. "My friend and preceptor, Althotas, my second father, is an inoffensive old man who has never seen you, let alone approached you, or if he did come near, he would not heed you, being absorbed in his work."

"His work—tell me what the work is!" muttered the Roman.

179

"He is seeking the elixir of long life, for which superior minds have been seeking these two thousand years."

"What are you working for?"

"Human perfection."

"A pair of demons!" said Lorenza, lifting her hands to heaven.

"Is this your fit coming on again? You are ignorant of one thing: your life is divided into two parts. During one, you are gentle, good and sensible: during the other, you are mad."

"And you shut me up under the vain pretext of this malady."

"It had to be done."

"Oh, barbarian, be cruel, without pity! imprison me, and kill me, but do not play the hypocrite and pretend to feel for me while you tear me to pieces."

"Do you call it torture to live in a luxurious suite of rooms?" said Balsamo with a kindly smile and not at all disturbed.

"With bars to all the issues!"

"Put there for the sake of your life, Lorenza."

"Oh, he roasts me to death at a slow fire, and he talks of my life's sake!" exclaimed the Italian.

Approaching, he offered to take her hand, but she repelled his as if it were a serpent.

"Do not touch me!" she said.

"Do you hate me so much, Lorenza!"

"Ask the victim how he likes the executioner."

"It is because I do not want to be one that I restrict your liberty a little. Could you come and go as you like, who can tell what your folly might drive you to."

"Wait till I am free some day, and see what I shall do!"

"Lorenza, you are behaving badly toward the husband whom you chose. You are my wife."

"That was the work of Satan."

"Poor crazy creature!" said the mesmerist, with a tender look.

"I am a daughter of Rome," continued she, "and some day I shall take revenge."

"Do you say that merely to frighten me?" he asked, gently shaking his head.

"No, no; I will do what I say."

"What are you saying—and you a Christian woman?" exclaimed Balsamo with surprising authority in his voice. "Is your creed which bids you return good for evil but a hypocrisy, that you pretend to follow it, and you boast of revenge—evil for good?"

"Oh," replied Lorenza, for an instant struck by the argument. "It is duty, not revenge, to denounce society's enemies."

"If you denounced me as a master in the black art, it would be not be as an offender against society, but against heaven. Were I to defy heaven, which need but comprise me as one atom in the myriads slain by an earthquake or pestilence, but which takes no pains to punish me, why should weak men like myself undertake to punish me?"

"Heaven forgets, or tolerates—waiting for you to reform," said the Italian.

"Meanwhile," said the other, smiling, "you are advised to tolerate your husband, friend and benefactor?"

"Husband? Oh, that I should have to endure your yoke!"

"Oh, what an impenetrable mystery?" muttered the magician, pursuing his thought rather than heeding the speaker.

"Let us have done. Why do you take away my liberty?"

"Why, having bestowed it on me, would you take it back? Why flee from your protector? Why unceasingly threaten one who never threatens you, with revelation of secrets which are not yours and have aims beyond anything you can conceive?"

"Oh," said Lorenza, without replying to the question, "the prisoner who yearns for freedom eventually obtains it, and your house bars will no more hold me than your wagon-sides."

"Happily for you, they are stout," replied Balsamo, with ominous tranquillity.

"Heaven will send another such storm as befel us in Lorraine, and some thunderbolt will shatter them."

"Take my advice to pray for nothing of the kind, Lorenza; distrust these romantic transports: I speak to you as a friend—listen to me."

Stunned at the height of her rebellion, Lorenza listened in spite of herself, from so much concentrated wrath being in his voice, and gloomy fire in his eye, while his white but powerful hand opened and shut so strangely as he slowly and solemnly spoke:

"Mark this, my child, that I have tried to have this place fit for a queen, with nothing lacking for your comfort. So calm your folly. Live here as you would do in your convent cell. You must become habituated to my presence. As I have great sorrows, I will confide in you; dreadful disappointment, for which I will crave a smile. The kinder, more patient and attentive you are, the more of your bars I will remove, so that in some months—who knows how soon?—you will become perhaps more free than I am, in the sense that you will not want to curtail my liberty."

"No, no," replied the Italian, unable to understand that firm resolution could be allied to such gentle words, "no more professions and falsehoods. You abducted me, so that I am my own property still; restore me to heaven, if you will not let me be my own mistress. I have borne with your despotism so far from remembering that you saved me from the robbers who would have ruined me; but this gratitude is much enfeebled. A few days more of this captivity against which I revolt, and I shall no longer feel obliged to you; a few more, and I shall perhaps believe you were in concert with those highwaymen."

"So you honor me with a captaincy of brigands," sneered Balsamo.

"I do not know about that, but I noticed secret signs and peculiar words."

"But," replied the other, losing color, "you will never tell them; never to a living soul? You will bury them in the remotest place in your memory so that they shall die there, smothered."

"Just the other way," retorted Lorenza, delighted as angry persons are at having found the antagonist's vulnerable point. "My memory shall piously preserve those words, which I will repeat over and over again when alone, and say aloud when the opening comes, as already I have done."

"To whom?"

"To the princess royal."

"Lorenza, mind this well," said he, clenching his nails in his flesh to subdue his fury and check his rushing blood at the thought that his brothers were in danger through the woman whom he had selected to aid them all, "if you said them, never again will you do so. For the doors will be kept fastened, those bars pointed at the head, and those walls reared as high as Babel's."

"I have already told you, Balsamo, that any soul wherein the love of liberty is reinforced by the hate of tyranny must escape from all prison houses."

"Well and good; try it, woman; but mark this well: you will only twice try it. For the first time I will punish you so severely that you will weep all the tears in your body; and for the second I will strike you pitilessly that you will pour forth all the blood in your veins."

"Help, help, he is murdering me," shrieked the woman, at the last paroxysm of wrath, tearing her hair and rolling on the carpet.

For an instant Balsamo considered her with mingled rage and pity, the latter overcoming the other.

"Come, come, Lorenza, return to your senses, and be calm. A day will come when you will be rewarded amply for what you have suffered, or fancy."

"Imprisoned," screamed the Italian, "and beaten."

"These are times to try the mind. You are mad, but you shall be cured."

"Better throw me into a madhouse at once; shut me up in a real jail."

"No, you have warned me what you would do against me."

"Then," said the infuriate, "let me have death straightway."

Springing up with the suppleness and rapidity of the wild beast, she leaped to break her head against the wall. But Balsamo had merely to stretch out his hands toward her and utter a single word rather with his will than with his lips, to stop her dead. She stopped, indeed, reeled and dropped sleep-stricken in the magnetiser's arms.

The strange enchanter, who seemed to rule all the material part of the woman though the mental portion baffled him, lifted up Lorenza in his arms and carried her to the couch; there he laid a long kiss on her lips, drew the curtains of bed and windows, and left her.

A sweet and blessed sleep enveloped her like the cloak of a kind mother wrapping the willful child who has much suffered and wept.

CHAPTER XXXIX

THE PREDICTED VISIT

Lorenza was not mistaken.

A carriage, going through St. Denis gateway, and following the street of the same name, turned into the road leading out to the Bastille.

As the clairvoyant had stated, this conveyance enclosed the Cardinal Prince of Rohan, Bishop of Strasburg, whose impatience had caused him to anticipate the hour fixed for his visit to the magician in his cave of mystery.

The coachman, who had been inured to obscurity, pitfalls and dangers of some darksome streets by the prelate's love adventures, was not daunted the least when, after leaving the part of the way still populated and lighted, he had to take the black and lonesome Bastille Boulevard.

The vehicle stopped at the corner of St. Claude Street, where it hid along the trees twenty paces off.

Prince Rohan, in plain dress, glided up the street, and rapped three times on the door, which he easily recognized from the indication the count had afforded.

Fritz's steps sounded in the passage, and he opened the door.

"Is it here resides Count Fenix?" inquired Rohan.

"Yes, my lord, and he is at home."

"Say a visitor is here."

"Shall I announce his Eminence Cardinal Prince de Rohan?" asked Fritz.

The prince stood aghast, looking round him and at himself to see if anything about him in costume or surroundings betrayed his rank. No; he was alone and in civilian dress.

"How do you know my name?" he inquired.

"My lord told me just now, that he expected your Eminence."

"Yes, but to-morrow, or the day after?"

"Not so, please your highness—this evening."

"Announce me, any way," said the prelate, putting a double-louis gold piece in his hand.

Fritz intimated that the visitor should follow him; and he walked briskly to the door of the ante-chamber, which a large chandelier with a dozen tapers illuminated. The visitor followed, surprised and meditative.

"There must be some mistake, my friend," he said, pausing at the door, "in which case I do not wish to disturb the count. It is impossible he can expect me, as he could not know I was coming."

"As your highness is Cardinal Prince Rohan, you are certainly expected by my lord."

Lighting the other candelabra, Fritz bowed and went out. Five minutes elapsed, during which the prelate, the prey to singular emotion, scanned the elegant furniture of the room, and the half-dozen paintings by masters on the tapestried walls. When the door opened, Count Fenix appeared on the threshold.

"Good-evening to your highness," he simply said.

"I am told that you expected me," observed the visitor, without replying to the welcome. "Expected this evening? impossible!"

"I ask your pardon, but I was expecting your highness," returned the host. "I may be doubted, seeing how paltry is my reception, but I have hardly got settled yet, from being but a few days in town. I hope for your eminence's excusing me."

"My visit expected? Who could have forewarned you?"

"Yourself, my lord. When you called your footman to the carriage door, did you not say to him: 'Drive to St. Claude Street, in the Swamp, by St. Denis Street and the Boulevard?'—words which he repeated to the driver?"

"Yes; but how could you see this and hear the words, not being present?"

"I was not there, but I saw and heard at this distance, as I am, you must not forget, a wizard."

"I had forgotten. By the way, am I to entitle you Baron Balsamo or Count Fenix!"

"In my own house I have no title—I am plainly The Master."

"Ah, the title in alchemy. So, my master in hermetics, if you expected me, the fire would be lit in the laboratory!"

"The fire is always kept burning, my lord. And I will have the honor to show your highness into the place."

"I follow you on the condition that you do not personally confront me with the devil. I am dreadfully afraid of his Satanic Majesty Lucifer."

"My lord, my familiar friends," replied Balsamo, "never forget how to deal with princes, and they will behave properly."

"This encourages me; so, ho! for the laboratory."

CHAPTER XL

THE ART OF MAKING GOLD

The two threaded a narrow staircase which led, as did the grand stairs, to the first floor rooms, but a door was under an archway there, which the guide opened and the cardinal bravely walked into a dark corridor thus disclosed.

Balsamo shut the door, and the sound of the closing made the visitor look back with some emotion.

"We have arrived," said the leader. "Only one door to open and shut behind us. Do not be astonished at the noise it makes, as it is of iron."

It was fortunate that the cardinal was warned in time, for the snap of the handle and the grinding of the hinges might make nerves more susceptible than his to vibrate.

They went down three steps and entered a large cell with rafters overhead, a huge lamp with shade, many books, and a number of chemical and physical instruments—such was the aspect.

In a few seconds the cardinal felt a difficulty in breathing.

"What does this mean, my lord?" he asked. "The water is streaming off me and I am stifling. What sound is that, master?"

"This is the cause," answered the host, pulling aside a large curtain of asbestos, and uncovering a large brick furnace in the centre of which glared two fiery cavities like lions' eyes in the gloom.

This furnace stood in an inner room, centrally, twice the size of the first, unseen from the stone-cloth screen.

"This is rather alarming, meseems," said the prince.

"Only a furnace, my lord."

"But there are different kinds of furnaces; this one strikes me as diabolical, and the smell is not pleasant. What devil's broth are you cooking?"

"What your eminence wants. I believe you will accept a sample of my produce. I was not going to work until to-morrow; but as your eminence changed his mind, I lit the fire as soon as I saw you on the road hither. I made the mixture so that the furnace is boiling, and you can have your gold in about ten minutes. Let me open the ventilator to let in some air."

"What, are these crucibles on the fire——"

"In ten minutes they will pour you out the gold as pure as from any assayer's in christendom."

"I should like to look at them."

"Of course, you can; but you must take the indispensable precaution of putting on this asbestos mask with glass eyes; or the ardent fire will scorch your sight."

"Have a care, indeed! I prize my eyes, and would not give them for the hundred thousand crowns you promised me."

"So I thought, and your lordship's eyes are good and bright."

The compliment did not displease the prince, who was proud of his personal advantages.

"He, he!" he chuckled; "so we are going to see gold made?"

"I expect so, my lord."

"A hundred thousand crowns' worth?"

"There may be a little more, as I mixed up liberally the raw stuff."

"You are certainly a generous magician," said the prince, fastening the fireproof mask on, while his heart throbbed gladly.

"Less than your eminence, though it is kind to praise me for generosity, of which you are a good judge. Will your highness stand a little one side while I lift off the crucible covers?"

He had put on a stone-cloth shirt, and seizing iron pincers, he lifted off an iron cover. This allowed one to see four similar melting pots, each containing a fluid mass, one vermilion red, others lighter but all ruddy.

186

"Is that gold?" queried the prelate in an undertone, as if afraid by loud speaking to injure the mystery in progress.

"Yes, the four crucibles contain the metal in different stages of production, some having been on eleven hours, some twelve. The mixture is to be thrown into the first mass of ingredients—the living stuff into the gross—at the moment of boiling—that is the secret, which I do not mind communicating to a friend of the science. But, as your eminence may notice, the first crucible is turning white hot; it is time to draw the charge. Will you please stand well back, my lord?"

Rohan obeyed with the same punctuality as a soldier obeying his captain. Dropping the iron pincers, which had already heated to redness, the other ran up to the furnace a carriage on wheels of the same level, the top being an iron block, in which were set eight molds of round shape and the same capacity.

"This is the mold in which I cast the ingots," explained the alchemist.

On the floor he spread a lot of wet oakum wads to prevent the splashing of the metal setting the floor afire. He placed himself between the molds and the furnace, opened a large book, from which he read an incantation, and said, as he caught up long tongs in his hand to clutch the crucible:

"The gold will be splendid, my lord, of the first quality."

"Oh, you are never going to lift that mass single-handed?" exclaimed the spectator.

"Though it weighs fifty pounds, yes, my lord; but do not fear, for few metal-melters have my strength and skill."

"But if the crucible were to burst——"

"That did happen once to me: it was in 1399, while I was experimenting with Nicolas Flamel, in his house by St. Jacques' in the Shambles. Poor Nick almost lost his life, and I lost twenty-seven marks' worth of a substance more precious than gold."

"What the deuse are you telling me? that you were pursuing the great work in 1399 with Nicolas Flamel?"

"Yes, Flamel and I found the way while together fifty or sixty years before, working with Pietro the Good, in Pela town. He did not pour out the crucible quickly enough, and I had a bad eye, the left one, for ten or twelve years, from the steam. Of course you know Pietro's book, the famous 'Margarita Pretiosa,' dated 1330?"

"To be sure; and you knew Flamel and Peter the Good?"

"I was the pupil of one and the master of the other."

While the alarmed prelate, wondered whether this might not be the Prince of Darkness himself and not one of his imps by his side, Balsamo plunged his tongs into the incandescence.

187

It was a sure and rapid seizure. He nipped the crucible four inches beneath the rim, testing the grip by lifting it just a couple of inches. Then, by a vigorous effort, straining his muscles, he raised the frightful pot from the scorching bed. The tongs reddened almost up to the grasp. On the superheated surface white streaks ran like lightning in a sulphurous cloud. The pot edges deepened into brick red, then browner, while its conical shape appeared rosy and silvery in the twilight of the recess. Finally the molten metal could be spied, forming a violet cream on the top, with golden shivers, which hissed out of the lips of the container, and leaped flaming into the black mold. At its orifice reappeared the gold, spouting up furious and fuming, as if insulted by the vile metal which confined it.

"Number two," said Balsamo, passing to the second mold, which he filled with the same skill and strength.

Perspiration streamed from the founder, while the beholder crossed himself, in the shadow.

It was truly a picture of wild and majestic horror. Illumined by the yellow gleams of the metallic flame, the operator resembled the condemned souls writhing in the Infernos of Dante and Michelangelo, in their caldrons. Add to this the sensation of what was in progress being unheard-of. Balsamo did not stop to take breath between the two drawings of the charges, for time pressed.

"There is little loss," observed he, after filling the second mold. "I let the boiling go on the hundredth of a minute too long."

"The hundredth of a minute?" repeated the cardinal, not trying to conceal his stupefaction.

"Trifles are enormous in the hermetical art," replied the magician simply; "but anyway, here are two crucibles empty and two ingots cast, and they amount to a hundred weight of fine gold."

Seizing the first mold with the powerful tongs, he threw it into a tub of water, which seethed and steamed for a long time; at length he opened it, and drew out an ingot of purest gold in the shape of a sugarloaf, flattened at both ends.

"We shall have to wait nearly an hour for the other two," said Balsamo. "While waiting, would your eminence not like to sit down and breathe the fresh air?"

"And this is gold!" said the cardinal, without replying, which made the hearer smile, for he had firm hold of him now.

"Does your eminence doubt?"

"Science has so many times been deceived."

"You are not speaking your mind wholly," said Balsamo. "You suppose that I cheat you, but do so with full knowledge. My lord, I should look very small to myself if I acted thus, for my ambition would then be restricted by the walls of this foundry, whence you would go forth to give the rest of your admiration to the first juggler at the street corner. Come, come! honor me better, my prince, and take it that I would cheat you more skillfully and with a higher aim if cheating was intended by me. At all events your eminence knows how to test gold?"

"By the touchstone, of course."

"Has not my lord made the application of the lunar caustic to the Spanish gold coins much liked at card-play on account of the gold being the finest, but among which a lot of counterfeits have got afloat?"

"This indeed has happened me."

"Well, here is acid, and a bluestone, my lord."

"No, I am convinced."

"My lord, do me the pleasure of ascertaining that this is not only gold, but gold without alloy."

The doubter seemed averse to giving this proof of unbelief, and yet it was clear that he was not convinced. Balsamo himself tested the ingots and showed the result to his guest.

"Twenty-eight karats fine," he said: "I am going to turn out the other twain."

Ten minutes subsequently, the two hundred thousand crowns' worth of the precious metal was lying on the damp oakum bed, in four ingots altogether.

"I saw your eminence coming in a carriage, so I presume it is in waiting. Let it be driven up to my door, and I will have my man put the bullion in it."

"A hundred thousand crowns," muttered the prince, taking off the mask in order to gloat on the metal at his feet.

"As you saw it made, you can freely say so," added the conjurer, "but do not make a town talk of it, for wizards are not liked in France. If I were making theories instead of solid metal, it would be a different matter."

"Then what can I do for you?" questioned the prince, with difficulty hoisting one of the fifty pound lumps in his delicate hands.

The other looked hard at him and burst into laughter without any respect.

"What is there laughable in the offer I make you?" asked the cardinal.

"Why, your lordship offers me his services, and it seems more to the purpose that I should offer mine."

"You oblige me," he said, with a clouding brow, "and that I am eager to acknowledge. But if my gratitude ought to be rated higher than I appraise it, I will not accept the service. Thank heaven, there are still enough usurers in Paris for me to find the hundred thousand crowns in a day, half on my note of hand, half on security; my episcopal ring alone is worth forty thousand livres."

Holding out his hand, white as a woman's, a diamond flashed on the ring-finger as large as a hickory nut.

"Prince, you cannot possibly have held the idea for an instant that I meant to insult you. It is strange that truth seems to have this effect on all princes," he added, as to himself. "Your eminence offers me his services; I ask you yourself of what nature can they be?"

"My credit at court, to begin with."

"My lord, you know that is shaky, and I would rather have the Duke of Choiseul's, albeit he may not be the prime minister for yet a fortnight. Against your credit, look at my cash—the pure, bright gold! Every time your eminence wants some, advise me overnight or the same morning, and I will conform to his desire. And with gold one obtains everything, eh, my lord?"

"Nay, not everything," muttered the prince, falling from the perch of patronage, and not even seeking to regain it.

"Quite right. I forgot that your eminence seeks something else than gold, a more precious boon than all earthly gifts; but that does not come within the scope of science as in the range of magic. Say the word, my lord, and the alchemist will become a magician, to serve you."

"Thank you, I need nothing and desire no longer," sighed the prelate.

"My lord," sighed the tempter, drawing nearer, "such a reply ought not to be made to a wizard by a prince, young, fiery, handsome, rich and bearing the name of Rohan. Because the wizard reads hearts and knows to the contrary."

"I wish for nothing," repeated the high nobleman, almost frightened.

"On the contrary, I thought that your eminence entertained desires which he shrank from naming to himself, as they are truly royal."

"I believe you are alluding to some words you used in the Princess Royal's rooms?" said the prince, starting. "You were in error then, and are so still."

"Your highness is forgetting that I see as clearly in your heart what is going on now as I saw your carriage coming from the Carmelite convent, traversing the town and stopping under the trees fifty paces off from my house."

"Then explain what is there?"

"My lord, the princes of your house have always hungered for a great and hazardous love affair."

"I do not know what you mean, my lord," faltered the prince.

"Nay, you understand to a T. I might have touched several chords in you—but why the useless? I went straight to the heartstring which sounds loudest, and it is vibrating deeply, I am sure."

With a final effort of mistrust the cardinal raised his head and interrogated the other's clear and sure gaze. The latter smiled with such superiority that the cardinal lowered his eyes.

"Oh, you are right not to meet my glance, my lord, for then I see into your heart too clearly. It is a mirror which retains the image which it has reflected."

"Silence, Count Fenix; do be silent," said the prelate, subjugated.

"Silence?—you are right, for the time has not come to parade such a passion."

"Not yet? may it expect a future?"

"Why not?"

"And can you tell me whether this is not a mad passion, as I have thought, and must think until I have a proof to the opposite?"

"You ask too much, my lord. I cannot say anything until I am in contact with some portion of the love-inspirer's self—for instance, a tress of her golden hair, however scanty."

"Verily you are a deep man! You truly say you can read into hearts as I in my prayer-book."

"Almost the very words your ancestor used—I mean Chevalier Louis Rohan, when I bade farewell to him, on the execution-stage in the Bastille, which he had ascended so courageously."

"He said that you were deep?"

"And that I read hearts. For I had forewarned him that Chevalier Preault would betray him. He would not believe me, and he was betrayed."

"What a singular connection you make between my ancestor and me," said the cardinal, turning pale against his wish.

"Only to show that you ought to be wary, in procuring the lock to be cut from under a crown."

"No matter whence it comes, you shall have it."

"Very well. Here is your gold; I hope you no longer doubt that it is gold?"

"Give me pen and paper to write the receipt for this generous loan."

"What do I want a receipt from your lordship for?"

"My dear count, I often borrow, but I never fail to write a receipt," rejoined the prince.

"Have it your own way, my lord."

The cardinal took a quill and scrawled in large and illegible writing a signature under a line or two which a schoolboy would be ashamed of at present.

"Will that do?" he inquired, handing it to Balsamo, who put it in his pocket without looking at it.

"Perfectly," he said.

"You have not read it."

"I have the word of a Rohan, and that is better than a bond."

"Count Fenix, you are truly a noble man, and I cannot make you beholden to me. I am glad to be your debtor."

Balsamo bowed, and rang a bell, to which Fritz responded.

Saying a few words in German to him, the servant wrapped up the ingots of gold in their wads of ropeyarn, and took them all up as a boy might as many oranges in a handkerchief, a little strained but not hampered or bent under the weight.

"Have we Hercules here?" questioned the cardinal.

"He is rather lusty, my lord," answered the necromancer, "but I must own that, since he has been in my employment, I make him drink three drops every morning of an elixir which my learned friend Dr. Althotas compounded. It is beginning to do him good. In a year he will be able to carry a hundredweight on each finger."

"Marvelous! incomprehensible!" declared the prince-priest. "Oh, I cannot resist the temptation to tell everybody about this."

"Do so, my lord," replied the host, laughing. "But do not forget that it is tantamount to pledging yourself to put out the match when they start the fire going to burn me in public."

Having escorted his illustrious caller to the outer door, he took his leave with a respectful bow.

"But I do not see your man," said the visitor.

"He went to carry the gold to your carriage, at the fourth tree on the right round the corner on the main street. That is what I told him in German, my lord."

The cardinal lifted his hands in wonder and disappeared in the shadows.

Balsamo waited until Fritz returned, when he went back to the private inner house, fastening all the doors.

CHAPTER XLI

THE WATER OF LIFE

He went to listen at Lorenza's door, where she was sleeping evenly and sweetly.

He opened a panel and looked in upon her, for some while in affectionate reverie. Closing the wicket, he stole away to his laboratory, where he put out the fire, by opening a register plate which sent most of the heat up the chimney, and ran in water from a tank without.

In a pocket-book, he carefully fastened up the receipt of Cardinal Rohan, saying:

"The parole of a Rohan is all very well, but only for me, and the brothers will want to know yonder how I employ their money."

These words were dying on his lips when three sharp raps on the ceiling made him lift his head.

"Althotas wants me, and in a hurry. That is a good sign."

With a long iron rod he rapped in answer. He put away the tools, and by means of an iron ring in a trap overhead, which was the floor of a dumb-waiter, as then they called elevators, he pulled this down to his feet. Placing himself in the center of it, he was carried gently, by no spring but a simple hydraulic machine, worked by the reservoir which had extinguished the fire, up into the study reserved for the old alchemist.

This new dwelling was eight feet by nine in height, and sixteen in length; all the light came from a skylight, as the four walls were without inlet. It was, relatively to the house on wheels, a palace.

The old man was sitting in his easy-chair on casters, at the middle of a horseshoe-shaped table in iron, with a marble top, laden with a quantity of plants, books, tools, bottles, and papers traced with cabalistic signs—a chaos.

He was so wrapt in thought that he was not disturbed by the entrance.

A globe of crystal hung over his yellow and bald pate; in this a sort of serpent, fine and coiled like a spring, seemed to curl, and it sent forth a bright and unvarying light, without other apparent source of luminous supply than the chain supporting the globe might contain to transmit.

He was "candling" a phial of ground glass in his fingers as a good wife tries eggs.

"Well, anything new?" said Balsamo, after having silently watched him for a while.

"Yes, yes; I am delighted, Acharat, for I have found what I sought."

"Gold—diamonds?"

"Pooh! They are pretty discoveries for my soul to rejoice over."

"I suppose you mean your elixir, in that case."

"Yes, my boy, my elixir—life everlasting."

"Oh, so you are still harping on that string," said the younger sage sadly, for he thought his senior was following an idle dream.

But without listening Althotas was lovingly peering into his phial.

"The proportions are found at last," he mumbled. "Elixir of Aristæus, twenty grams; balm of mercury, fifteen; precipitate of gold, fifteen; essence of Lebanon cedar, twenty-five grams."

"But it seems to me, bar the Aristæan elixir, this is about what you last mixed up."

"That is so, but there was lacking the binding ingredient, without which the rest are no good."

"Can one procure it?"

"Certainly; it is three drops of a child's arterial blood."

"And have you the child?" gasped Balsamo, horrified.

"No, I expect you to find one for me."

"Master, you are mad."

"In what respect?" asked the emotionless old man, licking with his tongue the stopper of the phial, from which a little of the nectar had oozed.

"The child would be killed."

"What of it—the finer the child, the better the heart's blood."

"It cannot be; children are no longer butchered, but brought up with care."

"Indeed! how fickle is the world. Three years ago, we were offered more children than we knew what to do with, for four charges of gunpowder or a pint of traders' whiskey."

"That was on the Congo River, in Africa, master."

"I believe so: but it does not matter if the young is black. I remember that what they offered were sprightly, woolly-headed, jolly little urchins."

"Unfortunately we are no longer on the Congo. We are in Paris."

"Well, we can embark from Marseilles and be in Africa in six weeks."

"That can be done; but I must stay in France on serious business."

194

"Business?" sneered the old man, sending forth a peal of shrill laughter, most lugubrious. "True, I had forgotten that you have political clubs to organize, conspiracies to foster, and, in short, serious business!" And he laughed again forced and false.

Balsamo held his peace, reserving his powers for the storm impending.

"How far has your business advanced?" he inquired, painfully turning in his chair and fixing his large gray eyes on the pupil.

"I have thrown the first stone," he replied, feeling the glance go through him. "The pool is stirred up. The mud is in agitation—the philosophic sediment."

"Yes, you are going to bring into play your utopias, fogs and hollow dreams. These idiots dispute about the existence or non-existence of the Almighty, when they might become little gods themselves. Let us hear who are the famous philosophers whom you have enlisted!"

"I have already the leading poet and the greatest atheist of the age, who will be coming into France presently, to be made a Freemason, in the lodge I am getting up in the old Jesuits' College, Potaufer street. His name is Voltaire."

"I do not know him. The next?"

"I am to be introduced to the greatest sower of ideas of the century, the author of the Social Contract, Rousseau."

"He is not known to me either."

"I expect not, as you only know such old alchemists as Alfonso the Wise, Raymond Lully, Peter of Toledo and Albert the Great."

"Because they are the only men who have really loved a life, sowed ideas that live, and labored at the grand question of to be or not to be."

"There are two ways of living, master."

"I only know of one—existing. But to return to your brace of philosophers. With their help you intend to——"

"Grasp the present and sap the future."

"How stupid they must be in this country to be lured away by ideas."

"No, it is because they have too much brains that they are led by ideas. And then, I have a more powerful help than all the philosophers—the fact that monarchy has lasted sixteen hundred years in France, and the French are tired of it."

"Hence, they are going to overturn the throne, and you are backing them with all your forces! You fool! What good is the upsetting of this monarchy going to do you?"

"It will bring me nothing, at the best, but it will be happiness for others."

195

"Come, come, I am in a good humor to-day, and can listen to your nonsense. Explain to me how you will obtain the general weal and what it consists of."

"A ministry is in power which is the last rampart defending the monarchy; it is a cabinet, brave, industrious and intelligent, which might sustain this wornout and staggering monarchy for yet twenty years. My aids will overturn it."

"Your philosophers?"

"Oh, no, for they are in favor of the ministry, for its head is a philosopher too."

"Then they are a selfish pack. What great imbeciles!"

"I do not care to discuss what they are, for I do not know," said Balsamo, who was losing his patience. "I only know that they will all cry down the next ministry when this one is destroyed."

"This new cabinet will have against it the philosophers and then the Parliament. They will make such an uproar that the cabinet will persecute the philosophers and block the Parliament. Then in mind and matter will be organized a sullen league, a tenacious, stubborn, restless opposition, which will attack everything, undermining and shaking. Instead of Parliament they will try to rule with judges appointed by the king; they will do everything for their appointer. With reason they will be accused of venality, corruption and injustice. The people will rise, and at last royalty will have arrayed against it philosophy, which is intelligence, Parliament, which is the middle class, and the mob, which is the people; in other words, the lever with which Archimedes can raise the world."

"Well, when you have lifted it, you will have to let it fall again."

"Yes, but when it falls it will smash the royalty."

"To use your figurative language, when this wormeaten monarchy is broken, what will come out of the ruins?"

"Freedom."

"The French be free? Well, then, there will be thirty millions of freemen in France?"

"Yes."

"Among them do you not think there will be one with a bigger brain than another, who will rob them of freedom some fine morning that he may have a larger share than his proper one for himself? Do you not remember a dog we had at Medina which used to eat as much as all the rest together?"

"Yes, and I remember that they all together pitched on him one day and devoured him."

"Because they were dogs; men would have continued to give in to the greediest."

"Do you set the instincts of animals above the intelligence of man?"

"Forsooth, the examples abound by which to prove it. Among the ancients was one Julius Cæsar, and among the moderns one Oliver Cromwell, who ate up the Roman and the English cake, without anybody snatching many crumbs away from them."

"Well, supposing such an usurper comes, he must die some day, being mortal, but before dying he must do good to even those whom he oppressed; for he would have changed the nature of the upper classes. Obliged to have some kind of support, he will choose the popular as the strongest. To the equality which abases, he will oppose the kind which elevates. Equality has no fixed water mark, but takes the level of him who makes it. In raising the lowest classes he will have hallowed a principle unknown before his time. The Revolution will have made the French free; the Protectorate of another Cæsar or Cromwell will have made them equal."

"What a stupid fellow this is!" said Althotas, starting in his chair. "To spend twenty years in bringing up a child so that he shall came and tell you, who taught him all you knew—'Men are equal.' Before the law, maybe; but before death? how about that? One dies in three days—another lives a hundred years! Men, equals before they have conquered death? Oh, the brute, the triple brute!"

Althotas sat back to laugh more freely at Balsamo, who kept his head lowered, gloomy and thoughtful. His instructor took pity on him.

"Unhappy sophist that you are, bear in mind one thing, that men will not be equals until they are immortal. Then they will be gods, and these alone are undying."

"Immortal—what a dream!" sighed the mesmerist.

"Dream? so is the steam, the electric fluid, all that we are hunting after and not yet caught—a dream. But we will seize and they will be realities. Move with me the dust of ages, and see that man in all times has been seeking what I am engaged upon, under the different titles of the Bliss, the Best, the Perfection. Had they found it, this decrepit world would be fresh and rosy as the morning. Instead, see the dry leaf, the corpse, the carrion heap! Is suffering desirable—the corpse pleasant to look upon—the carrion sweet?"

"You yourself are saying that nobody has found this water of life," observed Balsamo, as the old man was interrupted by a dry cough. "I tell you that nobody will find it."

"By this rule there would be no discoveries. Do you think discoveries are novelties which are invented? Not so—they are forgotten things coming up anew. Why were the once-found things

197

forgotten. Because the inventor's life was too short for him to derive from it all its perfection. Twenty times they have nearly consummated the water of life. Chiron would have made Achilles completely immortal but for the lack of the three drops of blood which you refuse me. In the flaw death found a passage, and entered. I repeat that Chiron was another Althotas prevented by an Acharat from completing the work which would save all mankind by shielding it from the divine malediction. Well, what have you to say to that?"

"Merely," said Balsamo, visibly shaken, "that you have your work and I mine. Let each accomplish his, at his risks and perils. But I will not second yours by a crime."

"A crime? when I ask but three drops of blood—one child—and you would deluge a country with billions of gallons! Tell me now who is the cannibal of us two? Ha, ha! you do not answer me."

"My answer is that three drops would be nothing if you were sure of success."

"Are you sure, who would send millions to the scaffold and battle-field? Can you stand up before the Creator and say, 'O Master of Life, in return for four millions of slain men, I will warrant the happiness of humanity.'"

"Master, ask for something else," said Balsamo, eluding the point.

"Ha! you do not answer; you cannot answer," taunted Althotas triumphantly.

"You must be mistaken on the efficacy of the means. It is impossible."

"It looks as if you argued with me, disputed, deem me a liar," said the old alchemist, rolling with cold anger his gray eyes under his white brows.

"No, but I am in contact with men and things, and you dwell in a nook, in the pure abstraction of a student; I see the difficulties and have to point them out."

"You would soon overcome such difficulties if you liked, or believed."

"I do not believe."

"But do you believe that death is an incontestable thing, invincible and infinite? And when you see a dead body, does not the perspiration come to your brow, and a regret is born in your breast?"

"No regret comes in to my breast because I have familiarized myself to all human miseries; and I esteem life as a little thing: but I say in presence of the corpse: 'Dead! thou who wert mighty as a god!

O Death! it is thou who reign sovereignly, and nothing can prevail against thee.'"

Althotas listened in silence, with no other token of impatience than fidgeting with a scalpel in his hands. When his disciple had finished the solemn and doleful phrase, he smiled while looking round. His eyes, so burning that no secrets seemed to exist for him, stopped on a nook in the room, where a little dog trembled on a handful of straw. It was the last of three of a kind, which Balsamo had provided on request of the elder for his experiments.

"Bring that dog to this table," said he to Balsamo, who laid the creature on a marble slab.

Seeming to foresee its doom and having probably already been handled by the dissector, the animal shuddered, wriggled and yelped at contact of the cold stone.

"So you believe in life, since you do in death?" squeaked Althotas. "This dog looks live enough, eh?"

"Certainly, as it moves and whines."

"How ugly black dogs are! I should like white ones another time. Howl away, you cur," said the vivisectionist with his lugubrious laugh; "howl, to convince Grand Seignior Acharat that you live."

He pierced the animal at a certain muscle so that he whimpered instead of barking.

"Good! push the bell of the air pump hither. But stay, I must ask what kind of death you prefer for him—deem best?"

"I do not know what you mean; death is death, master."

"Very correct, what you say, and I agree with you. Since one kind of death is the same as another, exhaust the air, Acharat."

Balsamo worked the air pump, and the air in the bell of glass hissed out at the bottom, so that the little puppy grew uneasy at the first, looked around, began to sniff, put his paw to the issue till the pain of the pressure made him take it away, and then he fell suffocated, puffed up and asphyxiated.

"Behold the dog dead of apoplexy," pronounced the sage; "this is a fine mode with no long suffering. But you do not seem fully convinced. I suppose you know how well laden I am with resources, and you think I have the method of restoring the respiration."

"No, I am not supposing that. The dog is truly not alive."

"Never mind, we will make assurance doubly sure by killing the canine twice. Lift off the receiver, Acharat."

The glass bell was removed and there lay the victim, never stirring, with eyes shut and heart without a beat.

"Take the scalpel and sever the spinal column without cutting the larynx."

"I do so solely because you say it."

"And to finish the poor creature in case it be not dead," said the other, with the smile of obstinacy peculiar to the aged.

With one incision Balsamo separated the vertebral column a couple of inches from the brain, and opened a yawning gash. The body remained unmoving.

"He is an inert animal, icy cold, forever without movement, eh? You say nothing prevails against death? No power can restore even the appearance of life, far less life itself, to this carcass?"

"Only the miracle of Heaven!"

"But Heaven does not do such things. Supreme wisdom kills because there is reason or benefit in the act. An assassin said so, and he was quite right. Nature has an interest in the death. Now, what will you say if this dog opens his eyes and looks at you?"

"It would much astonish me," said the pupil smiling.

"I am glad to hear that it would do as much as that."

As he drew the dog up to an apparatus which we know as a voltaic pile, he rounded off his words with his false and grating laugh. The pile was composed of a vessel containing strips of metal separated by felt. All were bathed in acidulated water; out of the cup came the two ends of wire—the poles to speak technically.

"Which eye shall it open, Acharat?" inquired the experimentalist.

"The right."

The two extremities were brought together, but parted by a little silk, on a neck muscle. In an instant the dog's right eye opened and stared at Balsamo, who could not help recoiling.

"Look out," said the infernal jester, with his dry laugh; "our dead dog is going to bite you!"

Indeed, the animal, in spite of its sundered spine, with gaping jaws and tremulous eye, suddenly got upon its four legs, and tottered on them. With his hair bristling, Balsamo receded to the door, uncertain whether to flee or remain.

"But we must not frighten you to death in trying to teach you," said Althotas, pushing back the cadaver and the machine; the contact broken, the carcass fell back into immovability.

"You see that we may arrive at the point I spoke of, my son, and prolong life since we can annul death?"

"Not so, for you have only obtained a semblance of life," objected Balsamo.

"In time, we shall make it real. The Roman poets—and they were esteemed prophets—assert that Cassidæus revived the dead."

"But one objection: supposing your elixir perfect and a dog

200

given some, it would live on—until it fell into the hands of a dissector who would cut its throat."

"I thought you would take me there," chuckled the old wizard, clapping his hands.

"Your elixir will not prevent a chimney falling on a man, a bullet going clear through him, or a horse kicking his skull open?"

Althotas eyed the speaker like a fencer watching his antagonist make a lunge which lays him open to defeat.

"No, no, no, and you are a true logician. No, my dear Acharat, such accidents cannot be avoided; the wounds will still be made, but I can stop the vital spirit issuing by the hole. Look!"

Before the other could interfere he drove the lancet into his arm. The old man had so little blood that it was some time flowing to the cut; but when it came it was abundantly.

"Great God! you have hurt yourself!" cried the younger man.

"We must convince you."

Taking up a phial of colorless fluid, he poured a few drops on the wound; instantly the liquid congealed, or rather threw out fibres materializing, and, soon a plaster of a yellow hue covered in the gash and stanched the flow. Balsamo had never seen collodion, and he gazed in stupefaction at the old sage.

"You are the wisest of men, father!"

"At least if I have not dealt Death a death-blow, I have given him a thrust under which he will find it hard to rise. You see, my son, that the human frame has brittle bones—I will harden and yet supple them like steel. It has blood which, in flowing out, carries life with it—I will stop the flow. The skin and flesh are soft—I will tan them so that they will turn the edge of steel and blunt the points of spears, while bullets will flatten against it. Only let an Althotas live three hundred years. Well, give me what I want, and I shall live a thousand. Oh, my dear Acharat, all depends on you. Bring me the child."

"I will think it over, and do you likewise reflect."

The sage darted a look of withering scorn on his adept.

"Go!" he snarled, "I will convince you later. Besides, human blood is not so precious that I cannot use a substitute. Go, and let me seek—and I shall find. I have no need of you. Begone!"

Balsamo walked over to the elevator, and with a stamp of the foot, caused it to carry him down to the other floor. Mute, crushed by the genius of this wizard, he was forced to believe in impossible things by his doing them.

CHAPTER XLII

THE KING'S NEW AMOUR

This same long night had been employed by Countess Dubarry in trying to mold the king's mind to a new policy according to her views.

Above all she had dwelt upon the necessity of not letting the Choiseul party win possession of the dauphiness. The king had answered carelessly that the princess was a girl and Choiseul an old statesman, so that there was no danger, since one only wanted to sport and the other to labor. Enchanted at what he thought a witticism, he cut short further dry talk.

But Jeanne did not stay stopped, for she fancied the royal lover was thinking of another.

He was fickle. His great pleasure was in making his lady-loves jealous, as long as they did not sulk too long or become too riotous in their jealous fits.

Jeanne Dubarry was jealous naturally, and from fear of a fall. Her position had cost her too much pains to conquer and was too far from the starting-point for her to tolerate rivals as Lady Pompadour had done.

Hence she wanted to know what was on the royal mind.

He answered by these memorable words, of which he did not mean a jot:

"I intend to make my daughter-in-law very happy and I am afraid that my son will not make her so."

"Why not, sire?"

"Because he looks at other women a good deal, and very seldom at her."

"If any but your majesty said that, I should disbelieve them, for the archduchess is sweetly pretty."

"She might be rounded out more; that Mademoiselle de Taverney is the same age and she has a finer figure. She is perfectly lovely."

Fire flashed in the favorite's eyes and warned the speaker of his blunder.

"Why, I wager that you were plump as Watteau's shepherdesses at sixteen," said he quickly, which adulation improved matters a little, but the mischief was done.

"Humph," said she, bridling up under the pleased smile, "is the young lady of the Taverney family so very, very fair?"

"I only noticed that she was not a bag of bones. You know I am short-sighted and the general outline alone strikes me. I saw that the new-comer from Austria was not plump, that is all."

"Yes, you must only see generally, for the Austrian is a stylish beauty, and the provincial lady a vulgar one."

"According to this, Jeanne, you would be the vulgar kind," said the monarch. "You are joking, I think."

"That is a compliment, but it is wrapped up in a compliment to another," thought the favorite, and aloud she said: "Faith, I should like the dauphiness to choose a bevy of beauties for maids of honor. A court of old tabbies is frightful."

"You are talking over one won to your side, for I was saying the same thing to the dauphin; but he is indifferent."

"However, she begins well, you think, to take this Taverney girl. She has no money?"

"No, but she has blood. The Taverney Redcastles are a good old house and long-time servants of the realm."

"Who is backing them?"

"Not the Choiseuls, for they would be overfeasted with pensions in that case."

"I beg you not to bring in politics, countess!"

"Is it bringing in politics to say the Choiseuls are blood-sucking the realm?"

"Certainly." And he arose.

An hour after he regained the Grand Trianon palace, happy at having inspired jealousy, though he said to himself, as a Richelieu might do at thirty:

"What a bother these jealous women are!"

Dubarry went into her boudoir, where Chon was impatiently waiting for the news.

"You are having fine success," she exclaimed; "day before yesterday presented to the dauphiness, you dined at her table yesterday."

"That's so—but much good in such nonsense."

"Nonsense, when a hundred fashionable carriages are racing to bring you courtiers?"

"I am vexed, sorry for them, as they will not have any smiles from me this morning. Let me have my chocolate."

"Stormy weather, eh?"

Chon rang and Zamore came in to get the order. He started off so slowly, and humping up his back, that the mistress cried:

"Is that slowcoach going to make me perish of hunger? If he plays the camel and does not hurry, he'll get a hundred lashes on his back."

"Me no hurry—me gubbernor," replied the black boy, majestically.

"You a governor?" screamed the lady, flourishing a fancy riding whip kept to maintain order among the spaniels. "I'll give you a lesson in governing."

But the negro ran out yelling.

"You are quite ferocious, Jeanne," remarked her sister.

"Surely I have the right to be ferocious in my own house?"

"Certainly; but I am going to elope, for fear I may be devoured alive."

Three knocks on the door came to interrupt the outbreak.

"Hang it all—who is bothering now?" cried the countess, stamping her foot.

"He is in for a nice welcome," muttered Chon.

"It will be a good thing if I am badly received," said Jean, as he pushed open the door as widely as though he were a king, "for then I should take myself off and not come again. And you would be the greater loser of the two."

"Saucebox——"

"Because I am not a flatterer. What is the matter with the girl this morning, Chon?"

"She is not safe to go near."

"Oh, here comes the chocolate! Good-morning, Chocolate," said the favorite's brother, taking the platter and putting it on a small table, at which he seated himself. "Come and tuck it in, Chon! those who are too proud won't get any, that's all."

"You are a nice pair," said Jeanne, "gobbling up the bread and butter instead of wondering what worries me."

"Out of cash, I suppose?" said Chon.

"Pooh, the king will run out before I do."

"Then lend me a thousand—I can do with it," said the man.

"You will get a thousand fillips on the nose sooner than a thousand Louis."

"Is the king going to keep that abominable Choiseul?" questioned Chon.

"That is no novelty—you know that they are sticks-in-the-mud."

"Has the old boy fallen in love with the dauphiness?"

"You are getting warm; but look at the glutton, ready to burst with swilling chocolate and will not lift a finger to help me out of my quandary."

"You never mean to say the king has another fancy?" cried Chon, clasping her hands, and turning pale.

"If I did not say so your brother would, for he will either choke with the chocolate or get it out."

204

Thus adjured, Jean managed to gasp the name:

"Andrea of Taverney!"

"The baron's daughter—oh, mercy!" groaned Chon.

"I do not know what keeps me from tearing his eyes out, the lazybones, to go puffing them up with sleep when our fortunes stagger."

"With want of sleep you mean," returned Jean. "I am sleepy, as I am hungry, for the same reason—I have been running about the streets all night."

"Just like you."

"And all the morning."

"You might have run to some purpose, and found out where that intriguing jade is housed."

"The very thing—I questioned the driver of the carriage lent to them, and he took them to Coq Heron street. They are living in a little house at the back, next door to Armenonville House."

"Jean, Jean, we are good friends again," said the countess. "Gorge as you like. But we must have all the particulars about her, how she lives, who calls on her, and what she is about. Does she get any love letters—these are important to know."

"I have got us started on the right road anyway," said Jean; "suppose you do a little now."

"Well," suggested Chon, "there must be rooms to let in that street."

"Excellent idea," said the countess. "You must be off quickly to the place, Jean, and hire a flat there, where a watcher can mark down all her doings."

"No use; there are no rooms to hire there; I inquired; but I can get what we want in the street at the back, overlooking their place, Plastrière Street."

"Well, quick! get a room there."

"I have done that," answered Jean.

"Admirable fellow—come, let me buss thee!" exclaimed the royal favorite.

Jean wiped his mouth, received the caress and made a ceremonious bow to show that he was duly grateful for the honor.

"I took the little suite for a young widow. Young widow, you, Chon."

"Capital! it shall be Chon who will take the lodgings and keep an eye on what goes on. But you must not lose any time. The coach," cried Dubarry, ringing the bell so loudly that she would have roused all the spellbound servants of the palace of the Sleeping Beauty.

The three knew how highly to rate Andrea, for at her first sight she had excited the king's attention; hence she was dangerous.

"This girl," said the countess while the carriage was being got ready; "cannot be a true country wench if she has not made some sweetheart follow her to Paris. Let us hunt up this chap and get her married to him offhand. Nothing would so **** off the king as rustic lovers getting wedded."

"I do not know so much about that," said Jean. "Let us be distrustful. His most Christian majesty is greedy for what is another's property."

Chon departed in the coach, with Jean's promise that he would be her first visitor in the new lodgings. She was in luck, for she had hardly more than taken possession of the rooms, and gone to look out of the window commanding a view of the rear gardens than a young lady came to sit at the summer-house window, with embroidery in her hand.

It was Andrea.

CHAPTER XLIII

TWO BIRDS WITH ONE STONE

Chon had not been many minutes scanning the Taverney lady, when Viscount Jean, racing up the stairs four at a time like a schoolboy, appeared on the threshold of the pretended widow's room.

"Hurrah, Jean, I am placed splendidly to see what goes on, but I am unfortunate about hearing."

"You ask too much. Oh, I say, I have a bit of news, marvelous and incomparable. Those philosophic fellows say a wise man ought to be ready for anything, but I cannot be wise, for this knocked me. I give you a hundred chances to guess who I ran up against at a public fountain at the corner; he was sopping a piece of bread in the gush, and it was—our philosopher."

"Who? Gilbert?"

"The very boy, with bare head, open waistcoat, stockings ungartered, shoes without buckles, in short, just as he turned out of bed."

"Then he lives by here? Did you speak to him?"

"We recognized one another, and when I thrust out my hand,

he bolted like a harrier among the crowd, so that I lost sight of him. You don't think I was going to run after him, do you?"

"Hardly, but then you have lost him."

"What a pity!" said the girl Sylvie, whom Chon had brought along as her maid.

"Yes, certainly," said Jean; "I owe him a hundred stripes with a whip, and they would not have spoilt by keeping any longer had I got a grip of his collar; but he guessed my good intentions and fled. No matter, here he is in town; and when one has the ear of the chief of police, anybody can be found."

"Shut him up when you catch him," said Sylvie, "but in a safe place."

"And make you turnkey over him," suggested Jean, winking. "She would like to take him his bread and water."

"Stop your joking, brother," said Chon; "the young fellow saw your row over the post-horses, and he is to be feared if you set him against you."

"How can he live without means?"

"Tut, he will hold horses or run errands."

"Never mind him; come to our observatory."

Brother and sister approached the window with infinity of precautions. Jean had provided himself with a telescope.

Andrea had dropped her needlework, put up her feet on a lower chair, taken a book, and was reading it with some attention, for she remained very still.

"Fie on the studious person!" sneered Chon.

"What an admirable one!" added Jean. "A perfect being—what arms, what hands! what eyes! lips that would wreck the soul of St. Anthony—oh, the divine feet—and what an ankle in that silk hose?"

"Hold your tongue! this is coming on finely," said Chon. "You are smitten with her, now. This is the drop that fills the bucket."

"It would not be a bad job if it were so, and she returned me the flame a little. It would save our poor sister a lot of worry."

"Let me have the spyglass a while. Yes, she is very handsome, and she must have had a sweetheart out there in the woods. But she is not reading—see, the book slips out of her hand. I tell you, Jean, that she is in a brown study."

"She sleeps, you mean."

"Not with her eyes open—what lovely eyes! This a good glass, Jean—I can almost read in her book."

"What is the book, then?"

Chon was leaning out a little when she suddenly drew back.

"Gracious! look at that head sticking out of the garret window—"

"Gilbert, by Jove! with what burning eyes he is glaring on the Taverney girl!"

"I have it: he is the country gallant of his lady. He has had the notice where she was coming to live in Paris and he has taken a room close to her. A change of dovecote for the turtle-doves."

"Sister, we need not trouble now, for he will do all the watching——"

"For his own gain."

"No, for ours. Let me pass, as I must go and see the chief of police. By Jupiter, what luck we have! But don't you let Philosopher catch a glimpse of you—he would decamp very quick."

CHAPTER XLIV

THE PLAN OF ACTION

Sartines had allowed himself to sleep late, as he had managed the multitude very well during the dauphiness' reception, and he was trying on new wigs at noon as a kind of holiday when Chevalier Jean Dubarry was announced.

The minister of police was sure that nothing unpleasant had occurred, as the favorite's brother was smiling.

"What brings you so early?"

"To begin with," replied Jean, always ready to flatter those of whom he wanted to make use, "I am bound to compliment you on the admirable way in which you regulated the processions."

"Is this official?"

"Quite, so far as Luciennes is concerned."

"Is not that ample—does not the Sun rise in that quarter?"

"It goes down there very often, eh?" and the pair laughed. "But, the compliments apart, I have a service to ask of you."

"Two, if you like."

"Tell me if anything lost in Paris can be found?"

"Yes, whether worthless or very valuable."

"My object of search is not worth much," responded Jean, shaking his head. "Only a young fellow of eighteen, named Gilbert, who was in the service of the Taverneys in Lorraine, but was picked up on the road by my sister Chon. She took him to Luciennes, where he abused the hospitality."

"Stole something?"

"I do not say so, but he took flight in a suspicious manner."

"Have you any clue to his hiding place?"

"I met him at the fountain at the corner of Plastrière Street, where I suppose he is living, and I believe I could lay my hand on the very house."

"All right, I will send a sure agent, who will take him out of it!"

"The fact is, this is a special affair, and I should like you to manage it without a third party."

"Oh, in that case, let me pick out a becoming wig and I am with you."

"I have a carriage below."

"Thank you, I prefer my own; it gets a new coat of paint every month, so as not to betray me."

He had tried on his twentieth peruke when the carriage was waiting at the door.

"There it is, the dirty house," said Jean, pointing in the direction of a dwelling in Plastrière street.

"Whew!" said Sartines, "dash me if I did not suspect this. You are unlucky, for that is the dwelling of Rousseau, of Geneva."

"The scribbler? What does that matter?"

"It matters that Rousseau is a man to be dreaded."

"Pooh! it is not likely my little man will be harbored by a celebrity."

"Why not, as you nicknamed him a philosopher? Birds of a feather—you know——"

"Suppose it is so. Why not put this Rousseau in the Bastille if he is in our way?"

"Well, he would be more in our way there than here. You see the mob likes to throw stones at him, but they would pelt us if he was no longer their target, and they want him for themselves. But let us see into this. Sit back in the carriage."

He referred to a notebook.

"I have it. If your young blade is with Rousseau, when would he have met him?"

"Say, on the sixteenth instant."

"Good! he returned from botanizing in Meudon Wood on the seventeenth with a youth, and this stranger stayed all night under his roof. You are crossed by luck. Give it up or you would have all the philosophers against us in riot."

"Oh, Lord! what will sister Jeanne say?"

"Oh, does the countess want the lad? Why not coax him out,

and then we would nab him, anywhere not inside Rousseau's house?"

"You might as well coax a hyena."

"I doubt it is so difficult. All you want is a go-between. Let me see; a prince will not do; better one of these writers, a poet, a philosopher or a bota—stay, I have him!"

"Gilbert?"

"Yes, through a botanist friend of Rousseau's. You know Jussieu?"

"Yes, for the countess lets him prowl in her gardens and rifle them."

"I begin to believe that you shall have your Gilbert, without any noise. Rousseau will hand him over, pinioned, so to say. So you go on making a trap for philosophers, according to a plan I will give you, on vacant ground out Meudon or Marly way. Now, let us be off, as the passengers are beginning to stare at us. Home, coachman!"

CHAPTER XLV

TOO GOOD A TEACHER

Fatigued by the ceremonies of the dauphin's nuptials, and particularly by the dinner, which was too stately, the king retired at nine o'clock and dismissed all attendants except Duke Vauguyon, tutor of the royal children. As he was losing his best pupil by the marriage, having only his two brothers to teach, and as it is the custom to reward a preceptor when education of a charge is complete, he expected a recompense.

He had been sobbing, and now he slipped out a pockethandkerchief and began to weep.

"Come, my poor Vauguyon," said the king, pointing to a footstool in the light, while he would be in the shade, "pray be seated, without any to-do."

The duke sighed.

"The education is over, and you have turned out in the prince royal the best educated prince in Europe."

"I believe he is."

"Good at history, and geography, and at wood-turning——"

"The praise for that goes to another, sire."

"And at setting timepieces in order. Before he handled them, my clocks told the time one after another like wheels of a coach; but he has put them right. In short, the heir to the crown will, I believe, be a good king, a good manager, and a good father of family. I suppose he will be a good father?" he insisted.

"Why, your majesty," said Vauguyon simply, "I consider that as the dauphin has all the germs of good in his bosom, those that constitute that are in the cluster."

"Come, come, my lord," said the sovereign, "let us speak plainly. As you know the dauphin thoroughly, you must know all about his tastes and his passions——"

"Pardon me, sire, but I have extirpated all his passions."

"Confound it all! this is just what I feared!" exclaimed Louis XV., with an energy which made the hearer's wig stand its hairs on end.

"Sire, the Duke of Berri has lived under your august roof with the innocence of the studious youth."

"But the youth is now a married man."

"Sire, as the guide of——"

"Yes, well, I see that you must guide him to the very last."

"Please your majesty."

"This is the way of it. You will go to the dauphin, who is now receiving the final compliments of the gentlemen as the dauphiness is receiving those of the ladies. Get a candle and take your pupil aside. Show him the nuptial chamber which is at the end of a corridor filled with pictures which I have selected as a complete course of the instruction which your lordship omitted——"

"Ah," said the duke, starting at the smile of his master, which would have appeared cynical on any mouth but his, the wittiest in the kingdom.

"At the end of the new corridor, I say, of which here is the key."

Vauguyon took it trembling.

"You will shake your pupil's hand, put the candle into it, wish him good-night, and tell him that it will take twenty minutes to reach the bedroom door, giving a minute to each painting."

"I—I understand."

"That is a good thing."

"Your majesty is good enough to excuse me——"

"I suppose I shall have to, but you were making this end prettily for my family!"

From the window the king could see the candle which passed from the hands of Vauguyon into that of his guileless pupil, go the way up the new gallery, and flicker out.

"I gave him twenty minutes—I myself found five long enough," muttered the king, "Alas, will they say of the dauphin as of the second Racine: 'He is the nephew of his grandfather.'"

CHAPTER XLVI

A TERRIBLE WEDDING-NIGHT

The dauphin opened the door of the anteroom before the wedding chamber.

The archduchess was waiting, in a long white wrapper, with the strange anticipation on her brow, along with the sweet expectation of the bride, of some disaster. She seemed menaced with one of those terrors which nervous dispositions foresee and support sometimes with more bravery than if not awaited.

Lady Noailles was seated by the gilded couch, which easily held the princess' frail and dainty body.

The maids of honor stood at the back, waiting for the mistress of the attendants to make them the sign to withdraw. These were all ignorant that the dauphin was coming by a new way in. As the corridor was empty and the door at the end ajar, he could see and hear what went on in the room.

"In what direction does my lord the dauphin come?" inquired the Austrian's pure and harmonious voice though slightly tremulous.

"Yonder," replied Lady Noailles, pointing just the wrong way.

"What is that noise outside—not unlike the roaring of angry waters?"

"It is the tumult of the innumerable sight-seers walking about under the illumination and waiting for the fireworks display."

"The illuminations?" said the princess with a sad smile. "They must have been timely this evening, for did you not notice it was very black weather?"

At this moment the dauphin, who was tired of waiting, thrust his head in at the door, and asked if he might enter. Lady Noailles screamed, for she did not recognize the intruder at first. The dauphiness, worked up into a nervous state by the incidents of the day, seized the duchess' arm in her fright.

"It is I, madame; have no fear," called out the prince.

"But why by that way?" said Lady Noailles.

"Because," explained Louis the King, showing his head at the half-open door, "because the Duke of Vauguyon knows so much Latin, mathematics and geography as to leave room for nothing else."

In presence of the king so untimely arrived, the dauphiness slipped off the couch and stood up in the wrapper, clothed from head to foot like a vestal virgin in her stole.

"Any one can see that she is thin," muttered the king; "what the deuse made Choiseul pick out the skinny chicken among all the pullets of European courts?"

"Your majesty will please to observe that I acted according to the strict etiquette," said the Duchess of Noailles, "the infraction was on my lord the dauphin's part."

"I take it on myself. So, let us leave the children to themselves," said the monarch.

The princess seized the lady's arm with more terror than before.

"Oh, don't go away!" she faltered; "I shall die of shame."

"Sire, the dauphiness begs to be allowed to go to rest without any state," said Lady Noailles.

"The deuce—and does 'Lady Etiquette' herself crave that?"

"Look at the archduchess——"

In fact, Marie Antoinette, standing up, pale and with her rigid arm sustaining her by a chair, resembled a statue of fright, but for the slight chattering of her teeth, and the cold perspiration bedewing her forehead.

"Oh, I should not think of causing the young lady any pain," said Louis XV., as little strict about forms as his father was the other thing. "Let us retire, duchess; besides, the doors have locks."

The dauphin blushed to hear these words of his grandfather, but the lady, though hearing, had not understood.

King Louis XV. embraced his grand-daughter-in-law, and went forth, with Lady Noailles, laughing mockingly and sadly, for those who did not share his merriment.

The other persons had gone out by the other door.

The wedded pair were left alone in silence.

At last the young husband approached his bride with bosom beating rapidly; to his temples, breast and wrist he felt all his repressed blood rushing hotly. But he guessed that his grandfather was behind the door, and the cynical glance still chilled the dauphin, very timid and awkward by nature.

"You are not well, madame," he stammered. "You are very pale, and I think you are trembling."

213

"I cannot conceal that I am under a spell of agitation; there must be some terrible storm overhead, for I am peculiarly affected by thunderstorms."

Indeed, she shook by spasms as though affected by electrical shocks.

At this time, as though to justify her assertion, a furious gust of wind, such as shear the tops off mountains and heap up half the sea against the other—the first whoop of the coming tempest filled the palace with tumult, anguish and many a creaking. Leaves were swept off the branches, branches off the boughs and from the trees. A long and immense clamor was drawn from the hundred thousand spectators in the gardens. A lugubrious and endless bellowing ran through the corridors and galleries, composing the most awful notes that had ever vibrated in human ears.

Then an ominous rattling and jingling succeeded the roar; it was the fall of countless shivers of glass out of the window panes on the marble slabs and cornices.

At the same time the gale had opened one of the shutters and banged it to and fro like a wings of a bird of night. Wherever the window had been open and where the glass was shivered the lights were put out.

The prince went over to the window to fasten the broken shutter, but his wife held him back.

"Oh, pray, do not open that window, for the lights will be blown out, and I should die of fright."

He stopped. Through the casement beyond the curtain which he had drawn the tree tops of the park were visible, swayed from side to side as if some unseen giant were waving them by the stems. All the illuminations were extinguished.

Then could be seen on the dark sky still blacker clouds, coming on with a rolling motion like troops of cavalry wrapped in dust.

The pallid prince stood with one hand on the sash-handle. The bride sank on a chair, with a sigh.

"You are very much alarmed, madame?"

"Yes, though your presence supports me. Oh, what a storm! all the pretty lights are put out."

"Yes, it is a southwest wind, always the worst for storms. If it holds out, I do not know how they will be able to set off the fireworks."

"What would be the use of them? Everybody will be out of the gardens in such weather."

"You do not know what our French are when there is a show. They cry for the pyrotechnics, and this is to be superb; the pyrotechnist showed me the sketches. There! look at the first rockets!"

Indeed, brilliant as long fiery serpents, the trial rockets rushed up into the clouds, but at the same time, as if the storm had taken the flash as a challenge, one stroke of lightning, seeming to split the sky, snaked among the rockets ascending and eclipsed their red glare with its bluish flaring.

"Verily, it is impiety for man to contest with God," said the archduchess.

The trial rockets had preceded the general display by but a few minutes as the pyrotechnist felt the need of hastening, and the first set pieces were fired and were hailed with a cheer of delight.

But as though there were really a war between man and heaven, the storm, irritated by the impiety, drowned with its thunder the cheers of the mobs, and all the cataracts on high opened at once. Torrents of rain were precipitated from the cloudy heights.

In like manner to the wind putting out the illuminations, the rain put out the fireworks.

"What a misfortune, the fireworks are spoilt," said the dauphin.

"Alas, everything goes wrong since I entered France," said Marie Antoinette. "This storm suits the feast that was given me. It was wanted to hide from the people the miseries of this dilapidated palace of Versailles. So, blow, you southwest wind! spout, rain! pile yourselves together, tempestuous clouds, to hide from my eyes the paltry, tawdry reception given to the daughter of the kaisers, when she laid her hand in that of the future king!"

The visibly embarrassed dauphin did not know what answer to make to this, these reproaches, and particularly this exalted melancholy, so far from his character; he only sighed.

"I afflict you," continued she; "but do not believe that my pride is speaking. No, no, it is nowise in it. Would that they had only shown me the pretty little Trianon, with its flower gardens, and smiling shades—the rain will but refresh it, the wind but open the blossoms. That charming nest would content me; but these ruins frighten me, so repugnant to my youth, and yet how many more ruins will be created by this frightful storm."

A fresh gust, worse than the first, shook the palace. The princess started up aghast.

"Oh, heavens, tell me that there is no danger!" she moaned; "I shall die of fright."

"There is no fear, madame. Versailles is built on terraces so as to defy the storm. If lightning fell it would only strike yonder chapel with its sharp roof, or the little tower which has turrets. You know that peaks attract the electric fluid and flat surfaces repel them."

215

He took her frozen yet palpitating hand.

Just then a vivid flash inundated the room with its violet and livid glare. She uttered a scream and repulsed her husband.

"Oh, you looked in the lurid gleam like a phantom, pale, headless and bleeding!"

"It is the mirage caused by the sulphur," said the prince. "I will explain——"

But a deafening peal of thunder cut short the sentence of the phlegmatic prince lecturing the royal spouse.

"Come, come, madame, let us leave such fears to the common people. Physical agitation is one of the conditions of nature. A storm, and this is no more, is one of the most frequent and natural phenomena. I do not know why people are surprised at them."

"I should not quail so much at another time; but for a storm to burst on our wedding-night, another awful forwarning joined to those heralding my entry into France! My mother has told me that this century is fraught with horrors, as the heavens above are charged with fire and destruction."

"Madame, no dangers can menace the throne to which we shall ascend, for we royalties dwell above the common plane. The thunder is at our feet and we wield the bolts."

"Alas, something dreadful was predicted me, or rather, shown to me in a dish of water. It is hard to describe what was utterly novel to me; a machine reared on high like a scaffold, two upright beams between which glided an axe of odd shape. I saw my head beneath this blade. It descended and my head, severed from the body, leaped to the earth. This is what I was shown."

"Pure hallucination," said the scoffer; "there is no such an instrument in existence, so be encouraged."

"Alas! I cannot drive away the odious thought."

"You will succeed, Marie," said the dauphin, drawing nearer.

"Beside you will be an affectionate and assiduously protective husband."

At the instant when the husband's lips nearly touched the wife's cheek, the picture gallery door opened again, and the curious, covetous look of King Louis XV. penetrated the place. But simultaneously a crash, of which no words can give an idea, resounded through the palace. A spout of white flame, streaked with green, dashed past the widow but shivered a statue on the balcony; then after a prodigious ripping and splitting sound, it bounded upward and vanished like a meteor.

Out went the candles! the dauphin staggered back, dazed and frightened to the very wall. The dauphiness fell, half swooned, on the step of her praying-desk and dwelt in deadly torpor.

Believing the earth was quaking under him, Louis XV. regained his rooms, followed by his faithful valet.

In the morning Versailles was not recognizable. The ground had drunk up the deluge, and the trees absorbed the sulphur.

Everywhere was mud and the broken boughs dragging their blackened lengths like scotched serpents.

Louis XV. went to the bridal chamber for the third time, and looked in. He shuddered to see at the praying-stand the bride, pale and prone, with the aurora tinging her spotless robe, like a Magdalen of Rubens.

On a chair, with his velvet slippers in a puddle of water, the dauphin of France sat as pale as his wife and with the same air of having faced a nightmare.

The nuptial bed was untouched.

Louis XV. frowned; a never-before-experienced pain ran through his brow, cooled by egotism even when debauchery tried to heat it.

He shook his head, sighed and returned to his apartments full of grim forebodings over the future which this tragic event had marked on its brow.

What dread and mysterious incidents were enfolded in its bosom it will be our mission to disclose in the sequel to this book, entitled "The Mesmerist's Victim."